My Royal Story

Henry VIII's Wives

Alison Prince

While the events described and some of the characters in this book may be based on actual historical events and real people, Eva De Puebla, Elinor Valjean and Beatrice Townhill are fictional characters, created by the author, and their stories are works of fiction.

Scholastic Children's Books
Euston House, 24 Eversholt Street,
London, NW1 1DB, UK
A division of Scholastic Ltd

London ~ New York ~ Toronto ~ Sydney ~ Auckland
Mexico City ~ New Delhi ~ Hong Kong

First published in the UK by Scholastic Ltd, 2011

Text copyright © Alison Prince, 2011
Cover illustration © Richard Jones, 2011

ISBN 978 1407 11735 5

Beatrice Townhill. Her book.

12th June 1536

Today is my birthday. It did not seem a special day at first. Agnes helped me to dress as usual and brushed my hair, then sat with me while I had my breakfast. She'd had hers earlier, with the other servants. I don't like Agnes much. She cannot read, so it is safe to write these words, my first entry in this treasured present.

I had to go and see my mother. She was very ill when I was born and never got properly well, and I don't see her often. She was sitting by her window with its criss-cross diamond panes, looking out at the trees. Then she turned her head and said, "You are not very tall for ten years old. Do you eat your meals?"

I said I did, but my voice came out as a whisper. She scares me. Maybe death came so close when she gave birth to me that its cold hand is still on her. She opened the drawer in the table beside her and took out a pearl as big as a shelled almond on a gold chain. She put the chain around my neck and fastened it. The pearl dangled halfway down my dress.

"A gem like that should lie against the skin. I thought you would be bigger," she remarked.

I said, "I'm sorry."

I started to lift the chain off, but she stopped me.

"No, no, keep it. You will grow, I suppose." She laid her hand over her own jewelled necklace and breathed for a moment with her eyes shut. Then she asked, "Do you say your prayers?"

"Yes."

"Good. You must always say your prayers. And do what Agnes tells you."

She looked out at the forest again and said, "You must leave me now. I am very tired."

I curtsied, but she did not notice. Somewhere out in the forest my father was hunting with the King and his gentlemen. The sound of dogs yelping and horns blowing came faintly from far away.

Later this morning, Agnes said, "You are to have lunch with your father, Young Miss."

She always calls me Young Miss. Elinor and Tom and their family call me Bee. So does my friend Kitty. Her name is really Catherine, but there are so many girls called Catherine – or Anne or Jane or Mary. I am lucky to have a different name. Papa told me once that Beatrice means "a woman who blesses".

Mr Thornton says the art of writing is to get things properly in order. He is my tutor, so I am sure he is right. Kitty and this diary come later in the day, so I should put other things first.

Papa was hungry after the hunt and all the work of watering

the horses and rubbing them down and seeing to the skinning and paunching of the kill. There were seventeen stags today, Papa said, and the King was pleased. But I thought about the deer moving carefully in the forest and could not fancy the venison on my plate in its lake of gravy. I ate the cabbage and roast parsnips, and when my father saw I did not want the meat, he stuck his fork in it and ate it himself. But then there were strawberries, with thick cream from our cows. I love strawberries.

Papa helped himself to a big hunk of cheese. "You'll be wondering what I have for your birthday, Beatrice," he said. "Can you guess what it is?" He was looking very pleased.

I shook my head and ate another strawberry. Last year he gave me a puppy, but it choked on a chicken bone and died.

He told me I was to come with him and meet the King. "His Majesty King Henry the Eighth," he said proudly. "And his new queen, Jane Seymour. What do you think of that?"

My spoon stopped in mid-air. I had never seen King Henry close up, only between the trees when he rides out with my father and the other huntsmen. He's a very big man, I think – but maybe that's because the people with him look smaller and not so grand.

I said, "Thank you, Papa."

He gave me a new dress to wear for the visit. It is red velvet, with a lace collar, tight round my middle, with a long, embroidered skirt. My hair was tied up under a white cap. I felt very hot in the coach. It is not far to Greenwich Palace and I wished I could be riding there on my pony, but fine clothes and satin slippers are no good for riding. I kept thinking about meeting the King and Queen. My hands got more and more sticky, and I knew my face was hot and red.

I tried to take my mind off it by thinking about seeing Kitty again. These last weeks must have been dreadful for her. Anne Boleyn, the queen who has just been executed, was Kitty's aunt. When the poor lady was sent to the Tower and condemned to death, she wrote to her sister, Mary Boleyn – Kitty's mother – to ask if Kitty could come and keep her company. I heard Papa talking about it to one of the grooms. "Mary Boleyn should never have agreed to it. The child is younger than my Beatrice." But how could they refuse the Queen her last request?

Kitty's father was Sir William Carey, the Esquire of the King's Body, but he died of the sweating sickness when she was quite small. I heard Agnes telling the other servants his job was to provide white cloths to clean the King when he had used the royal chamber pot. They were all screaming with laughter. After he died, Kitty's mother married Sir William Stafford. Agnes says he is just a common soldier, so he is not welcome at court, but Kitty is still there most of the time. Her old nurse looks after her.

When we arrived at the palace we were shown into a grand room full of court ladies and gentlemen, talking to each other and drinking wine. King Henry and Jane Seymour sat side by side on a carpeted dais.

King Henry really is very big. Not just tall, but broad as well, with strong legs like pillars – though I could see there was a bandage on one of them, under his black silk stocking. The red and gold of his clothes shone like the sun, and the real sun in the window behind his great chair blazed through his bright hair. I felt so dazzled that I could hardly look at him.

When it was our turn to approach, he said, "So your name is Beatrice."

I curtsied low and whispered, "Yes."

Papa frowned at me and said, "Yes, *Your Majesty*!"

The King swallowed the last of the wine in his goblet and held out his cup without looking at anyone in particular. Then he asked, "Are you a good child, Beatrice?"

I said, "I try to be, Your Majesty," and curtsied again.

He turned his head and shouted, "More wine here – what are you idle fools doing?"

A servant ran forward and refilled his glass, and the King drank from it. Then he got up and walked away to join a group of gentlemen who were talking and laughing.

Queen Jane smiled at me and said, "Bless you, child." Then she held out her hand to bring me closer and asked, "How is your mother these days?"

I did not know what to say. Nobody tells me if my mother is better or worse. I looked at Papa and he answered, "Much the same, Your Majesty. Not very well."

The Queen asked if I wanted to be a court lady when I was older. I was not sure, but I said, "If it so please Your Majesty."

"Then we must see what we can do."

Queen Jane is not exactly beautiful. She has a rather pale face that could be quite severe, but I was not afraid of her. Then Papa said, "Beatrice, you can go and play with your friend now."

Kitty was standing near. She had a book under her arm – this book, but I didn't know that then. We used to be together every morning for lessons at Mr Thornton's house, before she had to go to the Tower to be with her aunt. Mr Thornton teaches Latin, French, theology and the study of nature. He is very kind. Apart from Elinor and Eva, I think he is my favourite person.

"It's hot in here," Kitty said. "Let's go out." We went down the hill among the trees to the river and sat down on the grass to watch the boats go by. And that's when she gave me this diary. I opened it and saw Kitty's rather untidy writing covering the first three or four pages, but she spread her hand across the words to stop me from reading.

"Tear those pages out, Bee. Burn them. I was going to, but somehow I couldn't do it. She won't mind if it's you."

There was only one person who could have known what was on those pages – Anne Boleyn, who had watched Kitty writing as the hours ticked away to her death. Maybe Kitty's mother gave her this book as something to occupy her in the dreadful days – or maybe the doomed queen herself. I thanked Kitty and said the book was wonderful. But my mind had jumped to that terrible room in the Tower. Kitty would have heard the sawing and hammering as men built the scaffold on Tower Green. If she had looked down through that high, barred window, she would have seen the block where her aunt would kneel for the headsman's sword. It was too horrible to think about.

We were quiet for a long time, but at last I had to ask. "Kitty – was it terrible?"

She frowned at the sparkling water, and I thought she might be about to cry. But Kitty never cries.

"It doesn't matter," she said. "It's over."

She started picking the little white daisies that grew in the grass, and we made them into daisy chains and hung them round our necks. When Papa came down the hill to tell me we were going home, I took my chain off and gave it to Kitty. He would not have liked to see common daisies mixed with my mother's pearl.

When we got back, there was no sign of Agnes, so I did what Kitty could not. I read the pages of writing for the first and only time, and shuddered. Then I cut them out very carefully with my embroidery scissors, folded them, slipped them up my sleeve where nobody could see, and went down to the kitchen. Luckily it was empty except for the dog in his treadmill. His running was supposed to turn the joint of beef impaled on its spit over the fire, but he was asleep in his wheel with his head on his paws. I did not disturb him. I pushed the papers into the hot embers under the beef, and they flared up. In a few moments they had died into white ash. I stirred them with the poker to make sure no words remained. The dog opened his yellow eyes and looked at me. But dogs tell no tales.

I went across the fields to Elinor's house, glad to be out in the long, cool grass, with the blue sky above me instead of a carved and gilded ceiling. On the way, I saw Agnes kissing Walter Pearson behind an oak tree, but they didn't see me. I walked on, thinking about what Agnes said to me once when she was in a bad temper and a bit drunk. "You were a brat conceived behind a cowshed. Your hoity-toity mother saw your pa at a joust and thought she loved him. Next thing, he had to marry her. Not that he minded – she brought a good house with her."

Why do grown-up people think love is so important? King Henry got engaged to Jane Seymour on the very next day after Anne Boleyn had been beheaded.

Elinor said, "Hello, Bee – I hear it's your birthday!" She bent down and gave me a kiss.

I've only known Elinor for a few weeks, since the day I found her moving into one of my parents' cottages with what seemed such a big family. I was out on my own, which is not allowed, but Agnes was sleeping after her lunchtime wine. I am not supposed to have anything to do with the tenants, and generally I have never wanted to as they'd seemed rough and not very friendly, but I knew from the first moment that Elinor was different. She accepted me as though I had been one of her own children, a big sister to Michael and Maria, and accepted my help to carry things in, too, with no fuss or questions. She treated me as a real person, and I loved her at once. I have been sneaking out to see her ever since, whenever I can.

Today all her family were together – Elinor and her husband, Tom, and her mother, Eva, who was telling a story to the children. Elinor's

10

brothers, Will and Daniel, were there, too. Will is the younger one —
he's seven years older than I am. He's my special friend because he's so
funny and nice. He said he'd heard it was my birthday, and he gave me
an orange from the royal kitchens at Greenwich Palace, where he works.
It is studded all over with a pattern of cloves and tied with white ribbon.
It has a wonderful scent.

"A pomander," he said. "Hang it in your closet, and it will keep the
moths away." Then he asked, "How was your meeting with His Majesty?"

I was surprised. "How did you know I was there?"

Will put a finger to the side of his nose as if he was confiding a
secret. "Servants at the court are like mice," he said. "We keep out of the
way, but we know everything."

I wish he could have been my big brother. Daniel is nice too but he
is older. He works with Tom, who is a blacksmith. They are building a
new smithy on the side of the barn.

Elinor said, "I'm sure your father was pleased, Bee. Presenting you to
the King is a first step towards making you a court lady."

"I don't think I want to be a court lady." Eva had told me that Anne
Boleyn started that way, as a servant to Catherine of Aragon, the first
queen. And just look how she ended.

I told Elinor about Kitty giving me a diary and she said, "Oh, what a
lovely thing to do. Diaries are so important. You look at them at a later
time and your own words remind you of how things were. Let me show
you something."

She went to the cupboard and brought out two old, shabby books. One of them had a tooled leather cover with a metal hasp so it could be locked. I looked inside, but it was written in a language I didn't understand.

"That is my diary, Bee," said Elinor's mother, Eva. "It is in Spanish. I came from Spain, you see, with Catherine of Aragon. We grew up together. My uncle Rod was the Spanish Ambassador. Doctor Rodrigo Gonsalez De Puebla."

She sounded very foreign as she said the name, and I was amazed. I thought she and Elinor were just ordinary people. I asked, "Is your uncle still the ambassador?"

"No. He died a long time ago. Eustache Chapuys replaced him." Eva said.

"And he's still here," said Will. "Tough as an old turtle."

Eva went on explaining. "Catherine was the daughter of the King and Queen of Spain. She and I were almost the same age. When she was sixteen, her parents sent her to England to marry Arthur, their eldest prince."

That puzzled me. "Not Henry?"

"No. Prince Henry was only ten years old at the time. Arthur was his elder brother. But he died only a few months later."

"That's a shame." I wished so much that I could read the neat lines of words in Eva's diary. I asked why she wrote in Spanish.

"My mother advised it, as a safeguard against prying eyes." Then she told me Spanish is easy to learn. "Especially for someone like you, Bee, who knows Latin."

I laughed. "I don't know if Mr Thornton would agree about that!"

Eva says she will teach me to read Spanish. I am so excited! I'll be able to read all about her life with Catherine of Aragon. I know something went wrong for that queen, but I've never understood why.

Elinor's diary is in English, and wonderfully, she let me borrow it.

"If you are to have anything to do with the court, Bee, you need to know something about it," she said. "But please take good care of it. Do not show it to anyone else. Promise?"

I made the sign of the cross and said I promised. I will hide her diary with my own, in the small space underneath the cupboard in my room. Agnes will never dream of looking there.

13th June 1536

Elinor's diary is wonderful. She began it when she was just a year older than I am now. It begins on loose bits of paper tucked inside the front cover. The first words are:

Richmond Palace, 13th August 1525
This is the diary of Elinor Valjean, aged eleven. Today is my sister
Rosanna's birthday.

Rosanna was sixteen then. I met her a few weeks ago, with her husband, Diego, but they have gone away to Spain. It's such a shivery feeling to read about things that connect with the present day. I am going to copy some of them into my own book, if they explain things I never knew.

Elinor writes about the way it all started:

I am going to write a diary as well, only I do not have a proper one, so I have to write it on these scraps of paper. I will keep them in the back of my Latin book, so they will be private. I am not jealous of Rosanna. Of course she must have nice things for her birthday. I gave her a beaded cap that I'd sewn myself, with some help from Mama. But I will have to wait a long time before I am sixteen, and I want to start writing my diary now.

"Mama" is Eva, of course. Then Elinor talks about her father.

Papa would laugh if he knew about my diary pages. He isn't unkind, but he laughs at everything. I suppose it is because he is the court jester, "Mr John", as they call him. He says he has to remember that things are funny, because if he starts to think they are serious or sad, he would lose his job. I want to be a jester, too, but I am a girl, so I have to wear long dresses that make it hard to jump and tumble as he does. I wish I had been a boy. My brothers have far more fun, learning archery and fighting with swords and quarter-staves. Little

William is not much good at it yet, being only four and not very
strong, but Daniel at seven thinks himself quite the man.

I never imagined Elinor might have wanted to be a boy. She seems
so completely a mother, though she still looks very young. There are
several mentions of Greenwich in her pages, and that's exciting because
Greenwich is where we live. King Henry was born in the palace not far
from here, where William works. I found an entry written just before
Christmas five years ago, when Elinor was in the service of Anne Boleyn.

Once again we are at Greenwich for Christmas. I like this place so
much better than Anne's palace at Whitehall. A grassy hill slopes
down to the river, and Tom and I walk among the tall trees where
the herons nest. Queen Catherine has joined us for Christmas,
so my family is together again. It is lovely to see Mama, and the
boys who both look so much bigger now. Daniel is twelve, a stocky
boy, much more likeable than he was when we were children, and
William has filled out and lost his paleness... I used to hold William
when he was small, but I had forgotten how solid and how charged
with life a baby feels. The little legs kick so strongly and fists wave in
the air with excitement, ready to grab at a finger. Rosanna insisted
on feeding him herself, though the other ladies were surprised. Most
of them hand their children to a wet nurse. I would not want to
do that. How does the baby ever know who his true mother is if
another woman feeds him?

Will as a baby, held by his big sister, Elinor, when she was no older than I am now! How funny.

I wanted to see when Elinor started working for Anne Boleyn and found it. When she says "the Queen", she must mean Catherine of Aragon.

15th November 1528

This is a dreadful day. The King has commanded that I must leave the Queen's service and join Anne Boleyn's household. He is moving her from Greenwich to a much grander house in the Strand, with a garden that runs down to the river. She has demanded that most of the younger ladies shall wait upon her, and I am among them. Rosanna was not chosen, so I will not even have the company of my sister.

I am full of resentment. It is a bitter thing to have to serve a fellow servant, no matter how she has risen in the world. I will have to leave Mama, too, for she, like Rosanna and Diego, will stay with the Queen. … I am glad Rosanna and Mama will be with her, even though I shall miss them.

So the first queen was replaced by a second. I do not quite understand why, but I know the diaries will tell me.

15th June 1536

Today I ran to Elinor's house as soon as I could escape from Agnes, desperate to know why Henry had sent Catherine of Aragon away. I could not see why he should get tired of a beautiful, clever Spanish princess.

"Ask Mama," Elinor said. "She was there. I hadn't been born then."

Eva says Queen Catherine only produced one living child, the lady Mary. She lost every baby before that, and after. One newborn son lived for a few days then died. "And the King had a frantic need for a son," she said. "To inherit the throne and keep the Tudor family in power."

I always thought that the Tudor royal line had been here for centuries, but I was wrong. It only started when the present king's father came from Wales with his army, to support a rebellion against King Richard III. Richard was a Plantagenet. "They really *had* been ruling for centuries," Eva added. "Ever since 1154."

Henry Tudor's men won the Battle of Bosworth Field in 1485. King Richard was killed in the fighting. Amid the wreckage of the battle, Henry Tudor, a young man then, grabbed the crown from where it had rolled into the mud, put it on his own head and was declared King Henry VII. His son is our King Henry VIII. So our king is only the second of the Tudors, and unless he has a son to inherit the Crown, he will be the last. He is terrified, Eva says, that the Plantagenet family will claim the throne again. He has executed as many of them as he can, on the grounds that they are traitors. In his view, no Plantagenet can possibly be loyal to a Tudor king. But Elinor says there are still some of them about.

16th June 1536

Agnes spends more and more time with Walter Pearson, the big drover she wants to marry. That is good because I can be at Elinor's house more often. The other servants know I go there, but it saves them work if nobody has to look after me, so they don't tell my father.

There were several court ladies with Elinor today. They were friendly with her when she worked with them in the service of Anne Boleyn, until just a few weeks ago. I expect they like to escape to the peace of her house, just as I do. They were full of excitement because the King's daughter Mary may be coming to court.

"Don't tell me her father has forgiven her!" Elinor exclaimed.

They all laughed. As far as I could understand, the lady Mary is going to change her religion. She was always a Catholic, but she has signed a paper to say she will accept the King's new Church.

"What a little hypocrite," commented Lady Rochford. "All that fuss about being true to the Catholic Church, then she tells him she has changed, to get back into his good books."

"In which she has succeeded," said another. "The King is riding down to Hunsdon to talk with her."

They went on gossiping. I sat on a low stool in the corner and said nothing. It seems that the new queen, Jane, is delighted by the chance to meet Mary. I went on listening.

Lady Rochford said, "Jane is sending her brother, Lord Beauchamp, to ask her for a list of the clothing Mary will need when she comes to court." Cattily, she added, "The girl has been living like a church mouse, I hear. Hasn't a rag fit to be seen in."

Then she noticed I was there. She raised her eyebrows at the others in warning and said, "*Pas devant les enfants.*"

How insulting – as if I did not speak enough French to know what that means. "Not before the children". I had brought Elinor's diary with me as well as my own, in an old bag that might look as if it held a loaf of bread or a dead rabbit, so I went outside. I sat under a big tree that hid me from the house, reading. On February 15th 1526 Elinor was not quite twelve, but she had been working at the court for two years.

It makes me feel very pampered, with no work to do but lessons, and yet in a way I envy her. She was so much at the centre of things, and I am outside, on my own. Papa does not have much time to talk to me. Agnes said once, "It would be different if you'd been a boy, Young Miss."

Writing about a joust on that February day, Elinor sounded as puzzled by the court goings-on as I would be.

When the King came riding in on his big, black horse, a murmur went up, because his tunic was stitched with the words, DECLARE I DARE NOT. All the ladies were giggling behind their hands, and I asked Mama what it meant. Her face had turned quite pink and she said, "Never mind," so I asked Rosanna later. She told me the words meant the King has a new love, but he dares not say her name. But everyone knows her name. It is Anne Boleyn.

I keep thinking about Anne, wondering what it must be like to be loved by a king who already has a wife. I came face to face with her this evening as she brought a flask of sweet wine to the queen's chamber. She is hardly taller than I am, a slender wisp of a thing. I suppose I must have been staring, because she asked me what I thought I was looking at. She sounded very annoyed.

It was no use pretending I hadn't been looking. I dropped her a respectful curtsey while I thought fast, then said, "I was looking at you."

"And why, pray?" she asked.

I told her, "Because you are so beautiful." Papa has always said a jester must look innocent.

It worked very well. "Bless the child," Anne said. She patted my cheek and smiled at me. Then she went on to the queen's door with her flask of wine.

20

A few pages on I found a bit about Elinor's sister Rosanna falling in love with Diego Luiz de Frontera. He's the son of one of the Spanish courtiers who came with Queen Catherine's entourage. I see now why Rosanna has left to go to Spain. It is her husband's home country.

I read on. Elinor was still helping Eva, in the service of Queen Catherine of Aragon. On her thirteenth birthday she was appointed a Lady of Court.

I feel very grown-up, with my hair braided neatly under an embroidered cap, a present from Rosanna. Mama gave me a new gown, much more elaborate than any of my childhood dresses, and although I have always preferred boyish things, I must admit, this lovely dress is a pleasure. …How strange it is to feel like a court lady! Suddenly I am included in the gossip instead of being sent away like a little girl…

That made me smile. I'd been sent out of Elinor's room because the ladies did not want to talk in front of a mere child. Then I found an entry about Mary, the very person they were discussing. Elinor was at Hampton Court (*I love this place,* she says), still in the service of Queen Catherine of Aragon. The lady Mary was ten years old, but there was scheming afoot to find a politically powerful husband for her.

A delegation is here from France, to talk about Mary's marriage to the French king. Their ambassador said an extraordinary thing. He asked whether Mary really is the King's legitimate daughter. The courtiers who were listening dared not even glance at each other, they were so embarrassed. How can anyone doubt that Mary is the child of Henry and Catherine of Aragon?

Rosanna explained later what the ambassador meant. Apparently the King is trying to claim that he was never legally married to Catherine. He has found a passage in the Bible that says it is unlawful for a man to marry his brother's wife – and Catherine was of course married to Henry's elder brother, Arthur, for a few months. Arthur then died, and Catherine waited for years before it was decided that she could marry Henry, who had always been her true love.

Everything has changed now. Henry is trying to wriggle out of his marriage so he can take Anne as his new wife. And the only way he can do this is to declare his marriage to Queen Catherine illegal. I have never seen Mama so furious.

Just a week later, on April 17th 1527, Elinor sounded shocked all over again.

King Henry has asked Anne Boleyn to be his wife! How can *he? Obviously, he thinks he can dissolve his marriage to Catherine, but that is hardly the point. His determination to marry Anne astounds everyone. He has had mistresses before, many of them, we are all used to that, but to take this girl as a wife seems extraordinary. She is no more than a court servant, like the rest of us.*

Reading on, very carefully so as not to miss anything, I found the lady Mary at court, ten years old and officially betrothed to the French king. She was dancing with her father, King Henry:

He suddenly pulled off Mary's jewelled cap and let the wavy length of her fair hair fall free, as if to show off her beauty. Everyone laughed and applauded. Poor Mary, though. I would not be in her place, bound to marry an old man whom she has never met.

On the next page came the answer to my question – the reason why the King thought he had a right to divorce his first wife, Catherine of Aragon. At the time, Elinor was as puzzled as I am now:

Tonight I asked Mama what it says in the Bible about a man who marries his brother's wife. She took down our own Bible and turned to Leviticus and ran her finger down the pages. We stared at the close-printed lines by the candle's light. Most of the chapters were about sacrifice and burnt offerings, but then she came to the rules by which a man must live if he is to be pure. "This is it," she said. We read the words of chapter 20, verse 21 together:

Qui duxerit uxorem fratris sui, rem facit illicitam, turpitudinem fratris sui revelavit absque liberis sunt.

And if a man shall take his brother's wife, it is an unclean thing; he hath uncovered his brother's nakedness; they shall be childless.

"You see?" Mama said. "Henry thinks he has sinned in marrying

Catherine, who was his brother's wife. And he fears that God's punishment for that is to deny him a son."

I found the whole chapter very frightening.

I can see why. But it was a powerful weapon for the King. On June 22nd, he went to see Catherine and asked her to divorce him and cease to be his queen.

Heavens, what a rumpus! The Queen wept like a thing demented, and screamed at him that she was and always would be his legal wife. Henry emerged from her chambers looking ruffled and angry. I do not feel much sympathy for him. From what Mama has told me, Catherine went through years of hardship and neglect before he married her, and she would rather die than let him cast her off. She is sending a messenger to ask her nephew, the Emperor Charles, if he will help her.

Rosanna was married on New Year's Day in 1528. Then something dreadful happened. The sweating sickness broke out, and the King insisted that the court must leave London. But before they could get away, it had struck Elinor's family.

On June 15th, she wrote:

Papa is ill. When we got up early this morning, he was shivering although his skin was burning hot. He tried to tell us it was nothing serious, but his teeth chattered as he spoke, and it was obvious that he could not manage two days of riding. Mama will stay with him, but I have been ordered to go with the royal party. Diego and Rosanna will be with us as well. I am scribbling this quickly, as we are almost ready to leave. My poor parents – I am frantic with worry about both of them.

I looked up from the book and thought, today is June 16th. Elinor will be remembering what happened eight years ago. Then I read more. Two days later, they had arrived in a place called Tittenhanger, in Hertfordshire, at the house of the Abbot of St Albans.

The King thinks we will be safe from the plague here. My mind is constantly with Mama and Papa, left behind to cope as best they can. A lot of the servants are still there, so at least somebody will fetch water and food for them, but I am full of fear.

Eight days after that, Elinor received the news she had been dreading.

A rider arrived in the middle of last night, to tell the King that Anne Boleyn has the sickness, but then he added the terrible, casual words, "And I regret to say, Michel Valjean has expired. Your good jester, sire."

I burst into tears. The other ladies took me out of the room and tried to comfort me. One of them ran for Rosanna and told her, and we wept together. She has Diego, though, she is not alone with her grief. It is late now, and the candle is almost burned out, but I cannot stop weeping. Papa seems so real in my mind, with his thin, lively face, but I will never see him again, never watch his quick fingers over the lute strings, never laugh at his wit, never marvel at a new story.

My own eyes blurred and it was a minute or two before I could go on reading. Then, on the next page, Elinor mentioned Kitty's father's death.

We hear that Anne Boleyn's attack was only a slight one, though her sister's husband, William Carey, died of the sickness. Anne had the best of attention. Henry's own doctor was out tending the sick, but he sent Dr Butts to her at once. This morning, he dispatched a rider with a haunch of venison to assist her recovery.

We are packing to go back to London, but it will be a sad return.

17th June 1536

Eva was simmering with anger after the ladies had gone. "They don't understand," she said. "Mary will never give up her true faith. But how can they blame her for making this offer to her father? He sent her away to live in penury and never answered her letters – how much more was she supposed to endure?"

We talked about the piece in the Bible that says a man may not marry his brother's widow. Elinor said that the King's entire hope of divorcing Catherine rested on those words. But the Catholic Church, of course, does not allow divorce, so Henry was locked in a struggle to break free of its authority. Elinor said, "Everyone called it 'The King's Great Matter'. It went on and on."

Eva was still angry. "He had no right," she said. "God forgive me for saying this, but our king is a philanderer. Everyone knows it. He was bedding Mary Boleyn for a long time – your friend's mother, Bee, and really quite an unprincipled young lady, I'm afraid. There are some who say that your friend Kitty may be the King's daughter. Had she been a boy, like the son he admits to, King Henry might have been pleased, but there is no value in owning to an illegitimate daughter."

I said I never knew the King had a son. Elinor said, "Oh, yes. His name is Henry Fitzroy, which means "the king's boy". His mother is a woman called Bessie Blount."

Eva went on. "So he had been unfaithful, but he expected the Church to grant him a divorce from his lawful wife, mother of his daughter, as though *she* had given offence? I cannot forgive him."

We turned back to the King's Great Matter. I understand it better now. Henry formed the new Church that Papa and I go to. Its head is not the Pope but is, and always will be, the reigning king – or queen – of

England. That is why it is called the Church of England. In other ways, it is not so very different from the old Church. A form of the Mass is still said, and Communion taken. But the King hates the decoration and gilding and stained glass that made the old churches beautiful. He is sending his soldiers out to destroy all such opulence. The new churches have to be plain and severe.

I cannot stop reading – each page of this diary is a fascination. I think Catherine of Aragon sounds wonderful. In October she took the trouble to comfort Elinor, who was still grieving for her adored father.

Queen Catherine spoke to me kindly today. "Your father would not want to see you so sad, Elinor," she said. My eyes filled with tears again, but she told me something I had never thought of. "Every woman carries grief," she said. "It is like a fire, painful at first. But when you become used to it, you will find it a source of strength." I thought of how much grief she has known in her life and made her a deep curtsey. "God go with you," she said, and blessed me.

And later, I found this.

I almost regret the years spent in learning my music and dancing, and the gaiety of heart that led me to laugh and make up stories. Look where it has led me! But I seem to hear Papa assuring me that music lasts longer than people do. He is right, of course. I will take up my lute and play for my own comfort, for there is no other.

A few pages further on, Elinor came here, to Greenwich Palace, in the service of Anne Boleyn. Catherine was here, too, as she was still the rightful queen, but Elinor noted that she was housed in a different part of the palace *…with Mama and Rosanna, thank goodness.* Then she added, *My spirit of goodwill is sadly lacking.*

18th June 1536

Kitty is coming to lessons with Mr Thornton again. This morning the servant came to fetch her at the proper time, but Agnes, not unusually, was late. I was glad because there was something I wanted to ask my tutor. He is thin and old, with a skinny neck like a plucked chicken, but very kind. I think he gets as bored with French verbs and Latin declensions as I do, because he never minds if I ask him questions about something else.

I know I must not tell him about Elinor's diary, but I had read something there that filled me with questions. While picking up Anne's discarded clothes, Elinor had found a book by a man called William Tyndale. It was called *The Obedience of a Christian Man, and How Kings Ought to Govern.* She had dipped into it and found that Mr Tyndale had translated the Bible into English. It quite scared her, because ordinary people are not allowed to read the Bible. In the Catholic religion it is only the priests who can tell them what its ancient language says. So Elinor returned it to the shelf and told nobody she had seen it. She wrote:

Latin has always been the language of religion. What will happen to the authority of the Church if people start to take the mysteries of God into their own hands?

That same question has been troubling me ever since, because English is used in our church services. I do not know if God likes that.

I asked, "Is the Church my father and I go to the true Church?"

Mr Thornton frowned a little. "It depends on what you believe," he said. "Why do you ask, Beatrice?"

"Ours is the King's religion," I said. "But is that the one God approves of?"

He looked even more worried. "Who can know what God approves of? It is not for us to guess."

I asked why he did not come to our church.

"Beatrice, this is a dangerous thing to speak about," he said. "You are right, I am of the old Church, but there is something you need to understand. Those who remain Roman Catholics have become the King's enemy, though we did not wish it. I serve the King as a faithful subject and respect him as my sovereign – but he sees all those who do not accept his new Church as members of a body that is opposed to him. So those of us who keep the old faith have to be very careful."

I told him that I had heard that the Bible had been translated into English, and he nodded.

"It has indeed," he said. "The King gave orders that it shall be placed in every church in the country. And yet, only fifteen years ago, he wrote a book attacking the views of Martin Luther. The Pope was so pleased that he gave King Henry the title of Defender of the Faith. It will be used by all the rulers who come after him."

I said I did not understand what Martin Luther stood for.

"He began this movement against the old Roman Catholic Church," Mr Thornton said. "That is why his followers are called Protestants, because they protested against the Pope's authority."

"So is the King a Protestant now?"

Mr Thornton shook his head. "He still calls himself a Catholic. He hears the Mass and takes Communion. But he, not the Pope, is the head of this Catholic Church. As a result, he has two sets of enemies, both the Roman Catholics and the extreme Protestants who do not want either the King or the Pope at the head of their Church."

I asked why the King is sending out his soldiers to smash the statues in the old churches and destroy their pictures and their lovely stained glass windows.

Mr Thornton sighed. "Because these things have always been part of the old Catholic way of worship. Artists and sculptors and musicians have made beautiful things for the glory of God. But because beauty celebrates the old beliefs, beauty now is described as heretical. So it has to go."

I heard Agnes at the door, explaining to the servant how rushed

31

off her feet she had been, and Mr Thornton said quietly, "I hope this conversation is entirely between ourselves, Beatrice. As you may realize, answering your question with honesty puts me at some risk. I hope I can trust you not to talk about my views to anyone else."

I gave him my promise.

23rd June 1536

Mr Thornton told me today that he is leaving soon on a long journey. He is not sure when he will be back. I asked where he was going, but he would not tell me.

"In case we do not meet again, Beatrice, I would like to give you a small gift," he said. "You mentioned that your friend Eva De Puebla is teaching you Spanish. This may help." He gave me a book that has tables of all the Spanish verbs, and the pages to explain the grammar. He has written on its flyleaf: *For Beatrice Townhill, a good pupil. Remember me. Benedict Thornton.*

3rd July 1536

Now that Mr Thornton has gone, Kitty and I have no lessons. Papa does not seem greatly concerned. Agnes said, "If you'd been a boy, Young Miss, it would have been different." She is right. My father does not have much use for a girl, even though I am as good on a horse as any man.

Kitty is quite pleased that lessons have stopped, as she prefers to make herself useful at court. She says that will be her future, so there is no point in bothering too much about education. Her mother thinks she should continue to learn, so it may be that she is casting around for a new tutor, but there is no news of that yet. I miss Mr Thornton. I pray that he will be safe, for I do not know what journey he is on or how it will end.

4th July 1536

Eva is teaching me Spanish, and I am slowly starting to translate her diary. It is slow work, except for moments when I come to an easy bit, but coming to understand the words is so rewarding. Mr Thornton's book is a great help.

Eva didn't like this country when she first arrived. On the long journey from Plymouth to London after their stormy sea voyage, she wrote:

These English are a mystery to me. How do they endure the cold? It is dirty, too. The floors are strewn with rushes, fresh ones being scattered over the filth and dropped food of the previous day ...

She had no great opinion of English courtiers cither.

They behave, it seems to me, very much as the dogs do which skulk round the tables and snatch at thrown scraps of meat.

Eva's Uncle Rod, the Spanish Ambassador, shared her secret contempt for the English. According to her, he called the Tudors "*an upstart lot with only a very slender claim to being royal at all.*" He told her:

King Henry's mother, Lady Margaret Beaufort, is of royal stock, but on his father's side he comes of unruly Welsh landowners with a taste for fighting and good living. The crown was put on his head in all the blood and confusion of a battle fought at Bosworth Field, where it had rolled from the head of the dead Richard III.

I know about that. King Richard was the last Plantagenet king.

That first winter must have been terrible for Eva. She wrote:

I am sick with longing for Spain, where the sun shines even in these short days, and at night there is a blaze of stars. Here there is nothing but clouds and greyness and mud and the smell of wet stone.

And yet she found something to admire as well:

How strange the English are. In some ways they seem brutish and crude, full of uncouth vulgarity, and yet one hears music sung and played everywhere, and their clothes and linens are a glory of fine, colourful work. They seem to take a lusty joy in beauty of all kinds, and for this one can forgive them much.

Prince Arthur died on April 3rd 1502, just as spring was coming. Catherine had only been married to him for five months, and now she was a widow, at sixteen years old. Nobody cared. She had no money to maintain her household, and as the months went by, they became desperately poor and shabby. At the beginning of August, Eva wrote that they were all penniless:

Catherine as well. Fewer candles burn in the big iron holders, and the cooks present us with thin soup and tough meat, and their faces are full of contempt. Uncle Rod warns me to be careful what I say.

8th July 1536

I grab every moment I can to read. Eva's diary gets more and more fascinating. For the next two years, Catherine and her little handful of Spanish servants struggled on in poverty. Then Queen Elizabeth, our Henry's mother, died in childbirth. Her baby girl also died. *Rain falls like tears,* Eva wrote, for she had loved and admired the Queen. *Pluvia cae como lágrimas.* I could already guess what that meant. *Pluvia* is Latin for *rain,* and *lachrimae* means *tears* – though the spelling varies.

A few months later, a treaty of marriage between Henry and Catherine was signed. But it meant very little. The King gave Catherine a small grant of money each month to relieve the poverty of her little household, but the waiting went on and on. All else apart, young Henry – known as Harry – was still barely twelve years old.

On December 12th, 1504, a further blow fell. News came from Spain that Catherine's mother had died.

We have just heard that Queen Isabella died two weeks ago, on November 26th. Catherine is huddled in her bed, weeping, and the courtiers stand in hushed groups, talking in low voices about what is to happen now. My uncle has gone to Windsor, to consult with the King.

Without her powerful and adored mother to back her up from Spain, Catherine's hopes of marrying Henry must surely fail. And sure enough, here it is, on June 27th 1505.

Our fears were well founded. Prince Harry has backed out of the marriage agreement, though rumour has it that he looks guilty and wretched, and he was talked into it by the King and his close adviser, a man called Thomas Wolsey. The excuse is that Harry was under legal age when he made the agreement, so it is not binding, but it's quite obvious that his father has decided to seek a better match for his son and heir than Catherine.

Harry will be fourteen tomorrow. In law he will be a man; and he looks a man, taller than most even now, and broad and strong. I had let myself dream that Catherine would marry him on this day, but all those hopes are ruined now. Harry himself has probably had no say in it. For the last year or more, his father has kept him tightly secluded, shut in a small room beyond the King's own chamber, and all the reports we have of the boy say he looks sulky and resentful, far from his old gaiety.

Then it goes on:

Catherine has said nothing about the new announcement. Her face is pale, but her mouth is firmly set and her fierce look deters anyone from mentioning it. This evening, as we struggled to find something

edible on a couple of herrings that had been far too long out of the
sea, she said to me quietly, "Harry and I will be married, Eva. But
first the old king will have to die." I suppose the words shocked me,
for she smiled as she broke off a piece of bread and glanced round
to make sure nobody else had heard. "Time is on my side," she said.
"You'll see."

After his wife's death, Henry's father thought he might marry Catherine himself. But Catherine was having nothing to do with that. She told Eva:

I will be queen one day, but not through marrying Henry. He is 46
and I am seventeen. With his bad chest and his gout, he might die
within a couple of years, and then where would I be? A dowager
whom nobody wants. Even if I bore his child, it would not be heir
to the throne, for that position is Harry's. So I must be Harry's wife,
not his father's.

How determined she was! I admire her so much.

23rd July 1536

There is sad news today. Henry Fitzroy, the King's illegitimate son, is dead. He was only seventeen. He had consumption, which is a disease of the lungs. Some say it's the same illness that killed Prince Arthur and murmur that the royal family may be prone to it.

Will says the King has shut himself away and will speak to nobody. All his plans are in ruins. He had begun an Act of Parliament that would name his son by Bessie Blount as his heir instead of little Elizabeth, Anne Boleyn's daughter. At one point he had even planned to marry young Fitzroy to his older daughter, the lady Mary, so as to give him royal status, although they were half-brother and half-sister. That wouldn't have happened, because the King stopped recognizing the lady Mary as an heir to the throne after he divorced her mother, Catherine. None of it matters now, but it leaves King Henry even more desperate to produce a son.

Everyone keeps a watchful eye on Jane Seymour, his present queen, for any sign that she is pregnant. Will said, "If a royal seed does become implanted, those hawk-eyed ladies at the court will know it before the Queen does."

26th July 1536

It was a pathetic little funeral for Henry Fitzroy. Will says the Duke of Norfolk gave orders that his body should be wrapped in lead and taken for burial in a closed carriage, but Fitzroy's servants didn't bother with that. They loaded the dead boy into a cart filled with straw, and only two mourners followed it to Framlingham Church in Suffolk. How strange it is that the King sent nobody to represent him, though he seems to have cared so much for his only son. I suppose he saw no point. Young Fitzroy is dead, and all useful plans for him have died as well.

Agnes passed on a dreadful bit of gossip about the King's "bastard son" as she calls him. She says she heard that Anne Boleyn poisoned him. I said that was ridiculous. Anne Boleyn has been dead for more than a year – how could she have poisoned him?

"She was putting something in his food that stayed in his stomach and killed him in its own time," Agnes said darkly.

When I was reading Elinor's diary later, I thought of that again when I found an entry about John Fisher, the Bishop of Rochester, whom the King hated because he had said the divorce from Catherine of Aragon was illegal.

I did not realize just what danger John Fisher was in. Yesterday, everyone in his household collapsed at the table in terrible pain after eating the soup. Several of them are dead. Fisher himself had taken only a spoonful or two, but he was seized with agonizing stomach cramps. He is still very ill, as are the other survivors. The cook, Richard Rouse, has been arrested and accused of putting a poisonous white powder into the soup, but nobody believes the man did this of his own accord, if he did it at all. Quite clearly, someone was bribed. And where did the poison come from? I hardly dare write the name. It is whispered that the powder was supplied by Lord Wiltshire. And he, of course, is Anne Boleyn's father.

We dare not guess whether the King was party to the plot to poison Fisher. He is determined to show his disapproval, so he has ordered a new punishment for poisoners. They are to be boiled alive. The unfortunate cook, Richard Rouse, is to suffer this terrible death.

A few months later, Elinor wrote:

Tom overheard an alarming rumour today while he was shoeing the Duke of Suffolk's horse. (It is strange how the nobility will talk to each other in front of some menial person, as though they were not being heard and understood.) Anne has warned John Fisher not to attend the next session of Parliament, lest he should suffer a repeat of the stomach pains that almost killed him in February.

Fisher refuses to support the King in his new control of the Church, and Thomas More agrees with him. More is one of Henry's oldest friends, but I wonder if even he is safe.

I can see why rumours still spread.

29th July 1536

I begin to feel as if I am living in a dream, with half my mind back in the days that connect with my own so strongly, and half in the present.

Yesterday Papa let me join a hunt. My pony, Russet, loved it. His ears pricked up when he heard the horns blowing and he was shivering with excitement. I rode faster than I have ever done before, and had to duck sometimes when Russet charged through overhanging trees. Strangely, when the first stag went down from a well-aimed arrow, I did not flinch from looking as the men loaded it across the strong carrier horse to bring it home. And yet, when it was all over and Agnes brought me a bowl of warm water to clean my scratched and dirty face, the hunt was left behind in some other part of my mind. I was longing to find out what happened to Eva and Catherine. So after supper I said I was tired from the hunt, and retired to bed early – and went on reading.

To my great relief, everything changed when the old king died. It was

1509, and Prince Harry was eighteen years old. Eva was mending an old and much-worn dress when Catherine burst into the room and seized her hands, whirling her into a dance:

"Eva! Do you know what the King's last words were? He said Harry and I must wed! We must marry before the coronation, so the people will have a new king and his queen. I have won, Eva! I've won, I've won!"

The old king's funeral took place, five black horses drawing his carriage through black-shrouded streets. And then, on June 24th 1509, after a private marriage ceremony here at Greenwich, Henry and Catherine were crowned as England's new king and queen. The people in the streets, Eva says:

…roared their approval of her all the way to Westminster Abbey. We, her ladies, rode beside her on white horses, and our robes of blue velvet, edged with crimson, set off her silken whiteness perfectly. The streets were hung with scarlet cloth, thousands of yards of it, and the entire court was dressed in scarlet robes, richly furred.

Three days later, Eva was still full of joy:

The feasting goes on and on, in joyous celebration – and there is a sense of relief, too, as though we have all escaped from a crabbed hand that kept us from happiness. There is a new gaiety about the jousting and carnival, a new sense of youth and high spirits. Energy seems to radiate from Henry, who is free at last from that stuffy room with no door except the one into his father's chamber. He is laughing and tireless, charging across the tiltyard on the great stallion he rides, banqueting and dancing – but all the time his eyes seek Catherine's in an intimacy that almost makes me blush, and he constantly returns to her side to run his hand down her back and touch his lips to hers. She is his first love, and he cannot get enough of her.

Catherine was 24, six years older than her young husband. She knew far more about endurance and tenacity than he did, but she was too happy to think she would ever need these qualities.

1st September 1536

I have been so busy learning Spanish and reading Eva and Elinor's diaries that my own diary has been sadly neglected. My private game of avoiding Agnes gets better all the time, because she plays it too, though she does not know it. She avoids me so as to see more of Walter Pearson, and that suits me perfectly. I have been helping Elinor to pick fruit and make jam, and slice beans to pack in jars of salt for the winter. Her waist is becoming thicker now with her coming baby, and I want to help her as much as I can.

There is still no sign of a royal child. I privately wonder how Jane Seymour can bear going to bed with the King. The huge bulk of him seems so revolting, and the ulcer on his leg that constantly seeps through its dressing smells bad. Elinor says that will not deter Jane Seymour. She has known her for a long time, as they were both Maids of Honour to Catherine of Aragon, together with Anne Boleyn.

"I've always thought that Jane is like a sheep," she said. "Meek to look at, but knows exactly what it wants. That pale face and the neat little mouth, very sheep-like. And the not-so-stupid eyes, working out how to get into the next field where the grass is greener."

I thought back to my birthday visit with Papa and said Queen Jane seemed a kind lady, but Elinor said, "She has what she wants now. She can afford to be kind."

Eva said, "The man we should beware of is her brother, Edward Seymour. And Thomas Cromwell, with all his scheming and planning. He is a truly bad shepherd."

8th September 1536

Plague has broken out in London. Greenwich is quite a long way from the city, so I hardly understand the panic, but the King has given orders that the royal household must move at once to Hampton Court. Elinor says he has always been terrified of disease. And he will be anxious that Jane Seymour runs no risk of illness, for she must remain healthy if she is to produce the son he wants so much.

20th October 1536

Will has gone to Hampton Court, and so has my father, together with the hunting dogs, caged in several big carts, and most of the horses. I live in the house with Agnes and the servants and my mother upstairs in her room, and it all seems very quiet. But, thank goodness, there is still Elinor.

A rider from Hampton Court sometimes comes with messages for the servants who remained at Greenwich, and if there is anything for

Elinor he brings it across the fields to her house. Today he came with some letters, and told us that a rebellion has broken out. People in the town of Louth, in Lincolnshire, are so upset about the destruction of statues and pictures and old stained glass in their churches that a whole army of them are marching south. They want to see the King and persuade him to heal his rift with the Church of Rome. The man said, "His Majesty threatens to lead an army north to wipe out the protest."

Neither Elinor nor Eva made any comment, but when the messenger had gone Eva said, "The King will not want to do that. With his leg the way it is, he's in no state for days of hard riding and nights in some muddy field."

Elinor agreed. "He will find some other way to deal with this," she said.

She and Eva looked at each other and nodded. And neither of them smiled.

27th October 1536

I am almost at the end of Elinor's diary. She only finished it earlier this year, when she left the court and came to live in the cottage after Anne Boleyn's execution. Catherine of Aragon was alive until last January. It's all much more recent than I'd imagined. Elinor noted the King's interest in Jane Seymour just a year ago, on October 29th, yet she is now the Queen of England. I turn back to Elinor's first mention of her.

The King has fallen in love with yet another serving lady. This time it is Jane Seymour, who was in Catherine's service with me. She left when the Queen was sent away to The More. I remember her telling me at the time that she was fond of Catherine, but she thought it more sensible to stay in the King's court. Jane has always been very sensible. She is rather plain and has no sparkle at all, which is probably why Henry likes her. She is as different from Anne as any woman could be.

We stayed at Wulfhall during the summer travels, the house of Sir John Seymour, Jane's father. He does not sparkle, either. He is sheriff of Wiltshire, Dorset and Somerset and owns a lot of land, but he is no aristocrat, merely a wealthy farmer. He was greatly excited to have the King of England under his roof, and could not do enough to make us all comfortable...

Since our return, the King has been paying Jane Seymour a lot of attention, and most people assume she will soon become his new mistress. I am not so sure. Jane lowers her eyes modestly at Henry's advances. She seems quite incapable of flirting, and just looks very sensible and very good. This may be due to the advice of her brothers, Thomas and Edward, who are both at court. They know perfectly well that Anne Boleyn became queen by remaining virtuous, and clearly hope their sister can do the same thing. I groan at the thought. Do we have to go through another tedious and troublesome royal divorce? Life at this court is constantly packed with drama, and there are times when I long for simple peace.

Poor Elinor! She had come to a kind of liking for Anne Boleyn, and it must have been dreadful to see the Queen being arrested and taken away in hysterical tears to the Tower while the King pursued his plans to marry Jane. No wonder she longed for "simple peace". In May of this year, six days before Anne went to the block, Elinor wrote:

The King commanded today that Anne's household at Greenwich is to be broken up and dispersed. Those of us who served her are all dismissed.

I do not know what Tom and I will do. Will the King want me to serve Jane Seymour? It is plain that he means to marry her as soon as Anne is out of the way. After little more than a week, he is tired of riding out from Hampton Court to see Jane in the Surrey house. He is removing himself to Whitehall tomorrow, and Jane is to take up residence at a house in the Strand, just a short walk away.

This may be the right time to leave the court and all its intrigues. I suspect that I am pregnant again, and I am in no mood to attend to the whims of yet another royal mistress.

Perhaps I am not by nature a court lady. Papa came from a family of troubadours, travelling from one country to another, with no expectation of becoming rich or powerful. When Mama first knew about Tom, she felt she had to remind me that a blacksmith would not bring me the advantages that would come through marrying an aristocratic husband – but she smiled as she said it, and I knew she was not very serious.

Tom and I share a dream that one day we will leave the King's service, if he will release us, and live in some small place of our own. Perhaps it will never be more than a dream, but we love thinking about it, planning what crops we will grow and where we will keep the pig and the cow, and whether we can afford a horse. The dream may never come true, but at least it makes us happy.

30th October 1536

We hear the rebellion is gathering strength. More people join the long procession in each town and village they come through. They carry flags and a big banner proclaiming it to be the "Pilgrimage of Grace". Eva says they are marching in defence of the true faith, but neither she nor Elinor believe the King will let it go on much longer.

2nd November 1536

A messenger brought Elinor a letter from Will today. Queen Jane has done something very rash. In front of all the courtiers, she fell on her knees before the King and begged him to give up destroying the churches and monasteries. She told him the rebellion might be a punishment from God for attacking His sacred places.

Elinor read Will's words aloud:

Henry was furious. He told Jane to get up and mind her own business. He told her she should remember that the last queen had met her end because she tried to interfere in state affairs. The Queen ran from the room.

Elinor looked up and said, "What a stupid thing to do! Jane knows very well how queens are made, and how easily they can be broken. For all her smug innocence, she played her part in the breaking of Anne Boleyn."

I knew what Elinor meant. When I came back to the house, I turned to the words she had written in March of this year, when Henry had turned Thomas Cromwell out from the rooms next to his own so that Jane could occupy them.

Anne is hysterical with fury. She slapped Jane's face yesterday, not
for the first time. She has the right to chastise her servants, but this
was sheer jealousy. Jane seems unperturbed. This morning, she was
provocatively opening and shutting a locket containing Henry's
miniature, and Anne snatched it from her neck so roughly that she
cut the side of her own hand on its gold chain. I had to bandage
it for her. She was weeping as I did so, and she leaned her head
towards me a little, as if she would have liked an arm round her
shoulders in comfort.

Jane knows very well that any wife of King Henry's is only safe as
long as she produces children and gives him no cause for offence. And
since she is still not pregnant, she is in no position to annoy her royal
husband.

Eva said, "She's right about the rebellion, though. More and more
people are joining it."

William's letter said there are hundreds now in the Pilgrimage of
Grace, and they are getting near to London. They feel passionately that
the King is destroying their religion and their churches, so in the name
of their God, they must protest. Their leader is called Robert Aske.
I keep wondering if Mr Thornton is with them.

10th November 1536

The King has sent the Duke of Norfolk to speak to Robert Aske. Norfolk is to promise the rebels that their demands will be met. Jane Seymour's official coronation ceremony is to be held in York rather than London – not that it's a big concession. William's letter had a funny drawing of the Duke holding out a large, ornate plate to Aske and his followers, with one tiny dumpling on it labelled Wedding. But the rebels are happy to think they have gained a victory. They have gone home, relieved that they will celebrate Christmas in their own houses – hovels though they may be – rather on the roadside in sleet and rain. Will said Queen Jane is as quiet as a mouse now and agrees with every word her husband says. She has obviously learned her lesson.

I can see why the rebels are marching. There are beggars everywhere because the monasteries are being destroyed, one after another. Those great institutions with their houses and chapels, their cloisters and gardens and kitchens, used to provide work and housing for countless people. Now, those people have no living and no roof over their heads.

12th November 1536

I asked Elinor if she knew the Duke of Norfolk, who has gone to speak to the rebels.

"Oh, yes," she said grimly. "Everybody knows the Duke. He's the most calculating man I have ever met. Anne Boleyn was his niece. She never liked him. She said he was treacherous to his fingertips, and she was right." She shook her head. "That terrible day when they arrested her still haunts me. We were watching a tennis match, happy and light-hearted."

"Heavens, yes!" I remembered reading about it in her diary. "Was that the same Duke of Norfolk?"

"The very same," said Elinor.

I re-read that entry again this evening. It comes near the end of the book, written only six months ago. But now it has fresh meaning.

Anne seemed to believe that everything could be explained and smoothed over, and recovered something of her old spirit. We accompanied her to the dining chamber, escorted by the man stationed as a guard, and she set about her food with normal appetite.

She was still at the table when the door was flung open. The Duke of Norfolk came in, together with Cromwell and several other courtiers. Anne rose and asked their business, and her uncle unrolled a parchment he carried. He told her it was a warrant for her arrest. She was to go to the Tower and remain there "to abide during his Highness's pleasure."

I thought it astonishing that Anne remained so calm. Her voice was quite steady as she answered. "If it be His Majesty's pleasure, I am ready to obey," she said. And they took her away. We were not even allowed to pack some clothes for her.

Only ten days later, Elinor was at the Great Hall of the Tower for the Anne's trial. And it was the Duke of Norfolk, the Queen's own uncle, who presided. *He sat on a throne under a grand canopy, for he represented the Crown.*

Anne denied all the charges and protested her innocence, but all 26 of the noblemen found her guilty. Her uncle read out the sentence. True, Elinor's account says his voice cracked at the last moment. *After all, Anne is his sister's child*, she wrote. But he managed to read the official words that followed:

Because thou hast offended our sovereign lord the King's Grace in committing treason against his person, the law of the realm is this: that thou shall be burnt here within the Tower of London on the Green, else to have thy head smitten off, as the King's pleasure shall be further known of the same.

How *could* he? But I see why the King has sent him to deal with the rebels in the North. The Duke of Norfolk is a merciless man, bent on his own advancement, and he will do as King Henry asks him, regardless of what it is. He is also, Eva told me, a formidable soldier. He was a leader of the army that Catherine of Aragon sent to Scotland, to inflict the terrible slaughter at Flodden in which the Scots King James died. A man to be feared.

1st December 1536

A letter from Papa this morning says the court is moving to Windsor, as the plague in London seems to have burned itself out. Then they will be spending Christmas here in Greenwich. That's wonderful news. Christmas just with my parents would not be a great deal of fun. Papa always has to be at court, hunting with the King and dealing with the animals they kill. Then he is expected to be part of the roistering and celebration that goes on afterwards. Although he is not a member of the aristocracy, the King likes him. My uncle and aunt from Norfolk are coming to see my mother, but they are a severe, joyless couple. At Elinor's house there will be lots of laughter, especially when Will is there. A good place to escape to.

Papa has written to confirm that he will be back soon. He says I am to join Kitty at court for lessons with her tutor after Christmas. *"Unfortunately,"* he wrote, *"Mr Thornton seems to have thrown in his lot with this rabble of protesters who are causing so much trouble for the King. I hear there is a warrant out for his arrest."*

God protect my gentle tutor – if indeed there is one true God who remains above all the argument about how He should be worshipped.

21st December 1536

I have been with Kitty to see the small room in Greenwich Palace where we are to study. She has met the new tutor and says he is very strict. I am rather overawed by the thought of going to the Palace every day, but I will enjoy being with Kitty again. She told me all about the lady Mary's visit to court to be reunited with her royal father. She arrived with her ladies, all of them dressed in beautiful gowns, and walked in procession between the courtiers to meet the King and Queen. Mary curtsied twice, Kitty said, then knelt before the King. He gave her his blessing and raised her to her feet, and he and the Queen both kissed her – then she suddenly collapsed in a faint. People fanned her face and loosened her clothes, and she revived after a few minutes. Kitty said it was probably because there was a blazing fire in the room, so it was very hot for her after the bitter cold outside.

This looks like being a terribly hard winter. Elinor has taken to wearing a thick shawl. Her new baby is due in February and she is careful about going out in the snow, for fear of slipping and falling. Tom or Daniel break the ice in the cattle trough twice a day so that the cattle can drink. Most amazing of all, the great river Thames is freezing over.

3rd January 1537

What a Christmas it has been! I was at the court several times with Papa. One day my mother came as well, though it took several servants to help her down the stairs and into the coach. She travelled with her eyes closed, giving little moans of discomfort every time the coach lurched into a rut, and Papa held her hand and kept looking at her anxiously. She is fatter than when I saw her last, with puffy wrists and a double chin, but she managed to curtsey unaided when she was presented to the Queen. Her new gown of silver and pale green was very becoming.

The Thames froze completely solid, and the King and Queen and Lady Mary galloped their horses across the ice from one bank to the other. Little Elizabeth was there too. She is the daughter of Anne Boleyn, and although she is only three years old, I have an uneasy feeling that she knows what happened to her mother. I saw her being carried in from the coach so that her fine shoes would not get wet with the snow, and her quick eyes under a shock of red hair were noticing all that went on around her. She seems a clever little girl, too wise to say much unless asked. Henry has ignored her all this time because of his casting off of her mother, but during these days he seemed amused by her, and played with her a lot. Mary loves her small half-sister, and the two of them seemed to form a friendship at straightaway. Kitty whispered to me, "Isn't it wonderful to see the royal family all together like reasonable people for once!"

Robert Aske, the rebel leader, was at the court as well. He smiled at people nervously and seemed astonished to have been invited. The King has officially pardoned him, but Will shook his head. "Pardoning is not the same as forgiving," he said. "The old devil always has something up his sleeve."

Jane Seymour's father died just before Christmas, at his home in Wulfhall, but nobody seemed much concerned, least of all Jane. They say she had hardly seen her father in recent years. She did not go to the funeral. Her one aim now is to please the King, and she was certainly not going to interrupt his Christmas celebrations for something as trivial as a farewell to her father.

19th January 1537

Kitty was right about the new tutor, Mr Kershaw. He is much stricter than Mr Thornton. I don't mind much, as I like having work to think about, but Kitty finds the lessons boring. She hopes she will marry as soon as she is old enough, and sees no point in learning. I disagree with her about that, though we are good friends in every other way. If my mother had been a woman of learning and shared with me what she knows, my life would have been very different. But then, I would never have met Elinor. It is probably sinful to be discontented with one's life, because we are not given the power to see everything, and we do not know that our imagined changes would really be for the better. They might be infinitely worse.

All the same, I cannot suppress my small wishes and moments of envy. One of these overwhelmed me when I read in Eva's diary that Catherine of Aragon chose Lady Margaret Pole to be tutor to her daughter, Mary. I would love to have a woman as my tutor. Mr Thornton was always kind and wise, but Mr Kershaw is a dry man and I find him hard to like. I don't see why women are so often considered inferior to men in their thinking. They are just as clever, and if they had the good education enjoyed by their brothers, they could take a useful hand in all sorts of things that are barred to them now.

Margaret Pole had been one of Catherine's ladies-in-waiting in what Eva called "that dreadful Ludlow Castle", during the months of Catherine's marriage to Arthur. This evening, I asked Eva what she was like. She seemed surprised that I knew nothing about her and asked, "Didn't you see her when she came to court at Christmas? They say all the people were cheering as her carriage came through the streets. She has always been very popular."

"Oh," I said, "is *that* who it was."

She is clear in my mind – a tall woman with a thin, clever face, wrapped in a cloak against the falling snow as she trod the short distance from the coach to the entrance hall. The lady Mary's face lit up when she saw her, though she was careful to remain in her place beside her royal father until Lady Pole had been officially presented.

Eva said, "She was the lady Mary's godmother as well as tutor to the royal household." Then she sighed. "If things had gone the other way, one of her sons might have been on the throne now."

I was startled by this, so she explained.

"Margaret Pole comes of the Plantagenets – the royal family that had ruled England before the Tudors. But the first Henry, our king's father, arranged that Margaret should marry Sir Richard Pole, who was related to him."

I thought the King must have liked her if he wanted her to be part of his own family – but I had missed the point. Eva said, "Henry knew she had a claim to the throne, and he wanted her under the control of a husband who was a Tudor." Then she went on, "Lady Margaret never had any such ambitions, so he need not have worried. But he is still wary of her."

I didn't see why Henry allowed Lady Margaret Pole to be godmother to his daughter if he felt like that about her, but Eva says that was Catherine of Aragon's doing. Lady Margaret befriended the queen when she first came from Spain, and they'd always been close.

Then Eva sighed. "Poor Lady Margaret," she said. "She had been very happy with her husband, even though he was Henry's choice rather than her own. But he died, and she was left a widow with five children to bring up on her own. It was a terrible time. Her Plantagenet brother, Edward, had been attainted as a traitor and thrown into the Tower."

Eva says "attainted" means that if a man is declared to be a traitor, an Act of Attainder can be passed, without trial. Then he is imprisoned and can be executed and all his worldly goods and titles are confiscated by the King. Edward was a simple boy – not quite all there mentally. So when he was attainted he probably never understood what was happening. He might not even have known that, as a Plantagenet, he was next in line to the throne. He just found himself in prison, accused of treachery. And his sister Margaret was so destitute that she had to send her son Reginald into the care of the Church.

I asked what happened to Edward, and it's a sad story. A slightly crazy man called Perkin Warbeck claimed that he himself had a right to the throne. He was imprisoned of course, but his supporters tried to help both Perkin and Edward to escape. That gave the King the excuse he had been waiting for. He had both of them executed. After that, Catherine of Aragon found out what a dreadful state poor Lady Margaret Pole was in. She persuaded Henry to restore her title and family possessions, but everything has changed now. Catherine is dead, and the King dismissed Margaret Pole from court. This Christmas was the first time she has been invited back – and that was probably through Mary's begging and pleading.

I asked, "Are Lady Margaret's children grown up now?"

Eva nodded. "Long grown up. Margaret's son, Reginald, who was brought up by the Church, is a Cardinal now. But he is exiled in France. He published a book attacking the King's 'illegal' marriage to Anne Boleyn, and sent Henry a copy."

I couldn't believe it. "The King must have been furious," I said.

"Absolutely livid," Eva agreed. "Reginald will never dare to come back to England. And his brothers and friends are in danger, just for being who they are."

I think Reginald was insane to send the King a copy of his book – and, knowing what I do now, I am even more sorry for his mother, Lady Margaret. But she assured the King at the time that she did not agree with what her son had written, so perhaps he knows she means him no harm. She looks such a wise, peaceful lady. I am sure she would never hurt anyone.

17th February 1537

As soon as Christmas was over, Henry's soldiers went on stripping churches of their decoration and smashing their holy figures. More monasteries have been desecrated and destroyed, and the rebels have taken to the streets again, realizing that the King's promises meant nothing. Now that the holiday festivities have been enjoyed, the Duke of Norfolk has set out with a great army to Lincolnshire, with orders from the King to teach the people what it means to disobey their monarch. Norfolk is a Catholic, so you would think that he might have some sympathy for the rebels' distress about the destruction of the lovely old churches. But his religion comes a poor second to his desire to earn the King's approval. He has already hanged a great number of the protesters without trial. There is to be a Grand Assize next month that will try all the rebel leaders for the crime of treason. Robert Aske has gone into hiding.

18th February 1537

At last, the news everyone has been waiting for! Queen Jane is pregnant. It seems she conceived during the Christmas weeks. The King is to take her on progress through Kent, to revel in the congratulations of the people.

19th February 1537

We had hardly heard the Queen's good news when Elinor's baby was born – a little girl. She is to be called Isabella, after Catherine of Aragon's mother. Will calls her Bella, and although Elinor protested a bit, the name seems to have stuck.

I told Papa the news because I was so thrilled. He frowned. "Elinor?" he said. "Who do you mean?"

"Mrs Valjean. She lives in the cottage past the two meadows."

"Used to be one of Anne Boleyn's ladies?"

"Yes." I wished I had not mentioned it.

"She left the court, didn't she. Settled for being a farrier's wife. Why have you been seeing her? I don't want you mixing with the tenants."

I said I didn't "see her", I just happened on her sometimes. I felt disloyal, but I do not want him to forbid me to go to Elinor's house.

13th March 1537

The Assize has condemned 36 men to death. John Constable, one of the leaders, was hanged alive in chains over the gates of Hull. If they find Robert Aske he will suffer the same penalty. It disgusts me to think of him being invited here as the King's guest while such a horrible end was planned for him.

This icy winter has gone on and on. I have chilblains on my toes and fingers. I am weary of the whiteness everywhere, and long to see green grass. Thank goodness it is starting to thaw now.

Henry has taken Jane Seymour to Canterbury to make offerings at the shrine of Thomas Becket in the cathedral where that saint was murdered. How strange it is that the King goes to this holy place to pray for his unborn son while his men are destroying such shrines up and down the country. I keep thinking of Mr Thornton. I do hope he has found a safe place of refuge.

4th April 1537

The Queen's pregnancy has been officially announced, though it has been gossiped about for weeks. The Privy Council has ordered a Te Deum to be sung in every church in the country. Henry is in high spirits and Papa is constantly busy organizing hunts for him and his gentlemen. One bird they cannot bring back for the pot is the little creeping quail as it does not live in this country. Henry has sent to Lady Lisle in Calais for a supply, because Jane has a great craving for them. He will do anything for her, to ensure that the child she carries is safe and well.

There is much rivalry among the court ladies over who will be selected as Jane Seymour's chief lady-in-waiting. Apart from her sister Margaret, who is married to Thomas Cromwell's son, Gregory, the Queen has few people close to her, though a strong friendship has sprung up between her and the lady Mary. Kitty would love to be chosen, but she knows she is too young for such a trusted position – and besides, her mother is the sister of the executed queen, Anne Boleyn, which probably puts her out of the running.

Lady Lisle very much wants to establish one of her daughters in the English court, so she is doing anything she can to gain the King's favour.

It is she who is sending the supply of quails, and the service seems to be appreciated, for both of her girls are coming over from Calais to be inspected. They must bring clothes made of satin and damask, Kitty says, and applicants have to be "sober, sad, wise and discreet, lowly above all things, obedient…" I forget the rest of it, but the Queen seems to be very fussy.

14th May 1537

These spring days are very warm, and it is hard to concentrate on Latin verbs and declensions in the small, stuffy room. Mr Kershaw has a droning, nasal voice that makes me want to go to sleep. Kitty mopes and sighs, and quite often pleads a headache and goes out. I never have the courage to do that, so I struggle on with a story about Hannibal, who took three elephants across the Alps in the Punic Wars. *Trans Alpos tres elephantes duxit.* I have never seen an elephant, but some of the old pictures show a huge animal with a long nose that it can use to pick things up.

Things are very happy in Elinor's house. Bella is a joy. She is growing so fast – bigger every time I see her. She knows me now, and greets me with a beaming smile. We take her outside in her Moses basket while we sow peas and beans. We have set dishes of ale at the ends of the rows so that the slugs will die drunk there instead of attacking the young growth.

14th June 1537

I am eleven years old now. I did not go to the palace this year because the royal household is away at Hampton Court. Papa is with them, but he sent me a peacock and hen. They are beautiful birds, especially the male, who fans out his great tail into a wonderful display of blue and turquoise, but they screech like angry cats. My mother complains that she cannot sleep for their noise. When Papa comes back, I expect she will tell him to pen them somewhere at a distance from the house, but until that happens, I like watching them step about on the grass and the stone walls.

Agnes is married to her drover now. She is still employed to look after me, but in Papa's absence, she spends very little time here. I do not mind. It gives me more time to be with Elinor and little Bella.

16th July 1537

Mr Thornton is dead. It happened two weeks ago but I only heard this morning. Whenever I think of it, I start weeping again. I do not know what happened, only that the King's soldiers found them – he and Robert Aske in the same house – and arrested them, but not without a struggle in which Mr Thornton was killed. I thank God he died that way – quickly. It was worse for poor Robert Aske. He was taken to Hull and suffered the same dreadful fate as the men who were condemned six months ago. His shattered body still hangs in chains above London Bridge, as a warning to anyone else who thinks of opposing the King. God rest Mr Thornton's soul. He was a kind man and did what he thought was right.

21st August 1537

A letter from Kitty says the Queen has chosen Lady Lisle's elder daughter, Anne Basset, to be her companion during the time ahead when the royal baby will be born. But Jane Seymour did not like the French hood Anne was wearing, and said her undergarments of linen were far too coarse. She told her to provide herself with new ones made of fine lawn. She even said the girdle Anne was wearing had far too few pearls stitched to it, and told her that if she could not appear properly dressed, she would not be allowed to attend the royal christening. It sounds as if the Queen is getting very bossy and unreasonable – but Kitty says Jane Seymour is terrified of giving birth. She especially fears the childbed fever that kills so many woman, so she is dreading the time that is to come. Perhaps that is why she is so snappy and particular. I will pray for her.

4th September 1537

Plague is raging in London again, and a new letter from Kitty says Queen Jane is in a panic in case anyone coming from the city may bring the infection. It sounds as if the King is even more afraid, for at first rumour of the plague he at once removed himself to Esher, together with any members of the household who will not be needed at the time when Jane has her baby. Papa is with them, as the King spends his days hunting. He sends Jane the kill to add to her favourite quails. Henry said before he left that he would not be more than 60 miles away, should the birth begin. But 60 miles is two days' riding, even on a fast horse. Perhaps the King hopes to be in the quiet green of the forest when news of his newborn child reaches him.

1st October 1537

Elinor is worried about the Queen, who has not gone into labour yet. She says that if the child was conceived at Christmas, it should have been born by now. If the baby grows too big in the womb, Jane may have a hard time delivering it.

8th October 1537

The royal child has still not been born. Other babies have arrived with no trouble. We hear news that Frances Brandon, the King's niece, has given birth to a daughter. She is called Jane, after the Queen. Her full name will be Lady Jane Grey, which has a nice ring to it. And the Duchess of Suffolk has produced a healthy son. Why has the Queen not given birth? Kitty was saying a month ago that Jane Seymour could not unlace her dress any further over her great belly. Four weeks further on, I cannot imagine what a size she must be.

12th October 1537

At last! The royal baby is here – and, praise God, it is a boy! King Henry has his longed-for son, and there is great rejoicing. Bonfires have been lit in the streets, and the cannon at the Tower blazed round after round into the sky in celebration. People are hanging garlands at their doors, and Will in the kitchens at Hampton Court will be working non-stop to cater for the feasting and celebration.

Poor Queen Jane was in labour for three days and nights. Her doctors and attendants were in despair. The King rode home, confident that his son or daughter would be placed in his arms, only to find his wife still in agony and getting more exhausted with every minute. The doctors drew him aside to murmur that it seemed impossible for her to deliver the child in the normal way. They suggested that they might have to cut the baby from her, if it was to have any chance of surviving, though this terrible operation would cost the Queen's life. Henry had no doubt of which to choose. He said they must save his son. I cannot imagine that Queen Jane heard this, but as though aware of the dreadful threat, she gathered her failing strength for another desperate struggle and the baby at last burst out of her. They say Jane is able to sit up in bed now and has even been able to write a letter, so it seems she is recovering from the ordeal. The royal boy is to be called Edward.

25th October 1537

I can hardly bear to write this.

After her apparent good health following the birth, Queen Jane has died. Will rode from Hampton Court yesterday to tell Elinor. After the baby's christening last Monday, the Queen became ill with the childbed fever she had feared so much. There was nothing the doctors could do to save her. The King himself, for all his power, could only watch helplessly as her life ebbed away.

Jane's body is to be embalmed, for a queen is never buried straight away as common people are. The funeral will be a grand one, and such things take time to organize.

12th November 1537

Queen Jane has been laid to rest in Windsor Castle. They took her body back in grand procession to the place where she had lived as the King's wife for the two years of their marriage. Will was there in the crowd. He said Lady Mary was the chief mourner, riding a black horse draped in black velvet, and her face was wretched with grief. It must be so sad for her to lose her new friend so soon. Jane had been 29 years old, so that number of mourners followed her, in black habits, but wearing white headdresses to signify that she had died in childbirth. Then came 200 poor men, bearing lighted torches.

Jane Seymour was a kind lady, and very sensible, though she became strict and fussy in the second year of her short reign. She might have borne many more children for the King, and everything would have settled down. As it is, a single son will not be enough, for children's lives are never completely certain. It is God's will whether they go on living or not. So I suppose the search for a wife will have to start all over again.

25th November 1537

Yes, the search has started. Thomas Cromwell is urging King Henry to approach the French king, Francis, who has daughters of marriageable age. Kitty was telling me about it while we waited for Mr Kershaw to arrive in the small classroom. She said the French ambassador, Monsieur Castillon, suggested some possible brides. "And guess what?" she cried. "Henry asked if he could see them first and get to know them before making a decision. The ambassador was outraged." Kitty put on a French accent to imitate him. "Pair'aps, Sire, you like to try zem, one after ze ozzair, and keep ze one you find ze most agréable?" We collapsed in fits of giggles. Then Mr Kershaw came in and scolded us. Somehow we got through the lesson, but as soon as we had curtsied to our tutor and the door was safely shut, Kitty went on. "And Francis says the King actually *blushed*!"

28th November 1537

Whether King Henry blushed or not, he still wants to view the French princesses. He has met with Castillon again, and this time he suggested that the young women should be brought to Calais, where he would come and inspect them. Castillon told the French king, and he was not pleased either. He said with contempt that the English treat their women like horses. "Collect a number and trot them out to take which goes best!" So that has done Henry no good.

Papa is back here now. The court has moved to Whitehall, but King Henry is still in mourning for Jane, and hunting would be unseemly. Papa knew about the plan to hold a royal inspection of princesses, of course. I think he was a little shocked when I mentioned it, but then he looked at me thoughtfully and said, "I suppose you are old enough to hear of such things, Beatrice. How time flies." He must have decided I really am old enough, because he laughed and added, "So the French fillies are out of the race. Maybe he'll fancy a rank outsider."

16th December 1537

The Duke of Cleves has a daughter the English king might consider. I don't know if Papa would consider her a "rank outsider" but John Hutton, the English envoy in Brussels, says she has neither looks nor personality. He thinks Christina of Denmark, now the Duchess of Milan, might be a better choice. She has just arrived in Brussels from Italy, wearing black because her elderly husband died two weeks ago. She is only sixteen, and Hutton says she is very beautiful. Elinor's friends from court are full of gossip about her.

King Henry does not seem much interested in Christina, despite her beauty. He told Papa, "I am big in person, and have need of a big wife." And it is true, he is very fat now, though he disguises it by wearing jackets with padded shoulders that make him look powerful rather than corpulent. Perhaps he is afraid that a slender girl of sixteen might be scared to go to bed with him in case she should be crushed under his weight.

Papa tells me far more now than he used to. He says the King has heard of a Frenchwoman, Mary of Guise, whose husband died in June of this year. So he is back to the first idea of a connection with France. Cromwell is much in favour of it, because he thinks England needs a strong alliance with that country. Mary of Guise is 22 years old and not so slender as Christina. She is reported to be strongly built and very buxom. Her elderly husband married her when she was fourteen, and she bore him two sons. "Just what Henry needs," Papa said. "Not so much a filly as a brood mare." He says the King intends to ask Mary of Guise for her hand in marriage as soon as Christmas is over.

20th January 1538

Christmas this year was so quiet that it was hardly a celebration at all. The court is still in mourning for Queen Jane, so there were no great festivities. We stayed at home. My mother, with much help from the servants, was assisted down the stairs to join Papa and me in the dining room for Christmas dinner. She ate more than I thought she would, though often placing her hand on her heart and saying that such excess was too much for someone in her frail state of health. I did not manage to join Elinor and her family until the next day, but then we had a merry time with Will and Daniel and the children. Little Bella was immensely excited by it all. Eva gave her a silver rattle with dried peas inside it, and she keeps inspecting it and shaking it.

3rd February 1538

Mary of Guise has very firmly refused the King's proposal of marriage. Either the ambassadors had been scuttling around to come up with someone else or Mary had ideas of her own – either way, she told King Henry she is going to marry James V of Scotland in May of this year.

Will brought this news, and he was grinning all over his face. "Henry will be as sick as a dog with distemper," he said. I didn't see why, but Elinor says James is Henry's nephew. He's the son of Henry's sister, who married the Scottish king, James IV. That earlier James was the king whose gashed and bloodied coat Catherine had sent to Henry after the massacre at Culloden. His son, not surprisingly, has grown up with little love for the English, or for his Uncle Henry. Relationships with Scotland have become steadily worse during his rule – and now he has stolen Henry's hoped-for bride from under his nose. I can see why Will was laughing.

20th February 1538

The King's temper has not been good since his offer of marriage was rejected. Sleet and snow have prevented him from hunting, so he has nothing to do but eat and drink and grumble or sit slumped in miserable silence, all the while growing fatter and more unhealthy. His hair is thinning, Will says, and the abscess on his leg causes him constant pain. What's more, he must know that it won't be easy to find a girl who is willing to marry him. Mary of Guise will not be the only one who knows that Henry divorced his first wife and sent the second to the block. The parents of young, titled girls will think twice before considering a proposal from the King of England.

15th March 1538

It is only now, with the daffodils blooming and the trees coming into bud, that this cold and gloomy winter is at last ending. The baby Prince Edward thrives, God be thanked, despite his mother's death. His wet nurse, Mother Jack, is feeding him well. The few people who have seen him say he is a bonny child, very contented and happy, but he is shut away from the public gaze because the King is terrified that he may pick up some illness. At less than six months old, he has been given his own establishment at a manor house in a place called Havering, in Essex. King Henry goes there often to see his baby son and play with him.

The lady Mary went back to Hunsdon this winter. She took her half-sister, Elizabeth, with her because the little girl has lost the nurse who has always looked after her. Lady Bryan has cared for Elizabeth since she was born, but the King put her in charge of baby Edward and commanded her to move to Havering. He does not seem to care that there is nobody to look after Elizabeth. It is easy to see which of the three royal children is his favourite.

23rd March 1538

Once again King Henry seems to be thinking, perhaps more seriously, of marrying Christina of Denmark. This time he has not suggested that the potential bride should be brought here for his inspection. Instead, he has sent Hans Holbein to Brussels to paint a portrait of her. Maybe he hopes she is not as slim as people say.

Easter was better than the subdued Christmas that followed Jane's death. The King put aside his black mourning clothes and appeared in his favourite crimson slashed with gold. Others, too, were permitted to wear lighter colours. Mary came to court again, and she looked beautiful in white taffeta, though her face is always thin and rather tense. She brought little Elizabeth with her, and when she was busy one day she left the child with Kitty and me under the strict eye of Mr Kershaw. Elizabeth is four and a half years old now, and wonderfully clever. She sat stitching at a shirt she intends for her brother Edward when he is big enough to wear such things. She told me she thinks needlework boring, but her sewing is amazingly neat and precise for one so young. She is very pretty, too, with her mass of red hair that escapes from under her lace cap. She listened attentively to all that Mr Kershaw was saying, watching him with her bright, dark eyes as though she understood every word – and indeed she probably did. He turned to Kitty and me and said in his dry voice, "I only wish, young ladies, that you could display the attention that is so abundantly present in this child."

Afterwards Kitty said, "Just think, Bee – if anything happens to her brother, she may be the Queen of England." I made the sign of the cross at the thought of any harm to the King's precious boy, but what Kitty says is right. Elizabeth would probably run the country very well, given the chance. That seems unlikely, though. Elinor says Elizabeth can never be England's ruler because the King will not recognize the daughter of Anne Boleyn as his heir. Neither will he recognize Mary, whose mother he divorced. The throne of England waits for Edward.

19th May 1538

The King sent for barber-surgeons last week, to lance the abscess on his leg that gives him such constant trouble. Although the weather is fine and the other gentlemen are out hunting, Henry is unable to ride a horse these days and finds is painful even to walk.

Papa says the trouble began two years ago – it must have been just before I started keeping this diary. The King was thrown from his horse during a joust and lay unconscious for two hours. Everybody was frantic with worry that he was going to die. He came round at last, but he had a wound on his leg that became badly infected, and it has been a trouble to him ever since. The constant pain of it undoubtedly adds to his bad temper, which of late has reached new ferocity. Even from our small room upstairs where Kitty and I try not to die of boredom with Mr Kershaw, the sound of his shouting and rampaging can be heard. Thomas Cromwell, his Lord Privy Seal, bears the brunt of it. The ladies say they have several times seen Cromwell leaving the King's chambers unsteady on his feet, with his hair in disarray and the side of his face a livid red as though he had been slapped. Despite that, he still manages to produce one of his stiff little smiles if they greet him. Cromwell, like the Duke of Norfolk, will put up with anything from His Majesty because he wants power.

26th June 1538

The barber-surgeons have made no improvement to the King's infected leg, and he is in a furious temper and much pain. To make things worse, a treaty has been signed between France and Spain. It means that the two countries have agreed not to attack each other, and to stand together against any common enemy. And that enemy will be England.

Eva sighed when I told her what I had heard. "This is not the first time," she said. She fetched her diary and leafed through the pages until she came to October 12th 1510.

"Here we are," she said. "After Catherine's mother died, her father married again, this time to a Frenchwoman. Henry was frantic, convinced that the Spanish king had betrayed him."

I remembered the passage she meant, but I had not understood it very well.

"Catherine dealt with the King's fears so well," Eva said. "Listen to this." She read out in English what she had written.

Catherine looked at him calmly with her grey eyes. "My Lord," she said respectfully, "you are a great statesman; you will understand my father's motives. In his place, threatened by attack from France,

would you not play for time? Make a marriage, sign a pact, buy a
few months of safety? If you wish it, he will be on your side when the
time comes. Believe me." And he had no choice but to smile down
at her – *she comes barely to his shoulder* – then take her in his arms
and call her his clever little vixen.

Eva shook her head sadly. "Catherine was pregnant when I wrote
those words," she said. "Early the next year she gave birth to a boy who
was called Henry after his father, and all the church bells rang. But the
baby died seven weeks later."

I said the King could not blame the Queen for that, but Eva sighed
as she closed the book. "Yes, he could," she said. "In his view, everything
less than perfect about a child is the mother's fault. The father takes
credit for its virtues."

It seems so unfair.

8th July 1538

This summer has turned out to be a busy one for me. Now that I am
twelve, Papa says I am old enough to make myself useful at court.
Kitty has been working there more and more between lessons, hoping
she will be considered as a lady-in-waiting when the King at last finds

himself a new bride. She says it is only by helping with the work that she can make herself liked and useful. She is younger than I am, so I don't think she has much hope, but she knows a lot more about the court and its doings than I do, and she is very sensible and responsible, always there at hand if anything needs to be done.

Kitty helps the ladies, and I help Kitty. It's very interesting. I'm learning all the tasks, but the great benefit is that I am starting to recognize the faces of important people and know when to stand in the background, listening but saying nothing.

I overhear a lot. Fresh trouble is brewing about the Pole family because Lady Margaret Pole's eldest son, Baron Montagu, has been heard speaking in defence of his brother, Cardinal Reginald Pole. Reginald is the one who left the country for his own safety after he sent the King a copy of the book he had written, attacking Henry's proposal to divorce Catherine of Aragon. King Henry's loathing of the Plantagenets is at boiling point all over again. He suspects the younger brother, Geoffrey, of supporting Reginald as well, though there is no proof, and regards all of them as traitors.

Henry is so enraged that everyone here is working very quietly, not daring to meet anyone's eye, let alone smile. The only safety is to be as dumb as a piece of furniture. I do not know what is going to happen, but there is an oppressive feeling of gathering clouds, like before a thunderstorm.

29th July 1538

Since the treaty between France and Spain, Thomas Cromwell no longer wants a royal match with Christina of Denmark. Henry has no warmth for the scheme, either. Christina is the grand-niece of Catherine of Aragon, so she has strong connections with Spain. Now that the Emperor Charles of Spain has signed a treaty with France, he is head of a powerful Catholic alliance that is completely opposed to King Henry's new Church, so a Catholic wife for Henry has become a very unattractive idea. But the offer to Christina of Denmark has already been made, and Henry cannot take it back. He will have to wait for her response.

Cromwell has quickly switched to a different plan. He is now urging Henry to marry a German princess because Germany is a Protestant country. The Church set up by Martin Luther protests against the power of Rome and the Pope, and so does King Henry's Church of England. Cromwell wants the King to think again about the daughter of the Duke of Cleves. The German countries have no connection with Spain and France, so they would be valuable allies. But Cromwell sees any royal marriage as a political move. For the King, it is far more personal. He is looking for a wife who will give him pleasure and bear him a male child.

28th August 1538

The King's persecution of Lady Margaret Pole's sons continues. And it gets worse. Geoffrey Pole has been sent to the Tower, accused of helping his brother, Cardinal Reginald, to escape to France after the publication of his book. The King cannot see that episode as past history. To him, anyone connected with an act of disrespect remains potentially dangerous, and doubly so if they happen to belong to the Plantagenet family. There is a warrant out for the arrest of Reginald's other brother, Lord Montagu, though he had nothing to do with the book. He too is accused of treason.

27th September 1538

Horrible news today. They hunted down Lady Margaret Pole's son, Lord Montagu, and he has been executed, along with the Marquess of Exeter, another member of the Plantagenet family. The two men were accused of conspiring to kill the King, despite no evidence being offered. Exeter's young son, Edward Courtenay, has been thrown into the Tower, and it seems unlikely that he will ever see freedom again. Elinor says the King is determined to wipe out the entire Plantagenet family.

17th October 1538

Christina of Denmark, like Mary of Guise, turned King Henry down flat. She is only sixteen, but she told the English ambassadors that she has no intention of becoming the fourth wife of Henry Tudor. She said he is known all over Europe as the ruler who divorced his first wife, flouting the authority of the old Church in order to do so. He had his second wife killed for incurring his displeasure and, "lost his third for lack of proper care in childbed". She may not be right about that – the women who attended Jane Seymour did their best. But I can well see her objections.

Nobody knows what Henry said when the ambassadors broke the news – but Thomas Cromwell will be relieved. A marriage with Christina had become the last thing he wanted. Now she is out of the running, there is nothing to prevent an approach to the Duke of Cleves, who has not just one daughter looking for a husband, but two. It is true that John Hutton, the English envoy in Brussels, said neither of the young women had much beauty of face or of personality, but beggars cannot be choosers.

Heavens – can I really say that of the King of England? I get more like Kitty every day, ready to find something to giggle at.

20th November 1538

News has reached the Pope in Rome of the executions of Montagu and Exeter. His Holiness is very angry. He has reissued the Bull of Excommunication against Henry. Papa says France and Spain are now far more hostile towards Henry and his new Church, but the King does not seem bothered about that. Henry now believes that Cromwell is right to recommend marriage with one of the Cleves girls. It is a neat way to skate over the fact that two marriageable princesses have rejected him, because he can present it as a political decision to favour a different power group with his support. He is so pleased with Cromwell that he has granted him the post of Lord Great Chamberlain as a reward. A pat on the head for the bad shepherd, as Eva called him.

4th February 1539

I have been very ill. Wet cloths on my forehead. Pain.

Agnes had the sickness as well. Smallpox. But she is better.

Will came for me.

I am at Elinor's house.

9th February 1539

My parents are dead. Elinor told me this morning. They had the worst form of the illness. It infects all the internal organs.

Papa is not riding through the forest with his hounds. I can hear them howling in their pens from across the fields.

10th February 1539

Every time I wake I start to cry again.

I should grieve equally for Papa and my mother, but I cannot. She seemed so near to death all the time, yet Elinor told me she lived four days longer than my father.

17th February 1539

Aunt Gertrude has come, and Uncle John. They sent a message to say I must be brought back from Elinor's to my parents' house. Will wrapped me in a blanket and set me in front of him on the big cob, Bessie.

My aunt and uncle say I must go and live with them in a place called Kings Lynn in Norfolk. My mother was a Bedingfield like them. This house is theirs. They rented it to Papa, who was a mere commoner, with its lands and cottages. I did not know that. They do not want to live in it. They will find another tenant, they say.

18th February 1539

I told Uncle John I do not want to go to Norfolk. He stared at me as though I were mad and said, "What do you imagine you can do here?"

I said I might be one of the queen's ladies, and he laughed. "Have you seen yourself?" he asked. "No queen will want you anywhere near her."

Afterwards I crept into my mother's empty room, where there is a big mirror. My face is pitted and lumpy, scarred by the smallpox. I am hideous.

I wrote a note to Elinor and asked Agnes to take it across the fields to her house. Agnes had the illness, but it was a light attack and left no scars. She did not want to go to Elinor's house, but for the first time I said I was her mistress and she must do as I say. So she went.

Why could Agnes not have died instead of my father? God forgive me – it is not for me to judge.

11th February 1539

Elinor and Eva came to see my uncle and aunt, wearing beautiful dresses that I had not seen before. I suppose they were left from their days at the court. Tom was with them, in polished boots and a clean jacket.

Eva said, "I was with Queen Catherine of Aragon, from our childhood together until the last days before her death. And this is my daughter, Elinor, and her husband, Tom. Elinor was a lady-in-waiting to Anne Boleyn. After her execution, we left the court."

I saw my uncle and aunt exchange surprised glances.

"We know Beatrice well and love her like one of our own family," Tom said. "We would like her to live with us. We can give her a good home."

Uncle John noticed that I was standing there and sent me out. I listened outside the door of course. I think he and my aunt are relieved that someone else will look after me. They said they will provide money for my keep "as long as your demands are reasonable". I didn't hear the rest. I had started to shiver again, so I went upstairs and lay on my bed with a quilt over me.

I have no strength. If I try to walk far, my legs tremble like a newborn lamb. I know, too, that my uncle was right to say I am ugly. I will never be a lady-in-waiting now.

2nd March 1539

Will brought me back to Elinor's house. Russet is here, grazing in the field. I cannot imagine riding him. I can walk further now, but any effort makes me breathless and faint.

Elinor says my face will get better. I must try to believe her. Maybe this change is what God intended. I have been freed from Agnes, and from loneliness. Another pair of hands will be useful to Elinor. I thank the good Lord I was not here when the illness started. It would have been so terrible if the disease had struck this kind family.

4th March 1539

Kitty has been to see me. She had never been to Elinor's cottage before. She did not seem bothered about my face. "It is only a few pockmarks, Bee," she said. "There are hundreds of people worse off. Think of the cripples and the people born deformed. You are still pretty."

She says she will ask the ladies at court if there is a job I can do. Now that my parents are dead, I will need to work, she says. Work. Yes, I will work. But it still seems a long way off.

11th March 1539

I sleep in the alcove bed in the cottage kitchen. No servant brings my clothes in the morning, or brushes my hair, but I would not go back to that pampering. I feel stronger every day now. I can fetch water from the well and help with washing clothes and sweeping floors. This morning I saw hares dancing, as they always do in the spring, and had a moment of wonderful happiness.

19th March 1539

I spoke too soon of happiness. Lady Margaret Pole, that lovely, gracious woman who has done nobody any harm, is in the Tower of London. The King sent soldiers to ransack her house in search of "evidence", and they found what some say is an old banner, though others insist it was just a tunic. It was embroidered with designs that are supposed to be linked to the Pilgrimage of Grace that Henry put down with such savagery last year. Lady Margaret protested that she had nothing to do with that rebellion and has never been in any way disloyal to the King. She had remonstrated with her son over the views he expressed in his book, and even told the King she thought them traitorous. But her arguments were useless and she has been imprisoned like any common criminal.

Will knows the men who had to take her to the Tower. They told him Henry gave them orders to put Lady Margaret in a particularly cold cell on the north side of the Tower prison where it is sunless and draughty even in the summer months, and icy in the winter. Not content with that, the King has said she is to have scant food and no warm clothing. The men felt bad about it. "No need to be so cruel to her," they said.

Lady Margaret is 66 years old and she has spent her life in the service of the King and his family. I wondered if Thomas Cromwell might put in a word for her, but Elinor says Cromwell will never oppose the King. His aim now is to shepherd his royal master into a Protestant marriage, and the imprisonment of an elderly lady whose only crime is to be born a Plantagenet will not matter to him one way or the other.

Along with countless other people, I feel angry and helpless. Lady Margaret is much loved, but nobody will dare to intercede for her, and there is no queen who might plead with Henry. Cromwell, with the King's agreement, has sent two ambassadors to Düsseldorf to see the Cleves princesses, Anne and Amelia.

15th April 1539

Kitty was here today, full of the latest gossip. The envoys in Düsseldorf are Nicholas Wotton and Robert Barnes, and they are having a difficult time. The old duke has died, so his son William, the young duke, greeted them. But he was not at all helpful about his sisters. When they came into the room to be presented to the ambassadors, they were swathed in layers of heavy clothing, with hoods that came low across their faces. Wotton pointed out as diplomatically as he could that this prevented any clear view of the young ladies' appearance, and the young duke snapped, "Would you see them *naked*?" As Kitty remarked, it has obviously gone round the royal families that Henry Tudor likes to have prospective brides trotted out for his inspection like horses.

The envoys reported that, as far as they could see – which wasn't far – Anne is the better looking of the two sisters. So the King has sent Hans Holbein, whose last task was to portray Christina of Denmark, to paint a portrait of Anne of Cleves. He departed last week, with an envoy called Christopher Mont to ask the young Duke William if Holbein may paint a portrait of Anne.

20th May 1539

This is becoming rather comic. Kitty says Christopher Mont has been asking Duke William day after day if Holbein can begin work, and getting no further. The Duke kept refusing to answer – then at last he said if a portrait had to be painted, it would be by his own artist, Lucas Cranach. But Lucas, he said, "is not well, so he cannot consider it at present." Christopher Mont wrote to Cromwell with this frustrating news, and Cromwell wrote to King Henry, with a much more cheerful version of what he had been told. As Kitty said, "The King loves good news," so he was happy to read Cromwell's words to the gathered ladies and gentlemen. Cromwell claimed that everyone praised the beauty of Lady Anne and admired both her face and her figure. He declared that she excelled her sister, the Duchess of Saxony, "as the golden sun excels the silver moon."

I said, "But Cromwell has never seen the lady Anne."

"Exactly," said Kitty. "Everyone knew that, but we dared not raise an eyebrow."

Elinor was with us, and she said, "This is one of Thomas Cromwell's diplomatic games. Never mind about truth – he is determined to arrange this marriage and see England allied to Germany, so he will play any card he can. Regardless of what Anne really looks like, he needs Henry to believe that he is competing with other men for a girl of great beauty. It's a shrewd move, because if there's a prize at stake, the King will always fight to win it, even if he does not know its true nature. He is now convinced that Anne of Cleves is the princess every man wants, so he will have her at all costs."

Duke William is evidently playing the same horse-trading game, but on the other side. Without revealing anything much, he has managed to interest Henry in his sister, so he is driving a hard bargain. Last week he said he would not allow Anne to go to a court known for its bawdy behaviour and loose morals. Henry protested that the English court is a model of good behaviour. (That made Kitty giggle.) The Duke then said he had no money for his sister's dowry, which is a very clever move. Henry cannot turn Anne of Cleves down on those grounds, or everyone will say that he cannot afford her. Then he will be the laughing stock of Europe. And the Duke keeps his money intact.

23rd May 1539

The King has agreed to take Anne with no dowry. But he still only has Cromwell's word for it that Anne of Cleves is charming and beautiful. Henry knows this, for he has said he will only go ahead with the marriage if the Duke allows Holbein to start on the portrait of Anne and if he, Henry, likes the result. The Duke agreed at once, and there has been no more talk of the ailing painter Lucas Cranach. By now Hans Holbein will have started his painting.

11th June 1539

Kitty could not find me a job as a royal servant. She assures me that it is nothing to do with my pock-marked face, and now that I feel strong again, I can more easily believe she is right. I would not be the only one in the court who has a scarred face or the marks of an injury. It is more probably because I am not aristocratic enough. My mother comes of the Norfolk Bedingfields but she, like Kitty's mother, Mary Boleyn, "married beneath her". Never mind. Will has received permission for me to help him in the royal kitchens. "You might like it better than the catfights that go on in higher places," he joked.

I am glad it worked out that way. I go with Will to the court every morning, and working with him is like working in Elinor's house, only on a bigger scale and sometimes more frantic. I don't know about the catfights, but I rather enjoy the snatches of court gossip that come my way. I told Will and he laughed. "Of course you do," he said. "A Bee in a beehive."

19th July 1539

Hans Holbein has sent a miniature painting of Anne of Cleves. The King is so delighted with it that it is on open show for everyone to see. Will and I sneaked up from the kitchens to look at it – and it is indeed very beautiful. Anne gazes out from an ivory frame intricately carved in the form of a Tudor rose. Her face is dignified and virtuous, yet she clearly takes pleasure in worldly things, as the bodice of her gown is encrusted with fine jewels. There is no doubt now that she will be King Henry's new bride. But Kitty is not convinced that Anne really looks like that. "I mean," she said, "Holbein took his orders from Cromwell. A portrait that showed a plain girl would have wrecked all his plans."

Will agrees. Walking back to Elinor's house this evening, he said, "Have you heard the little rhyme that's going round about Anne's picture?" And he recited it.

"If that be your picture, then shall we
soon see how you and your picture agree!"

"Oh, wicked," I said.
"Isn't it," Will agreed. "It can't be true, though. Jem the butcher bet me

103

a pint of beer that the princess will turn out to have a face like a bulldog. I took him on because I reckon the King can't be that much of a fool. If he is, I'm poorer by a pint."

15th August 1539

Nicholas Wotton, who has just come back from Düsseldorf, told the King that Anne of Cleves speaks no English. Neither does she understand French, Latin or Spanish. She only speaks High Dutch, which is a form of German. What's worse, she cannot play a musical instrument of any sort and does not sing. In Germany such diversions are regarded as ungodly. Dancing is frowned on, and fashion in clothes is seen as immoral frivolity.

"Heavens!" Will said, fanning himself with a handy cabbage leaf. "Does the King really think he can marry this dumpling?"

We all looked at each other and held our hands up in a big shrug. For our king, music and dancing, rich clothes and theatrical extravagance are essentials. But he can't back out now. The marriage contract is to be signed on September 4th. After that, the young duke and his retinue will be coming here to meet the King. We are in a frenzy of cleaning and preparation.

Kitty says the lady Mary is dismayed to hear that Anne of Cleves is a Lutheran. I said I thought that Mary had accepted her father's new religion, but everyone seems certain that she remains deeply Catholic at heart. I cannot imagine how she will get on with her father's new bride.

28th August 1539

The coming visit has thrown everyone into a turmoil. Noblemen are ordering new clothes to be made, and there is fierce competition between the ladies for the privilege of serving the new queen. Kitty has her fingers crossed for luck.

Arguments are going on about the best route for Anne and her retinue to take to England for her wedding. Some think she should come by the quickest road route, north from Germany to one of the Baltic ports – but that would mean many days on a ship, and at this time of the year the weather may be rough. Anne has never been on the sea, so she will probably come overland to Calais and then across the English Channel.

17th October 1539

Heavens, how busy we have been! Banquet after banquet, with everything beautifully presented to impress the young duke and his courtiers. The work in the kitchens has never stopped. We are glad the visitors have returned home, as wc will have an even harder time of it when the new bride herself arrives, specially as she plans to be here for Christmas. Henry has sent a big contingent of people to escort her from Calais across the sea to England and at last to London. Magnificent royal beds are being sent to Dartford and to Rochester, where Anne will break her journey overnight. She is to travel with a retinue of 263 attendants and 228 horses.

21st October 1539

Kitty has her wish! She is to be a maid of honour to Anne of Cleves. Anne Basset, Lady Lisle's elder daughter, will be the new queen's chief attendant. She was lady-in-waiting to Jane Seymour in the sad days when she gave birth to little Prince Edward then lost her life. There seems to be truth in the rumour that the King likes Anne Basset, as he has given her a beautiful horse and saddle. Lady Lisle was so grateful that she gave the King some damson jam and quince marmalade that she had made herself. It seemed a small offering, but he was pleased. After some days, he had eaten all of it, and asked her if she had any more! He is in a very good mood now, with his new bride on her way to meet him.

11th December 1539

Anne of Cleves has reached Calais, and a grand reception is going on there, as although it is across the sea, it belongs to England. It looks as if the reception and the talking will go on for some time because the weather is dreadful and they say the sea is very rough. The King's plan for a Christmas wedding seems unlikely to happen.

Meanwhile, his daughter Mary, still deeply Catholic at heart, is supposed to be marrying the Protestant Duke Philip of Bavaria. Henry forced Mary to meet the Duke when he came to London, but she could hardly bring herself to be polite to him, and said afterwards that she would rather remain single all her life than enter into such a match. She has left the court now, saying she is ill, but everyone thinks she is lying low in the hope that Philip will look elsewhere for a bride.

31st December 1539

Christmas was busy, but not as frantic as it would have been had Anne of Cleves and all her huge retinue arrived. On December 26th the weather improved, so the royal party set sail. It was not too bad a voyage, as the ship arrived at Deal harbour at five in the morning, in just seventeen hours. Anne rested for a few hours in the great castle Henry has built there, and the same day they went on to Dover Castle. And then they set out for Canterbury. Poor things, they must have had a hard time of it because the weather turned to hail and sleet on a driving north wind, and it must have been horrible for both riders and horses. Now, on New Year's Eve, Anne is on her way to Rochester – and the King is so impatient to see her that he can wait no longer. He has summoned his men and is riding down to meet her.

2nd January 1540

The disaster we all feared has happened, and Will owes Jem the butcher a pint of beer. Anne of Cleves is no beauty. The King has come back from meeting her at the Bishop's Palace in a state of fury. He says he finds the German princess repulsive. He referred to her as "a Flemish mare".

I heard all this from Robin Perkiss, who brought his horse to Tom late last night because it had cast a shoe. He was among those who rode with the King to Rochester and he was full of the story. He said the King spoke politely to Anne, and had supper with her in the reception room, but at the end of it he came out bursting out into the corridor and turned on Sir Anthony Browne, who was waiting for him, hissing that Anne was totally unlike her portrait. "I love her not!" he raged. "I see nothing in this woman as men report of her, and I marvel that wise men would make such report as they have done!" He was so angry that he forgot to give Anne the gift of furs he had brought, and Sir Anthony had to give them to her the next morning, when Henry and his gentlemen were riding home.

Robin went on talking as Tom heated and shaped a new shoe for his horse. He said the wedding is still planned to go ahead. "But I tell you something," he said, after he had glanced outside the forge to make sure nobody was listening. He beckoned me and I stepped closer. He sniffed at me as though at a new-picked flower, then smiled. "The scent of youth," he said, "mixed with a little honest sweat. Beautiful. Many a man will forgive your pock-marked face for the sake of such freshness. I would myself."

I blushed, as it was the first time anyone has said anything about my scars, but he did not even notice. He lowered his voice and went on with what he had to say. "The lady of Cleves has a stink about her. When His Majesty came out from the chamber after he had given her a betrothal kiss, his face was screwed up as if he'd smelt a dead sheep in a ditch." Tom glanced up from nailing on the new shoe and grinned. Robin laughed. "I would not relish a wedding night with that lady!"

The King must know that he has been deceived – but who can he blame? It is not Holbein's fault. He is an artist and maybe saw a beauty in Anne that eludes other people. Or else Thomas Cromwell told him to make Anne look as attractive as he could. That seems more likely, since this marriage is part of his plan to link the King to a German ally.

At Christmas, Hans Holbein gave Henry a portrait of his little son, Prince Edward, who is now two years old. It makes the child look just like his father, very solid and handsome in a red velvet suit – and it was well timed. The King is so delighted with it that he cannot be too angry about the way he painted Anne of Cleves.

3rd January 1540

Today was the royal meeting of Henry and Anne of Cleves – a big public ceremony. Will said he could manage without me in the kitchens. "This will be quite a spectacle" he said. "Go with Elinor and Tom, and enjoy yourself."

And I did enjoy myself, though I wished Will could have been with us. The show was magnificent. The court is like a theatre company, always itching to start a new production. It is full of backbiting and malice when there is nothing better to do, but it loves plunging into spectacle and celebration, and does it brilliantly well.

The river is not frozen this year, so the King with all his nobles and the Lord Mayor and aldermen of London came sailing down from the City in barges decorated with streamers and banners. The lady Anne was on her way from Dartford, with a great train of attendants and horses. A pavilion made of cloth of gold was waiting for her, with smaller pavilions clustered near for her ladies. Braziers of scented wood burned everywhere, so that the travellers could warm their hands – but only until exactly twelve o'clock. With perfect timing, Anne led her retinue down Shooters Hill to meet the English nobles and hear a Latin address by the Archbishop of Canterbury.

I whispered to Elinor, "Where is the King?" She laughed and tucked my hand more closely under her arm. "Don't worry. You will know when he makes his entry."

She had hardly spoken when there was a fanfare of trumpets and everyone looked up the hill to see gorgeously caparisoned horses arriving. The lady Anne mounted her white palfrey with its gold-embroidered saddlecloth, and rode to meet the King, followed by a great procession of her courtiers and ladies. Pretty or not, she looked glorious, in white taffeta embroidered with gold and a cap clustered with pearls. Henry reined in his horse as he waited for her to draw level with him. Despite his size, he was magnificent, in a coat embroidered with cloth of gold, diamonds, rubies and pearls, topped by a collar richly encrusted with jewels and a jewelled sword. When his bride reached him, he doffed his velvet bonnet with a broad, courtly sweep of his arm that brought a roar of pleasure from all those watching, and leaned from his saddle to kiss her. I thought of what Robin had said about Anne having an unpleasant odour and wondered if it could be true. Nobody would have suspected it. After some conversation, the royal pair turned their horses and rode back towards the pavilions, so that the waiting crowds could get a closer view of the woman who is to be our new queen. I thought she looked pleasant enough – but then, any woman looks beautiful when she is sumptuously dressed and has met a king who wants to make her his wife.

Music was sounding from the river, where the voices of men and children rose in harmony from countless barges, and the royal procession started up the hill again towards Greenwich Palace. There will be a great banquet this evening, and I had a fresh pang of guilt about being out here instead of helping in the kitchens. Then, as the guns boomed a salute of explosions from one of the palace towers, startled ravens flew up in a cloud from the bare trees, and I was suddenly sad for Anne of Cleves. If she is not to the King's liking, this marriage can lead to nothing good. For all her jewelled clothes and her black-clad men-servants riding their massive horses, I would not be in her place.

6th January 1540

Today was the royal wedding ceremony. It had ended as I went out to fetch water from the pump – and Robin was leading his horse to the mounting block.

He said, "Well, my daisy-fresh girl, that was the most reluctant wedding I have ever seen."

He seemed a little drunk, but there were few people in the court who were not on such a day. He went on, "Do you know what His Majesty said to us before he entered the chapel?" He lowered his voice to sound like the King. " 'My lords, if it were not to satisfy the world and my realm, I would not do what I must do this day, for any earthly thing.' What do you think of that, my bonny Beatrice?"

I did not know what to say. Robin mounted his horse, then leaned down from his saddle, caught me by the sleeve and kissed me. Then he rode away.

Papa sometimes gave me a goodnight kiss when I was small, but Robin's kiss was different. Ever since, I look up for no good reason when a horse clatters across the yard and wonder if its rider is Robin.

11th January 1540

The King's new wife went to a tournament held in her honour today. I hope her scanty English protected her from the jokes being cracked around her. The King has not been discreet. He said to Cromwell for everyone to hear, "I have left her as good a maid as I found her." Cromwell looked dismayed – as well he might. Henry's main reason for seeking a fourth bride was to find a wife who would bear him more children, but if things are as distant between him and Anne as he claims, this will never happen. She, in her innocence, still strives to be kind and dignified. She has landed herself in a dreadful pickle, but, poor woman, she does not know it.

16th January 1540

The King's little daughter, Elizabeth, has written a letter to Anne of Cleves. The Queen found it so delightful that she has been showing it to everyone. I can well see why – for a child of only six years old, she writes amazingly well. I had taken a tray of sweetmeats upstairs and carried them round for the ladies, and the lady Anne gave me a smile, so I ventured across and read the little girl's words.

Permit me to show, by this billet, the zeal with which I devote my respect to you as queen, and my entire obedience to you as my mother. I am too young and feeble to have power to do more than felicitate you with all my heart in this commencement of your marriage. I hope that Your Majesty will have as much goodwill for me as I have zeal for your service.

I think the lady Mary, who has been looking after her since the birth of Prince Edward, may have helped her with the courteous words, but Elizabeth had written carefully and well. I hope the King will permit her to meet his new wife.

17th January 1540

The King did not permit it. When Anne showed him the letter, he handed it to Cromwell. I was clearing away some plates and wineglasses and heard what he said.

"Tell her that she had a mother so different from this woman that she ought not to wish to see her."

Anne looked at him blankly, and I wondered if she had understood, for her English is still very poor. But had I myself understood? Did the King mean that "this woman" was better than Elizabeth's mother or worse? Either way, it was a cruel rebuke to his little daughter. She does not deserve such a rebuff.

4th February 1540

Anne has not yet been officially crowned as Queen of England, but today she and the King went by royal barge up the river to Westminster for a grand civic reception. It was the usual dramatic affair, with boats full of liveried servants, music playing, guns firing from the Tower and people cheering on the banks. The royal couple will be staying in Whitehall for a few days.

Meanwhile, Lady Lisle's daughter, Anne Basset, has arrived from Calais to take up her appointment as lady-in-waiting to the Queen – only to be told that Anne of Cleves brought so many German servants with her that there is no room for any new English attendants. Lady Lisle is furious. She has had a word with Lady Rutland, wife of the Lord Chamberlain, but Lady Rutland confirms that the King will not allow any more servants to be taken on until some of the existing ones have left.

Kitty is afraid that she may be dismissed, as she is the youngest of the Queen's ladies. She has a very good reason for wanting to stay at the court – Sir Francis Knollys has fallen in love with her. Kitty looks cheerful and contented, as though this is something she has always expected. Sir Francis is the treasurer of the royal household, so he is highly placed, and he is a Protestant. He was one of the men the King sent as an escort to bring Anne of Cleves to England. I am so glad Kitty is happy. After the dreadful business of her aunt's execution and seeing what a husband can do to a once-loved wife, she might have been mistrustful of all men, but she has always been very practical. As she said when I was so downcast after being ill, "You just have to get on, Bee. The main thing is, we're alive."

10th February 1540

Lady Rutland told Anne Basset she would speak privately to Mother Lowe, who is in charge of the maids who came here with the Queen. Mother Lowe is a very severe German lady. Nobody knows what Lady Rutland said to her, but it worked like magic. A place has been found for Anne Basset. If the King asks any questions, I expect he will be told that someone left in order to make space for her. We are all much relieved.

23rd February 1540

Kitty asked me to help sort out her embroidery basket, which was in a dreadful tangle. "You can do it while we are at needlework with the Queen," she said, "nobody will mind you being there."

It turned out to be an extraordinary morning. The Queen is trying hard to improve her English, so she talks a lot with her ladies. Kitty says she begs them to correct her mistakes, but they do not like to do this too often in case she gets discouraged.

Today Anne was saying how good the King is to her. In her funny, gutteral accent, she told us, "Ven he comes to bed he kisses me, and takes me by the hand, and bids me 'Goodnight, sweetheart.' Unt in der morning he kisses me and bids, 'Farewell, darling.' *Sehr gemütlich*. So nice."

A look ran between the ladies, and I knew what it meant. *Is that all the King does?* Kitty raised an eyebrow at me, but her mouth was tightly pursed to prevent a giggle. One or two ladies coughed slightly and exchanged glances, but none of them said anything. The Queen knew something was wrong. "I haf made mistake?" she asked. "You tell me, please." Glances were exchanged again, then Lady Edgecombe put her needlework down and met Anne's troubled gaze. She took a deep breath and said, "I think Your Grace is a maid still." And we all nodded.

The Queen was puzzled. She asked, "How can I be a maid when I sleep every night with ze King?" She repeated what she had said about the kiss and the touch on her hand, but this time Kitty let a squeak of laughter escape. Lady Edgecombe frowned at her and shook her head, but all the ladies were trying to hide their smiles. They quickly made their faces straight again, but the Queen knew something was amiss. She asked, "Is zis not enough?"

Lady Edgecombe bit her lip and glanced round for help, not wanting to be the one who would tell her.

Lady Rutland took up the challenge. "Madam," she said to the Queen, "there must be more than this, or it will be long ere we have a Duke of York, which all this realm most desireth."

Anne knew then that she had touched on something that everyone else knew and she did not. Her pale face flushed, but she tried to hold on to her dignity. She said, "I am contented. I do not vant to know more."

But it was too late. Like boys teasing an animal, a streak of cruelty had touched us. Her ladies wanted to see if she would be upset when we told her the truth – and, to be honest, I did, too, though I am ashamed of that now. Lady Rutland explained in common, simple words how a child is conceived. Anne stared down at her hands, motionless on the cloth she had been embroidering. Other ladies started adding details, competing with each other in airing their knowledge of the ways in which a couple can enjoy each other's bodies. I must admit, I felt my own face grow hot, as a lot of what they said was new to me and a bit shocking.

The Queen could not stop the torrent of gleeful information. She was like a she-wolf surrounded by a pack of hounds. But at last she held up her hand and everyone fell silent – after all, she is the Queen. She said that she received as much of His Majesty's attention as she wished, then she told us to leave her. I pushed Kitty's tangled skeins of silk back into the basket and the ladies collected up their fabric and threads and scissors, and we all went out. Nobody looked back. Poor lady. She now knows that her marriage is a farce.

24th February 1540

Elinor looked sad when I told her about the Queen's ignorance.

"So Henry is discarding yet another wife," she said. "He changed the religion of England to get rid of Catherine and executed Anne Boleyn. Jane, admittedly, died in giving him a son, and he did not wish that death. But now he is refusing to act as a proper husband to Anne of Cleves so that he can escape from her in turn. If the marriage has not been confirmed by the sexual act then the Catholic Church will not recognize it as legally binding. It is only a matter of time before they agree to a divorce."

Eva took a different view. "In the eyes of his maker he is merely a man," she said, "and should try to keep the Commandments. But he sees himself as the right hand of God, in the same position as His Holiness the Pope, and that surely is a mortal sin."

Elinor warned, "Be careful what you say outside these walls, Mama." And Eva said she had been careful for years. I thought of Mr Thornton, my gentle tutor, who died for what he believed.

Sir Francis Knollys is close to the centre of things, and Kitty is close to Sir Francis, so she understands very well what is going on. The Catholics at court, led by the Duke of Norfolk, are delighted that the King is seeking to divorce Anne because she is a Lutheran. And things are looking bad for Thomas Cromwell. He pushed King Henry into marrying Anne because he thought an alliance with Germany against the Catholic countries was needed. It might have been fine if the marriage had worked – but it has not worked. Henry is not interested in the politics behind it. He simply sees that Cromwell lied to him and landed him in a marriage he hates. The French ambassador told Francis last week, "Cromwell is tottering."

4th March 1540

I can see why the Catholics at court are so angry with the King and his new religion. The continuing destruction of the great monasteries is terrible. Henry's soldiers have overrun the abbeys of Waltham, Christchurch and Rochester, and their desecration of the cathedral of Canterbury was so awful that even the men commanded to carry it out were uneasy. The King ordered them to dig up St Thomas's body from its resting place in the nave and throw the saint's bones on the dungheap, because St Thomas had questioned the authority of Henry 11 in 1170. That's nearly 400 years ago, and the king of the time sent his men to hack Thomas to death in the cathedral. Was that not punishment enough? And does it have anything to do with the Tudor family? I can only suppose King Henry's action is meant as a warning to anyone who thinks of opposing him. I cannot forget that he took Jane Seymour to Thomas Becket's shrine in Canterbury such a short time ago, to give thanks for her pregnancy. Today he flaunts on his thumb the great ruby ring that was the centrepiece of Becket's tomb, while the tomb itself is rubble and dust.

Elinor says the monasteries are a rich source of plunder for the King. He has given their extensive lands to his friends, who are busy building themselves great houses with the tumbled stones of ancient places of worship.

Eva told me a terrible prediction. When Henry cast off Catherine of Aragon, a friar named Peto said that if the King married Anne Boleyn, the dogs would lick his blood. I try to ignore it. How could dogs ever lick the blood of a king? But it still sends shivers down my back.

5th March 1540

Kitty is to marry Sir Francis Knollys next month. She was smiling when she told me, but she seemed matter-of-fact about it. "I always knew I would get married," she said. "It's not the day that matters, or the ceremony. It's the future. And I think Francis is a good man."

She is younger than I am, and yet she has always seemed more grown-up and experienced. Soon she is to be a married woman. How strange that seems. I cannot imagine myself married. But I am thirteen now, and I understand more about love than I used to.

Whenever Robin sees me carrying full dishes up to the great rooms, or empty ones down, he smiles at me and blows me a kiss. Last week he caught me when I had only a cloth in my hands and pulled me close to him for a longer kiss. I keep thinking about it. I watch all the time for a glimpse of him among the other men. He is tall and curly-haired, and his smile shows teeth that are wonderfully strong and white. Will had to go to the barber-surgeon to have a painful tooth pulled out last week. Kitty says Robin kisses all the girls and I should not waste my time with him, but for some reason, whenever I see him a kind of delicious shock runs through me.

9th March 1540

The King has told the council that his marriage is unconsummated and therefore can be dissolved. He also reminded them that there had been an earlier agreement that Anne of Cleves should marry the Duke of Lorraine's son. It was an idea that never came to anything, but he thought it might serve as an additional reason to declare his marriage invalid. The council has said it will investigate. So we wait to see what will happen.

17th April 1540

Today the King promoted Cromwell to the grand status of Earl of Essex. That seems very strange. I thought Kitty must have been wrong when she told us Cromwell was in disgrace and the King would discard him. She has not changed her mind, though. She said, "This is all part of Henry's plan. He told the Duke of Norfolk he means to force Cromwell to help him divorce Anne of Cleves. I know this because Norfolk told Francis and Francis told me. The King wants Cromwell to believe he is still trusted and valued because that way, he'll go on trying to make himself useful."

I didn't see that Cromwell could be of any use now, but Kitty smiled. "Oh yes, he can," she said. "There will be a court hearing about the divorce, and the King needs to be sure that he has at least one witness who will say exactly what he is told to say. After that, Henry will get rid of him. He is fattening Cromwell for the kill, like a Christmas goose. You'll see."

19th April 1540

The Duke of Norfolk has his own ideas about how to hasten the departure of Anne of Cleves. As Anne Boleyn's uncle, he had a lot to do with introducing her to the King. He saw her die as a result, but it has not deterred him from doing the same thing again. He has now produced a second niece to tempt King Henry's eye. She is Katherine Howard, a member of the leading Catholic clan of Howards. She is only about my age, but full of life and fun and naughtiness. Kitty says Katherine reminds her very much of her aunt, Anne Boleyn, who was cousin to Katherine. She has the same sharp-eyed beauty and liveliness.

Norfolk's plan seems to be going well. Katherine is delighted to find herself at court, and is flirting with the King with a pretty modesty that he finds irresistible. It is easy to see why she attracts him. Katherine could not be a bigger contrast to the kind but lumpish lady of Cleves.

Kitty is watching with grim amusement. She said today, "The King has risen to the bait like a trout to a fly. He's goggle-eyed with lust, and he can't keep his hands off her."

We can all see that is true. Henry doesn't seem to care that the girl is from the family of his Catholic enemies. But then, as Kitty pointed out,

"He's had a whole winter with nothing more than holding hands and a goodnight kiss."

Elinor knows all about Katherine Howard. Poor girl, her mother died when she was small, so she went to live in a large house in Lambeth owned by her grandfather's second wife, Agnes Tilney. She's the Dowager Duchess of Norfolk, stepmother to the Duke of Norfolk. I may be prejudiced against women called Agnes, let alone against men called Norfolk, but it really does seem that the Dowager Duchess made a very bad job of bringing up Catherine or any of the other children in her house. All of them came of aristocratic but poor families who could not afford to support their offspring. Mostly girls, they were supposed to be trained in proper court behaviour so that they could take their place in royal circles, but the Dowager Duchess didn't have much to do with them as she was nearly always at court. The children were left to the care of various attendants, who evidently didn't care what they got up to. Katherine was no more than twelve when she had an affair with her music master, Henry Manox. More recently, Elinor says, there is talk of a man called Francis Dereham. He and Katherine were so close that she looked after his money for him, and he would slap her on the bottom and call her "wife".

"Bee, you must not speak of this," Elinor warned me. "If the King ever finds out, Heaven only knows what will happen. The affair between Katherine and Dereham is over, so with any luck, it should remain safely buried." Elinor seemed about to say something else, but then she shook her head and said, "I must not tell you anything more. For your own safety, it is better that you don't know."

Elinor has never said such a thing before. I feel as if we are surrounded by mysterious and terrible danger.

21st April 1540

Katherine grows ever closer to the King, accepting his caresses and sitting on his lap. I cannot understand how she can bear to be fondled by a dangerous, grossly fat man three times her age, with a stinking ulcer on his leg that has to be dressed daily. The thought of it makes me shudder. They say that Henry weighs 21 stone. Kitty says they had to measure him the other day for a new suit of armour, and were forced to join two tapes together, for he is 54 inches round his middle. But I suppose Katherine is enchanted by the idea that she may be queen.

26th April 1540

Today was Kitty's wedding. To put it correctly, Catherine Carey took Sir Francis Knollys as her lawful wedded husband. Compared with the panoply that accompanies royal weddings, theirs was a modest affair.

I was among her guests, and Elinor lent me one of her court dresses that fitted me well once we had done up its laces tightly.

It was beautiful to come out of the chapel in the procession of lords and ladies who followed the bride and groom. After the subdued light of the stone building, the sunshine of this spring day came as a blessing, with the birds on the trees rejoicing in song. Kitty looked lovely, in white silk embroidered with pale-green leaves, and Sir Francis is very handsome, a dignified, kindly man. I think she will be happy with him. He chose Kitty for good reasons, and she accepted him with equally good sense, for he represents exactly what she has always wanted.

She says she will try to find a place for me as a maid of honour. She thinks it is high time I stopped spending half my life in a cottage "stuck out in the fields" and the other half in a hot kitchen. But I am very aware of my scarred face and lowly status, and cannot imagine that I will ever achieve her kind of success.

7th May 1540

May Day was a merry affair, to all appearances, with jousting that went on for five days, and banqueting and handing out of prizes. Anne of Cleves accompanied Henry to all the events, and neither he nor she gave the slightest sign that anything was wrong. Thomas Cromwell, on the other hand, is looking grim. Yesterday he spent a long time with Sir Thomas Wriothesley (whose name sounds like Rithsley or Ridley), who was his right-hand man during the months of negotiation to bring about the Cleves marriage. The pair of them are clearly worried about this Catholic girl who has taken the King's fancy.

The King is now trying to blame Anne of Cleves for the failure of the marriage. At dinner the other day he said she is "wilful and stubborn" with him. In other words, if the marriage truly is unconsummated (which he wants to establish as a fact), he is not to blame. The failure has to be due to Anne's unwillingness, not his. I think this is very unfair. Cromwell went to see Anne this afternoon and warned her not to antagonize the King. He told her she must do her very best to "render herself more agreeable". Perhaps he thinks he can still save this marriage, and continue his plan to link Henry with the German states. He seems not to understand that his plan is already in tatters. Or perhaps he knows and is desperately trying to salvage it.

As for the Queen – I admire her more and more, because she is behaving with wonderful dignity. After the sudden lesson from her ladies, she understands that her husband was going through a pantomime of celebration and love when all the time he disliked her, yet she has shown nothing but respect for him, coupled with unruffled good humour. Cromwell has no sense of humour, but you'd think even he would see that she cannot possibly make herself "more agreeable" to the King. Does he really imagine that she can perform a dazzling seduction at this stage? It is the last thing either of them could want.

10th June 1540

The whole court is buzzing with excitement. Thomas Cromwell has been thrown into the Tower of London. Apparently he arrived at the council chamber as usual this morning, where the councillors were seated in preparation for the day's business, but the minute he came through the door, the Duke of Norfolk stepped forward and arrested him "in the name of the King". Soldiers were waiting to bundle him into a barge and take him down the river to the Tower. Cromwell's initial bluster turned to a white-faced silence.

The Catholic lords are jubilant. There will be no more efforts from Cromwell to preserve a marriage to a Protestant princess that they feel should never have happened in the first place. The way is now open for Henry to devour the choice little dish they are wafting under his nose. The King is walking about with a smile like a happy tiger, revelling in the coming public demonstration that he has a new love in his life. There is a legal reason behind this move, too. It gives him another reason for divorcing Anne of Cleves – he can add the fact of his own infidelity.

A Bill of Attainder has been drawn up, confiscating all Cromwell's possessions and property and stripping him of his titles. So much for the recent honour Henry bestowed on him. Kitty was right – the King was fattening him like a Christmas goose. Cromwell is charged with both treason and heresy. That means he will die the terrible death reserved for those who oppose the King's will. He is to be hanged, drawn and quartered. I have never liked the bad shepherd, but I would not wish such torture on anyone.

14th June 1540

Today I am fourteen years old. Kitty came into the kitchens, caught my hands that were wet from washing turnips, and kissed me. "Come with me," she said, "I have a surprise for you." I followed her upstairs, and there Lady Edgeworth told me I have a place among the Queen's maids of honour.

"It may be a brief appointment," she warned. "You will understand, Beatrice, that the lady Anne may not be the King's wife for very much longer. But it is a chance for you to prove yourself. You will go to the Queen later today to be sworn in." She looked me over and added, "You will need better clothes."

I curtsied and thanked her. Outside the door, I hugged Kitty and thanked her too.

"It should have happened ages ago," she said. "You should thank Francis, not me. He had a word with the King."

I do not have to live at the court yet, and I am glad of that. When I got back to Elinor's house tonight, we had a birthday celebration, and then she opened a chest in the corner of the upstairs room and pulled out dress after dress. I put on a pale blue one embroidered with small flowers and stared down at myself in wonder.

When Will saw me, he doffed his cap with a courtly sweep that reminded me of the King meeting Anne of Cleves at the top of Shooters Hill. "Lady," he said, "I am ever at your service." He gave me a brotherly hug and kiss, and suddenly I thought of Robin and felt the same excitement for Will – but it seemed slightly disgraceful. He laughed at my pink face and asked, "Why are you blushing?" I just said the new dress was very warm.

24th June 1540

The King has sent Anne of Cleves away to the palace at Richmond, so my work in her service has not lasted long. She has taken only her German servants, so none of the English ladies who had served her are needed. Henry told her she was being moved because there is plague in London, but we all know that is untrue. Had there really been plague, he himself would have been the first to leave the city.

I don't think Anne believed his story either. I helped to carry her things down to the waiting coaches and riders, and saw her look steadily at the King. Her gaze held no anger, but neither did it hint at a smile. He raised her hand to his lips and kissed it briefly, then turned away and went back into the palace.

I am not sure what will happen next, but I do not mind too much if my brief taste of being a court lady is over. Little Bella runs about all over the place now, and Elinor will welcome some help to look after her and tend the garden and the house. But I am to stay at the court until the end of the week.

25th June 1540

Kitty was waiting for me this morning.

"The King wants you to stay at court, Bee!" she said. "He says there will be a need of servants for the new queen. You will have my old room that has been empty since I married. What do you think of that!"

Papa used those very words after he told me I was to visit the King, four years ago, and I felt the same mixture of excitement and fear. But there is some irritation, too. I will be serving Katherine Howard, a girl little more than my own age and far less educated.

Kitty took me to see the King. I knelt before him and repeated the vows to be obedient, chaste and faithful.

26th June 1540

Work has begun straight away. Katherine Howard is to go to the palace of Lambeth, and we are all to go with her. It is only a few miles upriver, but we have been busy all day loading clothes and finery into boxes to be carried down the hill to the waiting barges. It was late afternoon by the time we were done, and the sails were hoisted, with men at the long oars to take us out from the jetty. I have not had a chance to go down to the kitchens and tell Will, but I'm sure he knows what is happening. As he said all those years back, "Servants know everything."

I am going to miss him so much.

28th June 1540

The King has been every day to see Katherine Howard, even in broad daylight. He does not seem to care that people line the riverbank to stare at the royal barge and make ribald jokes about the King and his new wench.

Twice Henry and Katherine have dined with Bishop Gardiner at Southwark Palace, but nobody is fooled into thinking the King comes here for that purpose. Unlike Anne of Cleves, Henry has emerged from his latest marriage with no dignity at all – but he does not seem to care. He has power, and that matters to him far more than dignity.

I myself have "moved up in the world" as they say, but I do not respect myself. Serving this silly girl is irksome, and I often have to refrain from sighing or rolling my eyes when she is being particularly empty-headed.

Kitty is here, too, as Katherine particularly asked for her, but Francis must remain at Greenwich with the King's court. Kitty makes no objection, though she wishes it did not have to be that way. She and her husband will be together once the royal marriage has taken place and the King and his new queen are under one roof. Kitty thinks it will not be long. Meanwhile we just have to put up with Katherine with as much grace as possible.

29th June 1540

The Bill of Attainder against Cromwell is now law. He has written to the King, begging him to spare his life, but nobody thinks that Henry will be merciful. He knows that Cromwell manoeuvred him into marriage with Anne of Cleves like a sheepdog herding a ewe into a pen, and this is his revenge.

Cromwell's thin beard and baggy, calculating eyes have always repelled me, but I hate the thought of the death that is waiting for him. As a traitor he will be hanged, then cut down while still alive, disembowelled and hacked into four quarters. But it will not happen quite yet, as Henry has not finished with him. As we all expected, there is to be a meeting of Church dignitaries to decide whether his divorce from Anne of Cleves can be allowed to go ahead, and Henry will have to present a strong case if he is to persuade them to agree. Cromwell's evidence will be important, so the King will keep him alive until he has performed this last service.

Kitty said, "Everything in Cromwell's life has been for calculated gain. The only thing he can gain now is mercy from the King, which he may get if he is a good enough witness. Everyone will be sure he is telling the truth. They'll think a man condemned to death would never risk eternal damnation of his soul by lying to a court of law."

Cromwell is probably more frightened of the King than he is of hell, so I am sure Kitty is right.

I wonder if all powerful men and women live for calculated gain? I remember the calm look Anne of Cleves gave the King when he sent her away to Richmond. It expressed a kind of settled satisfaction. Perhaps the gain she had always wanted was to escape her overbearing brother, Duke William. Cromwell used her as a pawn in the marriage game, but what if she was in fact using him? Other women had refused to marry Henry because of his age and size and dangerous temper. Anne could have refused him, too, but she took him on. Nobody ever asks a bride why she has agreed to a marriage, but Anne of Cleves could have had her own reasons. She must have realized that marriage to the English monarch would mean she would leave Germany and say goodbye to her brother, probably forever. If that is what she wanted, she has done well. She does not even have to cope with the unpredictable King. I think she may be a very clever woman.

2nd July 1540

One of the ladies-in-waiting here is called Katherine Parr, and tonight she did a very brave thing. When the King was relaxed and cheerful, she asked him humbly if he would consider releasing her cousin, Sir George Throckmorton, from the Tower. Sir George, a devout Catholic, had been appalled when Henry closed the convent of which his aunt was abbess, making 25 nuns homeless. Later he was found to have in his house a copy of the demands made by Thomas Aske, leader of the Pilgrimage of Grace. Although he had never met Aske and had nothing to do with the pilgrimage, Henry had thrown him into prison, and he has been there ever since.

Katherine Parr is a very gracious, well-read woman, and she put her case gently and with such dignity that the King perhaps felt he would look churlish if he refused it. Or perhaps he was cheerful enough about his intended new marriage to be smiling and benevolent. Whatever the cause, he agreed, and the other ladies all clustered around Katherine afterwards, congratulating her.

6th July 1540

The privy councillors went to Richmond today, to ask Anne of Cleves for her consent to the divorce. Unlike Catherine of Aragon, she made no objection at all. Eva's diary records how Henry's first queen fought like a tiger for her marriage. Even when she had been cast off and the King had married Anne Boleyn, she protested her rightful place as Henry's wife and the Queen of England. Anne of Cleves is no doubt delighted to have escaped so quickly and painlessly.

Katherine Howard clapped her hands like an excited little girl when she heard that the divorce will go through. The King comes to dine with her almost every night now. He takes her on his knee and kisses and fondles her, but she slaps his hand away playfully if he attempts to undo her bodice or raise her skirts. Henry does not seem to care that we witness this. Neither does Katherine, as she is making it very plain that she will not give in to his physical demands until they are married. Like

Anne Boleyn before her, she is making him wait. The Duke of Norfolk and the Catholic lords have no doubt told her that her virginity (if she is still a virgin, which some doubt) is her ace card, and she must not play it until the game has been won.

9th July 1540

The Church council agreed in just two days that the King's marriage to Anne of Cleves can be annulled. They gave three reasons. The first is that there might have been an agreement for Anne to marry the Duke of Lorraine's son. The second is that his marriage to Anne has not been consummated. The third is that Henry had never given his consent to the match. We were all surprised by that one. If it is true then the only person who can testify to it is Thomas Cromwell.

There is something strange about this business of whether the King gave his consent to the marriage, all the same. There was no need to consider it. The Catholic Church had accepted non-consummation of the marriage as legal grounds for annulment, and Henry had offered evidence of his own adultery as an additional reason. There was no doubt that the divorce would go through.

Kitty thinks that the Duke of Norfolk may have engineered the question of the King's consent. The Catholic duke has always loathed

Thomas Cromwell, and would have found great pleasure in making him tell the court that he had not asked the King's agreement before trapping him in a match he never wanted. It served a double purpose, confirming Henry's innocence and forcing Cromwell to condemn himself. Norfolk must be rubbing his hands with glee.

A deputation from the Privy Council went this afternoon to tell Anne of Cleves that her marriage is at an end. She is permitted to call herself the King's sister, but she is no longer his wife. It must have come as a huge relief to the King that the divorce went through so easily, and that Anne was so agreeable. He is going to give her 4,000 pounds a year. What a fortune for one woman to spend on herself! And she is to have three handsome houses to call her own – Richmond Castle where she is at present, a manor at Bletchingly and Hever Castle, which used to be Anne Boleyn's home.

Nicholas Wotton has gone to Germany to break the news of the divorce to the young Duke William. Anne asked Wotton to be sure to tell her brother that she is not going back. She wants him to know she likes it in England and intends to stay here for the rest of her life. So if that really was her plan all along, it has worked out well. She put up with a humiliating marriage, but only for seven months, and now she is a free woman, with abundant money and three beautiful houses. The King has told her she will be welcome to come to court whenever she chooses. Meanwhile, silly little Katherine Howard is willing and eager to take on the privilege, as she sees it, of being Henry's next wife.

12th July 1540

Katherine was frowning over the pages of a letter this morning. Poor thing, she does not read very well. She looked up and said as an excuse, "It's such untidy writing, I can hardly make out the words." So I read it to her, stopping from time to time to agree that it was dreadful scribble. In fact it was very neat, though small and inclined to use flowery phrases that Katherine would not have understood.

It was from a woman called Joan Bulmer. She had served in the Duchess of Norfolk's household, where Katherine had spent her early years, so she and Katherine knew each other well. Joan had acted as Katherine's secretary, writing letters at her dictation. I suspect that nobody knew about this, as there was a hint in her letter that Katherine might not like her to say what she knew.

Joan had left the Duchess's house when she got married and moved to Yorkshire, but her letter made it clear that she had not liked either the county or her husband. Her pages of flowery writing spoke of the "unfeigned love" she had always felt for Katherine and complained at length that her marriage had brought her into "the utmost misery of the world and most wretched life". And then she came to the point. She asked Katherine to find her a place at court, adding, "If you do not help me, I am not like to have worldly joys." She ended with the words, "I know the Queen of Britain will not forget her secretary."

I did not like the tone of this veiled threat. Neither did I like the idea of this woman coming to court. She might know a lot more about Katherine than the fact that she could not write well. I thought of Elinor's hint that people from Katherine's past could be dangerous, and felt I should try to discourage this idea of employing Joan Bulmer. I suggested that Katherine should ask her uncle's advice before promising anything, but she flinched from that idea and said it was nothing to do with him. That increased my unease because if the Duke of Norfolk does not know about certain things in his niece's previous life, there are obviously dangerous secrets lurking somewhere. Katherine set about answering the letter at once. She did not suggest that I should write it for her, but she asked several times for help with spelling. Judging from the words she stumbled over, I saw that she was promising to use all possible influence to find Joan Bulmer a post at court.

17th July 1540

When Nicholas Wotton arrived in Germany and delivered his news of Anne's divorce, Duke William immediately sent an emissary to London.

Anne joined him and the Lords of the Council for dinner, and Kitty says she was very cheerful and told them she was "honourably treated". She returned the King's wedding ring, and he has written to thank her. He is now saying he is happy to be Anne's "perfect friend" and will regard her as his "dearest sister".

Today Thomas Wriothesley went to Richmond to close down Anne's former household. She will be keeping some of her German servants, and they have been sworn in to her service. The others have gone home, and the English ones were dismissed, but she thanked them kindly for all they had done. Anne spoke to Wriothesley of her gratitude for the King's kindness and generosity to her. She even told him she would let King Henry see any letters that passed between her and her brother and sister, or anyone in the German court. It seems a wonderfully kind assurance that she intends to be completely open and honest. I am sure the King will be pleased.

18th July 1540

Katherine now puts on all the airs and graces she thinks a future queen should display. The King finds this charming and funny. Kitty and I are careful to give no sign of what we really think. Kitty has taken a step up the social ladder now she is married to a high-ranking courtier.

She holds her head high and looks more serious. Our childhood giggles are left behind now. But Kitty and I will always be friends.

20th July 1540

Now that the divorce has gone through, the Duke of Norfolk and his cronies are urging the King to marry again without delay. They sent him a petition, asking that he should seek "the love and favour of some noble personage to be joined with him in lawful matrimony". I can hardly think of Katherine Howard as a noble personage. She comes of a titled family that is very close to the King, and is undoubtedly an aristocrat, but in all personal ways she is totally lacking in nobility. But King Henry needs to beget another son, and if this girl pleases and amuses him, and has no offensive body smell, that is enough. Cromwell is out of the way, locked up in the Tower for the dwindling remainder of his life, and the King is free to follow his own fancy. If some people are shocked because that fancy is for a girl who could be his granddaughter, so much the better. It suits his theatrical taste for causing outrage – and Katherine is at the beginning of her life as a potential mother. God willing, there is no reason why she should not give him the children he so much needs.

Prince Edward is two and a half years old now. He is a healthy little boy, by all accounts, though nobody sees much of him as he is kept in such careful seclusion. I do not see Will now that I am here at Lambeth, but I remember how he told me that a food taster has to sample every meal prepared for the child. "Who would take on that job?" he said. "Every mouthful you sample may be your last. And nobody will care if you die in agony, so long as the royal lad goes on eating and growing."

The King's son is as safe as human care can make him – but how can anyone be safe? Pestilence blows in the wind like unseen dust. Plague and the sweating sickness cannot be kept out by oaken doors and heavy curtains. I do not know where the smallpox came from that left me with these pits on my forehead and cheeks. It arrived like an evil spell. I was well and happy one week and near to death the next. A royal prince has no more protection against such chance than common people do – in fact, sometimes it seems to work the other way. Agnes survived the smallpox, and my mother and father did not. Tom told me he had noticed that people who milk cows never get smallpox. If only I had been born in a cottage, rather than a grand, chilly house, maybe the disease would not have laid its hand on me.

I miss Tom and Elinor so much. And Eva. And Will – oh, how I miss Will.

23rd July 1540

The King is not pleased at all with Anne's offer to let him see letters between her and her brother. Being suspicious to his very fingertips, he cannot see why his ex-wife should be so kind unless she has something to gain from it. Kitty says he thinks that Anne could be plotting with her brother to make war on Britain. If so, she could be trying to reassure Henry by showing him a few letters of sisterly chit-chat while she is sending quite different ones, unseen, to the Duke. That is the way the King's mind works. He can't believe that someone could make such an offer out of sheer consideration and gratitude. He sent a council deputation to see Anne today, to tell her she must give them a letter written to her brother in German, saying she is completely contented and has no cause for any grievance against the King. Once the councillors have translated and approved it, they will send it on to the Duke. I can imagine how Anne gazed at them in calm surprise. Then, of course, she will have sat down at her desk and written the letter they dictated to her. She has nothing to lose.

25th July 1540

Suddenly we had to pack everything up for a move to Oatlands Palace. We came here yesterday. It's a long way up the river, between Weybridge and Walton on Thames. To my delight, Will is with us, as the King is to marry Katherine Howard here in four days, and he demanded the services of his favourite chef.

Oatlands is very beautiful. Its warm, rosy-red bricks glow in the afternoon sun. At its centre there is a moated manor house that is over a hundred years old, and its cloistered courtyards are tranquil, with fountains playing at their centre. The King acquired it two years ago. It was a ruin then, but he rebuilt it before he married Anne of Cleves, when he still believed she would be his permanent queen. Its foundation stones came from Chertsey Abbey, one of the monasteries ruined at his royal command.

I would love to wander about at leisure, gazing at beautiful things, but we are much too busy. We are all sworn to secrecy about the wedding, for it is to be very private. Parliament will be dissolved tomorrow for the summer recess and it seems that Henry has let the members go without telling them of his intention.

This time there will be no grand, theatrical event staged in front of hundreds of people. No liveried servants, no gloriously caparisoned horses, no burning braziers, no dramatic meeting at the top of a green hill. The Bishop of London will come here and marry the royal couple in this quiet place, in front of no more than the necessary witnesses and family members. Nevertheless, we are in a frenzy of preparation, for even though it is on a small scale, this wedding must be perfect.

28th July 1540

And yes, it was perfect. Katherine looked radiant and absurdly young beside her corpulent, middle-aged husband. The King smiled with satisfaction, like a large cat that has eaten very well. We, his servants, found out the unpleasant secret that he had given orders for Thomas Cromwell to be executed on this very day. I suppose he relished the theatrical satisfaction of making a new marriage at the same time that he rid himself of the man he blamed for the failure of the old one. For us, the thought was so horrible that it cast a shadow over the bright sky.

I wish I hadn't known about it, but a man who came from London as one of Bishop Bonner's attendants told us. As we passed each other with trays and dishes for the royal couple and their party of select friends, we exchanged carefully blank glances. At one point the King thumped his glass on the table and called for more merriment, but it was hard to smile.

29th July 1540

Cromwell's death, we know now, was appalling. For his testimony in the divorce proceedings, the King had granted him the small mercy of beheading rather than the full horror of being hanged, drawn and quartered, but his end was not a clean and quick one. They took him from his cell and brought him out to Tower Hill, where a public scaffold had been erected and a crowd of thousands waited, laughing and shouting with the usual malevolent glee.

Cromwell's old friend Sir Thomas Wyatt was there. Wyatt himself had been imprisoned in the Tower after Anne Boleyn's arrest – Kitty remembers it. He had fallen in love with Anne Boleyn and was suspected of committing adultery with her. It was only through Cromwell's intervention that he was released, so it was doubly bitter for him to be present at this execution. Cromwell saw that Wyatt was weeping and called down to him, "Oh, Wyatt, do not weep, for if I were not more guilty than thou wert when they took thee, I should not be in this pass." So he knew he had played a dangerous game – and lost. He knelt and said his last prayers.

The executioner botched his job. It took two strokes of the axe to sever Cromwell's neck. I am glad we did not know about that while we were serving celebration food and drink at the King's wedding.

30th July 1540

For all his appearance of relaxed happiness with his new bride, King Henry has made it very clear that his power is absolute. Today three people were hauled from the Tower tied to hurdles and dragged through the streets to Smithfield, where they were executed for high treason. One of them was Richard Fetherston, who used to be the lady Mary's tutor. Another was Edward Powell, who had been in prison ever since he championed the cause of Catherine of Aragon. The third was Queen Catherine's former chaplain, Thomas Abell. And Robert Barnes, a Lutheran who had helped to arrange Henry's marriage to Anne of Cleves, was burnt at the stake as a heretic.

The King must have given orders for these things to be done when he was in the middle of planning his wedding. He is so cold now, even in the middle of enjoying festivities, that he frightens me. For all his outward good nature, his eyes are reptilian and calculating. I often wish I could leave all this behind and go back to Elinor and the little house standing among fields. After the execution of Anne Boleyn she must have felt as I do. That is why she fled. But for me, there is no going back. Elinor is my true mother in every way that matters, but I have to make my own life. I can only go forward, however reluctantly.

1st August 1540

The King is taking his new wife to Hampton Court. Perhaps in order to save money, or to travel without too much ostentation, very few servants will go with them. His marriage has not been announced to the public yet, though gossip among those in the know will surely have spread it around the titled families. Kitty and her husband will be with the royal party, but the rest of us have been told that we may have a few days' rest, to do as we wish. This has caused grumbling, as some people live at the court and have nowhere else to go, but I am happy. Will and I can go home to Greenwich and see Elinor.

4th August 1540

Eva was deeply saddened to hear about Robert Fetherston.

"God rest his soul," she said. "He was such a gentle, devout man. You know, Bee, the King himself appointed him as Mary's tutor. She'd have been seven years old then. Henry was still married to Catherine, and he was anxious to get good advice about the education of his little daughter. Catherine suggested asking Juan Luis Vives."

I sometimes forget that Eva is Spanish, but when she rolled off this three-part name it reminded me. When she was my age, she was still in Castile and English was a foreign language to her. She went on, "Juan Luis was famous for insisting that girls need to be well educated. He said the King and Queen could not do better than Robert Fetherston. So King Henry appointed him." She sighed. "It was before Henry began all this nonsense about a new Church. He was still a proper Catholic."

"Like Mr Thornton," I said. I have never forgotten my old tutor.

"The trouble started after he married Anne Boleyn. He wanted to weed out anyone who did not welcome his new wife and agree with the new religion. So he introduced the Act of Succession."

Eva put her hand over her eyes and shook her head. "March 1534. I will never forget it."

I didn't know about the Act of Succession. Eva said it ruled that only the children born to Anne Boleyn could inherit the throne, and Henry's daughter Mary was debarred from the succession. But more than that, Henry insisted that everyone in England must swear that they accepted him as the head of the Church. Any future monarch born to him and Anne Boleyn would in turn be head of the Church. Anyone refusing to take the oath would be accused of treason and executed.

I can see now why Mr Thornton had been so troubled. He could not possibly swear on the Bible that he accepted Henry as the head of the Church. For him, a belief in God would always mean a belief that the Pope represented God's will on earth and that priests had the power to pardon sin and give absolution.

Then Eva laughed. "You know, Henry sent his soldiers to Catherine's household to force everyone to take the oath. Henry knew Catherine would refuse – she had already said she would rather die. He thought he could frighten her servants into giving in, but Catherine was too clever for them. She told the soldiers none of her servants could speak English, and asked politely if the oath could be put to them in Spanish. The soldiers could not speak Spanish, of course, so they agreed that she could put the oath to her servants. So she questioned them seriously, and each one solemnly raised a hand and said *si*, and the soldiers went away satisfied. But they did not know what Catherine had asked them to agree to. She had said, '*El Rey se ha heco cabeza de la Iglesia*.' which means, The King has made himself head of the Church. This was a fact, and the servants had no difficulty in agreeing. But they had not been asked to accept Henry instead of the Pope."

I liked that story – but I wanted to know if the Act of Succession is still in force. Elinor said, "As far as I can see, it will always be in force. This is the new Church of England, and Henry's insistence will probably last forever. The reigning monarch will be its head throughout England's future."

Eva was still thinking of the past. "Robert Fetherston refused to swear. He said that before his God, he could not. So did Thomas Abell, who had been Catherine's chaplain. And Bishop John Fisher, who had done nothing wrong except defend a slightly crazy woman called the Nun of Kent, who had been preaching against the new religion. It was a terrible time."

Will came in and tucked a sprig of honeysuckle into my hair.

"There, my honey Bee," he said cheerfully, "a blossom for you." Then he added, "What would we have to complain about if times were not terrible? The King is a blessing to all grumblers." He joined his hands and gazed piously at the ceiling, then intoned, "Oh, Lord, we thank Thee for the great gift of Henry Tudor, who takes our minds off our own troubles by providing larger ones." We all cheered up.

8th August 1540

The King has at last announced to the public that he is married to Katherine Howard. He has sent envoys out everywhere to unroll a parchment and read out the words written there. I forget the beginning of the speech, but it ends by saying that he has found a wife who is "a perfect jewel of womanhood" and will, he hopes, produce "the desired fruits of marriage".

The royal couple are still at Hampton Court. Elinor warns me that the new queen may want to appoint her own friends as serving ladies. I think Katherine regards me as a distant friend, but Elinor is right, I may be discarded. I tell myself I would not mind – and yet I would miss the court. There is an excitement and danger about it that is strangely addictive. Perhaps I have become a court lady after all. But when the winter comes and I'm in some great stone palace with no view of the sky, I'll wish I was back here, gathering early blackberries in the sunshine.

15th August 1540

Katherine has asked for me to continue in her service. I will be among ladies who are very close to the royal family. Lady Margaret Douglas is the King's niece, and Lady Margaret Howard is Katherine's stepmother, and there is Katherine's sister, Lady Arundel. Lady Rochford is included, too. She was married to Anne Boleyn's brother, George, and during that queen's trial she said her husband had enjoyed a sexual relationship with Anne though she was his sister. Everyone knew it was untrue, but George Boleyn went to the block all the same, and Elinor told me Lady Rochford showed no sign of regret. Some say it was her only way out of a miserable marriage, but even so, she is not a woman I could ever trust.

The King intends to take Katherine on progress, showing her off to people in as many parts of the country as he can. I will be among the servants going with them. We are busy packing and preparing. It is a big task – King Henry constantly gives his young wife more clothes and jewellery. She wears a brand-new gown every day, each one more opulent and richly embroidered than the last. This morning she appeared in one that had words stitched in gold thread on its sleeves, saying, *Non autre volonté que la sienne.* I doubt if she speaks much French, but she will of course know that it means: No other will but his.

I wonder if Charles de Marillac, the French Ambassador, suggested it? He is very pleased with himself at the moment, as France is back in favour now that we have a Catholic queen. The court has gone collectively mad about all things French, and everyone is trying to appear in what they hope is the latest French fashion – not that King Henry will take his eyes off Katherine for long enough to notice anyone else. He showers his new bride with gifts. She wears a beautiful gold medal showing the Tudor rose entwined in a true lovers' knot, lettered with an inscription that says, RUTILANS ROSA SINE SPINA – a red rose with no thorn. Henry thinks Katherine is perfect, and she in turn is in a state of bliss. She dances around, flaunting her brooches, rings, necklaces and pendants as though every minute of her life was a special celebration.

The lady Mary is at court, but we can all see that she finds Katherine's ostentation offensive. Mary had become very friendly with Jane Seymour, who would never have dreamed of behaving in such a way. After Jane died and Henry remarried, Mary came to like Anne of Cleves too. But Jane and Anne were both well-educated, intelligent women, and their friendship with Mary never became over familiar or disrespectful. No matter how warmly they felt towards her, they always spoke to her courteously. Katherine, though charming in her kittenish way, does not understand courtesy. She knows how to please her doting husband – the Duke of Norfolk and his friends trained her well in that – but she treats everyone else with a commonplace good cheer that borders on vulgarity.

It is not her fault, I suppose. As a child she was left to the care of servants, and the refined conventions of the court are hard for her to understand. She is a kind girl at heart and means no harm. I should not blame her for enjoying the wonderful fortune that now lights up her days. She is full of happiness, and that in turn makes the King happy. Even though his lame leg and huge size prevent him from taking part in the dancing, he loves to watch Katherine dance with others, delighting in her quick feet and the elegant turn of her head in a chaconne or bourrée. She is, admittedly, very pretty, and she carries off her many absurdities with all the innocence of a naughty child.

There is no sign that she is pregnant, though her servants say the King visits her bed every night. A lot of vulgar joking is going on. Will is to come with us on progress and when someone wondered if the King still had it in him to beget a child with a wife as slender as Katherine, he said, "Useless. Might as well try to mate a bull with a ferret." The questioner laughed so much, he nearly choked on the apple he was eating.

10th September 1540

We have been on the road again, with the horses and luggage carts, riders and walkers. We spent some days in Northamptonshire, in a big manor house called Grafton. Luckily the threatened rain held off. The autumn sun and a light wind have made the travelling quite pleasant. We are at Ampthill in Bedfordshire now, and will be here for two weeks. Lady Edgecombe told me that Catherine of Aragon had been banished to this house when Henry dismissed her from the court, so Eva must have been here. Lady Edgecombe said she remembered Eva well and asked me to pass on her best wishes.

It was Lady Edgecombe who tackled Anne of Cleves on that extraordinary morning when she told the Queen that we thought she was still a virgin. She is the kind of person who knows everything and makes wise decisions, but she never does anything in a hurry. She is aware of the drinking and revelry that has been going on during this royal progress, but she said, "There is no need to do anything yet. Before long they will go too far."

11th September 1540

Yes, they did go too far. Edward Baynton, the Queen's vice chamberlain, was so drunk tonight before we had even finished dinner that the King could not fail to notice. He stopped smiling at Katherine and turned a cold gaze in Baynton's direction. Everyone fell silent, but the stupid man babbled on, too taken up by some drunken story he was telling to notice the warning signs. Then he saw he was being stared at and stammered to a halt, but it was too late. The King thundered that he expected better from a man entrusted with high office, and issued orders that henceforth, everyone would observe "the sober and temperate order" that was proper in the presence of himself and the Queen.

I thought back privately to times when I had seen the King himself drunk and roistering – but all that has changed now. His new queen is a young girl whom he believes to be pure and innocent, and he is protecting her fiercely from any form of crude behaviour. Afterwards, glances were exchanged that said without words what we all knew. Katherine is not the white lamb of her husband's imagination. It is common knowledge that she was only twelve when she had an affair with her music master, and everyone except the King knows Francis Dereham doted on her until the Duke of Norfolk thought up a different plan for his niece. Under the wide sleeves of my gown, I crossed my fingers and uttered a silent prayer that Henry never finds this out.

23rd October 1540

I am glad the travelling is over. From Ampthill we went to The More in Hertfordshire, where Thomas Wolsey, the Archbishop of York, used to live. I'd read in Elinor's diary how the King blamed him for not being able to persuade the Pope to sanction a divorce from Catherine of Aragon. Wolsey was arrested as a traitor, but he died on the way to London for imprisonment in the Tower. Perhaps it was a better death than the one in store for him.

We are in Windsor now. We were hardly unpacked and settled in when people starting asking if it's true that Anne of Cleves is pregnant. The King was appalled, and denied the rumours angrily. It turns out that she had been confined to her bed with an upset stomach for a day or two, so gossips immediately put it around that she had morning sickness and was expecting a baby.

27th October 1540

Now we have a new scandal. We had hoped to keep this from the King, but we all knew during the summer progress that Lady Margaret Douglas, Katherine's chief lady-in-waiting, had fallen in love with Charles Howard, the Queen's elder brother. Lady Margaret is the King's niece, and is almost as headstrong as her royal uncle. She caused outrage four years ago when she married Lord Thomas Howard without even mentioning it to Henry, let alone asking his permission. It was an extraordinary thing to do. The King was furious, of course. He sent both of them to the Tower. Lady Margaret was released after a time, but Thomas Howard became ill and died there. And now Margaret has upset the King all over again by having the cheek to fall in love with his new bride's brother! She will not get away with it so easily this time. Henry has packed her off to Syon Abbey, which used to house a community of nuns until they were driven out in the abolition of the monasteries, and Charles Howard has been forbidden to have anything further to do with her.

Katherine has sensibly said nothing. I can't guess whether she has been well advised or simply does not care what trouble her brother gets himself into. Either way, she has remained meek and quiet, and the King is still pleased with her.

16th November 1540

A strange gift arrived for Katherine today. A man called Richard Jones sent her a book of his own writing called *The Birth of Mankind*, all about the conceiving of babies and their safe delivery. He dedicated it to "our most gracious and virtuous Queen Katherine". We all thought she would be embarrassed by such a broad hint that the whole country was waiting for her to produce a child, but she just smiled and set the book aside. Its long words probably baffle her, so she may not understand what it is about.

2nd December 1540

We are away for a second time, though nobody expected it. When the days started to darken in November, and the London streets were full of mud as well as the usual filth, the King got it into his head that he needed to be in the country. So we packed up once again, and set off for Woking, in Surrey. Here he has taken to rising before dawn, at between five and six o'clock. He attends Mass at seven, then goes out hawking with his huntsmen. He stays out until dinner at ten in the morning, and declares that this new routine suits him well. His leg is better at the moment, and he can ride again. But he and Katherine have a fancy to go to Oatlands, where they were married. After that, it will be Hampton Court for the Christmas festivities. We will be on the road again next week.

7th January 1541

What a Christmas it has been! In contrast to last year, when the King was glumly facing a forced marriage to a woman he disliked, this was an overflowing of festivity and happiness. He gave Katherine gift after glorious gift. The diamond pendants were breathtaking, and I gasped at the sight of a heavy necklace of 200 perfect pearls. The thing I liked best, though, was the black-velvet muffler edged with sable fur and encrusted with rubies and pearls. The other ladies smiled dutifully but they did not seem particularly impressed. Lady Edgeworth told me afterwards that she had seen these beautiful things before. "They were given to other wives," she said, and gave me a glance that told the rest without words. These were gifts that had been reclaimed when those other wives were banished or dead.

Robin danced with me several times. "You have not lost your sweetness in growing to be a woman," he said as we passed each other. And next time we crossed, he kissed my cheek. Everybody saw. I would have been all blushes at one time, but I know now that Robin sets his cap at any girl who will return his smile. All the same, I sat down with my head high, as my uncle's words still ring in my mind – *Have you seen yourself?* I know I should put all that behind me, but it has been difficult to believe that people do not think I am ugly.

At New Year we were busier than ever. The lady Mary came, and so did Anne of Cleves. We all wondered if she would seem embarrassed now that the King has a new wife, but she carried it off beautifully. Before she arrived, she sent Henry a gift of two magnificent horses, complete with velvet trappings in a wonderful shade of deep violet, and he was delighted. Anne was charming to Katherine and they got on amazingly well. After the King had retired to bed because his leg was troubling him, his two wives, past and present, stayed up late, talking and dancing together.

The next day Henry gave Katherine yet more gifts – this time a beautiful ring and two little dogs. I am not sure that Katherine likes dogs, but the question did not arise as she graciously handed the new presents to Anne.

The festivities are over now. Most of the guests have gone home and the others will be departing soon. The King is making plans to go to London to attend to business with the Privy Council, but Katherine will stay here.

Late this evening, I found Will sitting on a bench in the kitchen, leaning back against the wall with his eyes closed. He opened them when he heard me come in, and gave a tired smile. "Thank Heavens that's over," he said. "If I'd had one more swan to stuff, I think I'd have booted it out of the back door."

I sat down beside him, and for some moments we were quiet. Then he asked, "What are you going to do, Bee? Are you going to marry Jolly Robin?"

I wondered if he had been up to the big hall and seen me dancing with Robin. I shook my head and told him, "That never meant anything. He kisses all the girls."

Will gave a small nod but said nothing. The quietness went on, and a kind of sadness came over me. I didn't know what I was doing in this grand palace. It was months now since I had seen Elinor. Months since I had walked across meadows, free of the smells of people and perfume and food and filth. Months since I had heard Bella chattering and the birds singing in the morning.

Will put his arm round me and whispered, "What's the matter, sweetheart?"

Tears had come, and I could not answer. Very gently he put his fingertips under my chin and turned my face to his. Then he kissed me.

I think about it again and again, and each time there is a warm surge of happiness. I feel as if I have come home.

12th February 1541

The King has sunk into a state of gloom. After Christmas his leg took a turn for the worse, and he hardly leaves his private chambers now. When he does, it is only to sit in his great chair, shifting uneasily and groaning. The Queen changes the dressings on his festering ulcer at least twice a day, with no complaint. I admire her for that. I have held the basin for her sometimes when she cleans the sore so I know it has a dreadful stink. I would hate to have to touch it. The King cannot go hunting, as riding a horse is out of the question, and that depresses him. He has not even tried out the beautiful chargers that were a gift from Anne of Cleves.

The French ambassador describes Henry's illness as *mal d'esprit* – a sickness of the spirit – and I think he may be right. The King is unable to take any interest in anything. He seems sunk in despair. Even Katherine no longer seems to amuse him. He is grateful – I think – for her ministrations as a nurse, but his delight in her has vanished. The only thing that still brings him any satisfaction is eating. Will is concerned about the huge quantities food and wine the King is devouring. "It's enough for five men," he said today. "But it's doing him no good. He just gets fatter and more miserable."

We are all involved in rehearsals for masques to be held later this month, in an effort to rouse the King from his lethargy. Will is devising words for songs, and all the prettiest girls will be dancing. I am not sure that it will work. Henry sits in his great chair with no more movement than a vast sack of potatoes. His baggy eyes glare out from a face so fat that its chin is lost in his bulging neck, which goes from his lower lip to the great jewel fastening his jerkin.

22nd February 1541

As I feared, the masques did not improve things. The King watched the dancers, actors and clowns unsmilingly, and seemed bored by the songs and music. Afterwards, Katherine was in tears because he had shut her out from his rooms, as he so often does now. She asked us if his bad mood was caused by something she had done, and we tried to assure her that it was not. Lady Edgeworth explained that the King often gets these long periods of black depression in the winter, particularly if his health is poor, but Katherine was not reassured. She cannot understand why her husband has turned so cold, and is sure he is tired of her. What started off as such exciting fun has changed into gloom, and it is very hard on her. Any other girl would seek comfort with some younger and more cheerful man. But that, of course, is impossible. Katherine is the King's wife. Whatever he does or does not do, it is her duty to accept it without question.

20th March 1541

With the blossoming of primroses and daffodils, King Henry's darkness is at last beginning to leave him. He has begun to move about more and this in turn seems to have improved his leg a little. He is even starting to speak to people again.

Katherine has just learned about Lady Margaret Pole, who has been imprisoned in a cold cell in the Tower for two years now, with no heating to protect her ageing bones against the bitter winter weather and only the most miserable food. Katherine, to her credit, was horrified. She went straight to her tailor (asking Henry's permission first) and ordered him to make a furred nightgown and petticoat, a bonnet and a warm worsted cloak. She has sent these to Lady Margaret, together with four pairs of shoes and some warm slippers and stockings, and paid for all of it out of her own purse.

She has also scored a remarkable victory over the case of Thomas Wyatt, who was at the execution of Cromwell, having only just himself been released from the Tower. He was restored to his duties as ambassador after being pardoned, but then he came under suspicion again because he was estranged from his wife, Margaret. The King thinks Wyatt may be a dangerous adulterer, so he has imprisoned him in the Tower again for treason. In fact Margaret is the adulterous one of the pair. Wyatt had been separated from her for fifteen years because of her infidelity, and during that time she had affairs with several other men. Kitty says Wyatt is a wonderful poet who has invented a new form of verse called the sonnet, but the King does not care about that. He says Wyatt has broken the conditions on which he was released – namely, that he must live with his wife again, permanently.

Katherine felt that this was unreasonable. Bravely, or perhaps rashly, she tackled Henry about it. The argument went on all last week. Katherine begged and cajoled and used all her charms, and at last she won, at least partially. The King has agreed to release Wyatt from the Tower – but he still insists that Wyatt must live with his adulterous wife again. It is amazing how prudish Henry can be about other people's lives when his own is such a patchwork of outrageous behaviour, but I suppose that is all part of his conviction that he is superior and all-powerful.

Katherine, needless to say, gets no credit for Wyatt's release. The public statement reads that the King, who is "of his own most godly nature inclined to pity and mercy, hath given him his pardon in large and ample sort".

"Pity and mercy?" Will said. "Pigs might fly."

Everyone is delighted that Wyatt has been pardoned, and Katherine is regarded with far more respect than before. The King is being congratulated on his wisdom and compassion (though we know he had to be talked into it) and he is looking pleased with himself.

10th April 1541

Katherine thinks she may be expecting a baby. We are all praying that it is true. The King is immensely pleased. He has issued a declaration that, if the pregnancy is confirmed, Katherine will be officially crowned as Queen of England at Whitsuntide.

22nd April 1541

Alas for all our hopes, the Queen was not pregnant. She might have had an early miscarriage, but the details hardly matter. There is no royal baby. The King has relapsed into his black mood, and sits scowling at nothing that we can see. Katherine is chastened and miserable – and to make things worse, a persistent rumour is going round that Henry intends to take Anne of Cleves back. Of course an official denial has been issued, but for some anxious days Katherine half-believed it. One morning I found her in tears. I put my arms round her, and though she is too much a queen now to admit that she had been listening to gossip, she laid her head on my shoulder. "He does not want me," she said.

Poor girl. Her light-heartedness has gone and there is a small frown between her dark eyebrows. Perhaps she thought the gaiety and opulence of Christmas was to be the daily pattern of her life. If so, she is sadly disappointed.

23rd April 1541

There is a new uprising against the King, this time in Yorkshire. Again, people want to see the old religion restored. It seems to be a minor affair compared with the Pilgrimage of Grace, but it is a new source of irritation to Henry. He dealt firmly with Jane Seymour when she begged him to see there might be reason in what the pilgrims were saying, and then dealt decisively and brutally with the rebels – but this new unrest worries him. He is back into an irrational terror that some member of the Plantagenet family may be trying to stir people up against him with a view to claiming the throne. It seems very unlikely, since the few remaining members of the old ruling family are either dead or exiled or in prison, but in his present mood of angry suspicion, any hint of disloyalty throws him into furious panic. So he regards the insurrection in Yorkshire as a serious threat.

Sir John Neville is responsible for that part of the country, and he should have reported that a conspiracy was brewing. He failed to do this, so the King holds him responsible for the uprising. Sir John has been committed to the Tower, accused of treason. The French ambassador cattily described him as "a man of mediocre ability and wit", and it is true that he is not a clever man. But a plea of mere incompetence will do him no good, for Henry is in a savage mood.

21st May 1541

Oh, this is terrible! The King's irrational terror of the Plantagenets has led him to order that Lady Margaret Pole must die. She is 68 years old and in all her life she has never criticized the King or expressed the slightest interest in becoming Queen of England. She said publicly that she disagreed with her son's opinions. I can't see how she could possibly have done anything treasonable, since she has been locked up in the Tower for the last two years. But she has a direct claim to the throne, so Henry regards her as an enemy.

Katherine, who persuaded the King to let her send Lady Margaret some warm garments only six weeks ago, is distraught. For days she has been begging him to show mercy, but he is unbending. His face is an expressionless mask, his small mouth set hard in a narrow line. He has commanded that the Act of Attainder, which two years ago condemned Margaret Pole to a traitor's death, shall be put into effect without delay. The poor lady is to be executed next week, and I feel sick to my soul.

28th May 1541

The horrible details of Lady Margaret's death are all round the court, whispered in revulsion by those who saw it. The Constable of the Tower had woken her early that morning and gave her a short time to get dressed and compose her soul for her coming death. Perhaps he thought it was merciful to do the thing as quickly as possible. She was escorted out to Tower Green, where a scaffold had been erected in the same place were Anne Boleyn had died. A large crowd of people had come to watch.

Lady Margaret did not submit. She protested her innocence (quite rightly – for she was innocent). She broke away from her captors, but they caught her and dragged her back. Even then, she resisted with all her strength. She refused to place her head on the block and had to be forced down. The executioner was not the usual one, but an inexperienced young man who was perhaps unnerved by the fight this elderly lady was putting up. He may have been horrified by what he had to do. Whatever the cause, while they held her down, still struggling, he struck at her blindly with the axe and gashed her shoulder. Desperately he went on hacking at her. The horrified watchers saw eleven blows before the terrible task was completed.

The men from the Tower themselves were aghast. They have had no hesitation in telling everyone about the rhyme that Lady Margaret had carved into the wall of her cell:

For traitors on the block should die;
I am no traitor, no, not I!
My faithfulness stands fast and so,
Towards the block I shall not go!
Nor make one step, as you shall see;
Christ in Thy Mercy, save Thou me!

I went down to the kitchens in tears, and Will put his arms round me as I cried. "We must leave this place," he said.

Yes. Oh, yes.

5th June 1541

The atmosphere in the court is very different now. Katherine is white-faced and silent, and there is unspoken sympathy for her.

She has seen for the first time the ruthless cruelty that lies below the King's smooth surface, and it has shocked her. She knows, as four women before her have found out, that Henry regards her as a cross between brood mare and plaything. It is not her place to think about what he does, let alone to voice the slightest criticism. He gave in to her plea to let her send clothes to Lady Margaret Pole because it seemed a soft-hearted feminine indulgence, but matters of life and death are nobody's business but his own. I can see that Katherine will never feel the same about him again. He is not the big, genial husband she took him for. He is dangerous.

15th June 1541

The King has plans to go to the eastern counties, and then north to Yorkshire, where a lot of people joined the Pilgrimage of Grace. Kitty tells me his purpose is to collect money. All the towns that supported the rebellion had huge fines imposed on them, and he wants to make sure they are paid. Also he will be meeting with his nephew, King James V of Scotland.

We have a few days off before the journey north, and I am at Elinor's house. I feel as I did when I was a child, running to this warm and comforting refuge. Eva is deeply grieved for Margaret Pole.

She said, "That sweet lady did nobody any harm. It was not her fault that her son was so reckless in opposing the King's divorce. Why could he not have listened to her assurances?"

Elinor said, "He has never listened to any woman."

Eva disagreed. "He listened to Catherine of Aragon. She earned his respect – but she was the only one. He has kept all his other wives in their place and made it clear that he did not want to hear their opinions. He had a nod of respect for Anne of Cleves, I suppose, who had the good sense to make no fuss when he divorced her. But Catherine was different."

I asked if that was because she was his first wife and the one he truly loved, but Eva said it was more than that.

"Catherine had fought her way into marrying him and he admired her intelligence and her grasp of politics. He left her in charge of the country when he went off to war with the French, and she conducted a war with the Scots and won." But then Eva shuddered a little. "Oh, that was horrible."

I asked what happened, and she shook her head. "I don't want to remember. It was the one time when I wished Catherine was not quite so passionate in her love for her husband."

I looked again at Eva's diary, wanting to know what it was that she refused to recall, and found it. I had read it before, but with patchy understanding because my grasp of Spanish was poor. This time I read her words carefully, using Mr Thornton's Spanish grammar book to make sure I had the meaning right.

On September 12th, 1513, Catherine was on her way back from Buckingham, where she had launched her army against the Scots. Eva wrote:

The Scottish army is utterly destroyed, and James is dead. Surrey met them in the Cheviot Hills, at a place called Flodden. …In three hours of fighting, 10,000 Scottish soldiers were killed. Ten <u>thousand</u>. There can hardly be an able-bodied man left in the country. The officers and nobility, too, were mown down, and at last James himself fell.

Eleven days later, Catherine was home, but her triumph had come at a cost.

On the night after her return, she lost the baby she had been expecting. Poor little future child – such an innocent casualty of war, and so deliberately put at risk, it seems to me. Catherine herself looks white-faced and exhausted, but she gave herself no rest after the miscarriage, and it has not stopped her from the grim business in which she is still taking part.

When she heard of James's death she ordered his body to be brought to London. I was with her when the captain of the travel-weary men came to report that this had been done. She went out with him, and bade me follow. I could not look at the wrapped and already stinking burden they carried, but she seemed exultant.

The body must be taken to Henry in France, she said, that he might see for himself that the Scots had been vanquished.

An uneasy glance ran between the men, and their captain begged Catherine to excuse them from such a task. She looked at him with contempt and turned on her heel.

Upstairs, she unwrapped the bundle of soiled clothing which the captain had given her, and held up a surcoat, gold-embroidered with the lion of Scotland. It was soaked with blood and slashed almost to ribbons. The captain had explained apologetically that after the battle the English troops had plundered the dead men who lay everywhere, stripping them of clothes and valuables. The body of the Scottish king, too, had been stripped, but the captain had managed to retrieve his coat. And as I watched her, sickened, Catherine smiled. "If I cannot send his dead enemy's body, Harry shall at least have his coat," she said. And in the afternoon of that same day, she dispatched it to France.

I saw why Eva did not want to think again about that day. That slashed and blood-soaked coat had been stripped from the King of Scotland, the father of our present James V of Scotland. It was he who married Mary of Guise, snatching her from under his uncle Henry's nose when he was seeking a wife before he married Anne of Cleves. And it is this James whom Henry expects to meet in Lincoln in a few weeks' time.

Eva does not think the Scottish king will come.

12th August 1541

There have been days of travelling along rough roads, mostly hot and dusty, though we had a week of pouring rain, when the horses were labouring through mud and everybody was wet and miserable. The royal progress is slow, limited by the lurching baggage carts and the weariness of the foot servants, and arrival in a town comes as a relief. Will is not with us and I miss him dreadfully, but Kitty has come. I am glad of her company.

We have stopped at Dunstable, Ampthill and Grafton, then Northampton. After that there were some days in the pretty town of Stamford, which Kitty and I liked for its river running through green fields. Then came Lincoln, with its cathedral reached by the narrow lanes that wind up the hill. We were lodged in the Bishops' Palace there, and it was very comfortable – but it was in that town that the Pilgrimage of Grace had started. The King gave orders for the townsfolk to be assembled. When they were all gathered, he delivered an unsmiling speech, announcing that he pardoned the people for having permitted an uprising in their midst. The unspoken message was clear. They should consider themselves fortunate to be forgiven, but no such rebellious movement was ever to occur again. Henry's words were heard in silence, though everyone dutifully joined in the cheers that were called for the King afterwards. They could hardly do otherwise.

Now we are in the port of Boston, where ships go in and out and canals wind across the flat country. From here we will head north again to York to meet King James, then all the way to Newcastle, which is quite near to the border with Scotland. Some of the men have been there before, carrying messages from the King, but Henry himself has never ventured so far north.

A rider came today with news that Spain and France are on the brink of war. Both are seeking English support. The King is looking pleased. There is no question of which side he will be on. He does not like Spain because of the link with the Spanish emperor, but he mistrusts King Francis even more and believes the French may launch an attack on England. That is why he has been building defences all along the south, including the massive castles at Deal and Walmer.

Henry is enjoying this progress. He particularly liked the maritime bustle of Boston and spent a long time watching the boats and talking with their captains. Katherine has cheered up too. In every village and town we have passed through, the people who turned out to line the roads have greeted her with applause and a warm welcome. She responds well, smiling and waving, open-handed in her gestures of affection. She is so young and pretty, they adore her at once. The King basks in her popularity, taking it as a compliment to himself that he has acquired such a beautiful young bride, so he in turn is genial and good-tempered. Long may it last!

20th August 1541

We are in a place called Pontefract. Something very disturbing has happened. A young man came up to us, asking to speak to the Queen. Lady Edgeworth asked who he was and what he wanted – but Katherine must have heard the man's voice, because she came running out. He greeted her with great familiarity, as though they were old friends. He is Francis Dereham.

A glance of alarm ran between us. It was bad enough when Joan Bulmer pushed herself into Katherine's household, but this is far worse. All of us – except the King – know that Katherine had an affair with Dereham before her uncle decided to put her forward as a possible future queen. If the King finds out… I cross my fingers and close my eyes at the very thought. Please God, let the King not find out.

Dereham had a polite manner and an easy smile that reminded me a little of the peddlers who used to come to our back door when I was a child. Agnes always sent them packing. He said he had been recommended by the Dowager Duchess of Norfolk, in whose house Katherine had grown up, and added that the Duchess was sure the Queen would be pleased to have him as a member of her household. There was silence as we watched Katherine and noted the faint flush that rose to her face. She responded with correct formality – but instead of turning the man down, as we expected, she said she would ask the King if he could be employed.

She put her request to the King over dinner tonight, almost casually. Henry asked her why she wanted to appoint Dereham, and she gazed at him innocently and said, "Because the Duchess of Norfolk asked me to be good to him – and so I will." And the King, being in a good humour, shrugged and said if that was what she wanted, he agreed. So Francis Dereham is to begin work as the Queen's secretary when we get back from progress. Joan Bulmer was also employed as "secretary". Could Katherine think of nothing more original?

Jealousies have broken out, of course. Katherine does not know it, but there are several young men in the court who find her extremely attractive and would give anything to be in her service. There is much grumbling going on, with demands to know why this upstart fellow has been taken into the Queen's service when so many of the loyal court servants are ignored.

When we were alone Kitty said, "Bee, this is so dangerous. There can only be one reason why Katherine agreed to Dereham's request. It's because she dares not refuse. She is terrified of what he may reveal."

Neither of us put words to our fears. We may be on the road to disaster.

18th September 1541

We arrived in York three days ago. Since then, the King has been waiting for his nephew, James V of Scotland, to arrive as promised, but as Eva predicted, he has not come. Henry is furious. He said the Scottish king can expect no favours from him in future. He has given order to set out tomorrow for Hull. The aim of going to Newcastle has been dropped as it should have been in the company of James and his retinue. From Hull we will be heading back through the many towns, aiming to reach Windsor by the end of October.

26th October 1541

We made good time on the return journey, spending no more than a single night in most of the places we passed through. Now we are at Hampton Court – and to my joy, Will is here. He was transferred from Greenwich when the other cook cut his hand with a cleaver. It turned septic and led to blood poisoning, and the poor man seems likely to die. I should not rejoice at anyone's misfortune, but I am disgracefully happy.

It seems that the failure of the Scottish king to keep his appointment with Henry was not his fault. His mother, Queen Margaret of Scotland, died in Methven Castle on the 8th of this month. King Henry snorted at such a feeble excuse, but I think it's obvious that James could not start out on a long journey to England at that point.

Henry has good reason to think that James is on the side of France. There has long been an alliance between the two countries. The Scottish king's present wife is French, and so was the previous one, Madeleine of Valois, who died of consumption. And James grew up in the shadow of his father's death at Flodden. There is no good reason why he should have any liking for Henry Tudor.

None of that mattered when we first came back, as the court doctors met us with the news that four-year-old Prince Edward was ill with a fever. Henry was desperately worried. Luckily, he did not hear Charles de Marillac, the French ambassador, remark with his usual waspishness that the boy was too fat and flabby to live long. God be thanked, the young prince is recovering now, so his father's panic has subsided.

27th October 1541

Our fears about Francis Dereham were well founded. Ever since he came here as Katherine's secretary, his mask of politeness has slipped away. He has been behaving with appalling arrogance. He treats the Queen with a familiarity that we all find offensive and worrying, and she does nothing but give him an anxious shake of the head and an imploring glance.

A few nights ago, things came to a head. Dereham remained sprawled in his seat at the dinner table while everyone else stood up, as is customary, when the Queen's Council rose to leave. Mr John, one of the gentlemen ushers, was so offended by this rudeness that he sent a messenger with a note to remind all members that they must observe the courtesy of rising when the leading dignitary leaves. When Dereham read the note, he told the messenger to go to Mr John and tell him that he, Dereham, had been one of the Queen's advisers before Mr John knew her, and would still be there after she had forgotten him.

When Mr John received this insolent reply he came in person to remonstrate. Dereham was still sprawled in his chair and did not bother to get up. Mr John, normally a courteous gentleman, was so outraged that he laid hands on the man to try to haul him to his feet. It led to a brawl that turned into an actual fist fight. Dereham, being the younger and stronger, walked away smirking while Mr John was left huddled and gasping, blood pouring from his nose. We were all horrified. Nobody has breathed a word to the King – there are strict rules against violent behaviour in the court.

There is much talk about why the Queen tolerates Dereham's rudeness and discourtesy. Everyone can see that she is afraid of him, and anyone who did not already know that she'd had a previous affair with him certainly knows now. Except the King.

Kitty said, "Katherine should have stood up to Dereham when he first arrived, when we were on progress. She could have told him she has the power to get him executed for his impertinence."

I said Katherine would not dare to do that if she was afraid Dereham might reveal things she did not want known. Kitty looked at me and sighed. "You may be right, Bee," she said. After a minute, she went on, "My aunt Anne's tragedy started in just the same way, with murmurs that she had been involved with other men. Henry had loved her and found her fascinating, just as he loves Katherine now. But his love quickly turns to hatred if he finds any fault in the woman he thought perfect."

It is the first time she has spoken of Anne Boleyn, in all these years.

1st November 1541

I keep hoping that there is nothing to worry about. The royal pair are getting on wonderfully well now. Henry's delight in Katherine is obvious. He smiles at the sight of her and cannot refrain from running his hand down her back when she is close enough to touch. Everyone feels a little more secure in the light of such loving sunshine, and the atmosphere in the court is cautiously contented, even though Dereham continues to be irritating.

Today there was a special service of thanksgiving for the royal marriage. It was held in the Chapel Royal at Hampton Court, where we are now. The King thanked God for the blessing of such a perfect companion. He said, "I render thanks to Thee, Oh Lord, that after so many strange accidents that have befallen my marriages, Thou has been pleased to give me a wife so entirely conformed to my inclination as her I now have." And he commanded every church in the kingdom to hold similar services of thanksgiving.

A strange thing happened, though. In the middle of the King's thanksgiving, Archbishop Cranmer entered the chapel quietly. We thought he had come to add his respects to the royal couple and join in the thanksgiving, but he did not sit down. Instead he put a sealed letter beside the King, who was still speaking. Then he went out again without a word.

Same day, later

I am in such a turmoil that I don't know where to start. Nothing will ever be the same again. Things are terrible – and yet I am so happy.

Will came to find me. "Come for a walk," he said. It was a night of hard frost, so I was surprised. I looked at him, but for once his face held no laughter. So I fetched my cloak and we went out. An almost full moon hung over the bare trees, and the grass was white, crunching under our feet.

Will said, "You were at the thanksgiving service, weren't you. Did you see Cranmer come in with a letter?"

I nodded. The quietness of the way the archbishop had laid the letter on the table was still in my mind. Then Will told me what had happened. The coachman who drove Cranmer to the court came down to the kitchens for something to eat before he was called for the homeward journey. And he told the servants that a man called John Lascelles had come to see Archbishop Cranmer. The household staff knew Lascelles – he had been there before.

"They knew his sister too," Will said. "Mary Lascelles. Mary Hall since her marriage. And Mary knows Katherine Howard. They'd both been brought up at the Duchess of Norfolk's house in Lambeth. They slept in the ladies' dormitory."

I thought I knew what he was going to tell me. "So she wanted a job at court, like Joan Bulmer?"

It seems it's worse than that, though it started the same way. Lascelles suggested to his sister that she might get a job in Katherine's service, but Mary refused to approach Katherine. She said she was very sorry for her. Lascelles asked why, but, as Will put it, "she clammed up and wouldn't explain." Lascelles told Cranmer about it. And Cranmer sent for Mary Hall.

I could see why – because she could not lie to an archbishop, or refuse to answer his questions.

"Exactly," Will said. "Mary poured out the whole story. And Cranmer's housekeeper had her ear pressed to the panelling. That room is not as soundproof as its owner thinks."

Mary Hall's story is the one we have all dreaded. She told the Archbishop about Katherine's affair with Henry Manox, the music master, and also about Dereham. He, too, was at the Dowager Duchess's Lambeth house. Mary told Cranmer how Dereham used to come into the ladies' dormitory at night and get into Katherine's bed. She said all the girls knew it. They tried to pretend they were asleep, but from the sounds coming from Katherine's end of the room, they knew exactly what she and Dereham were up to.

Cranmer is the archbishop of Henry's Church of England.

Will said, "He has never liked Katherine because she belongs to the Howard family – Catholics, all of them. Mary Hall handed him his chance to get rid of Katherine, and he took it."

"That's what was in the letter. He has told the King."

Will said, "I fear so."

We stared at each other. Our breath misted the darkness.

"What is going to happen?" I whispered.

"Nothing good," Will said. "If we are right, Henry knows that his rose without a thorn is not as pure as he believed."

I covered my face with my hands. Poor, silly Katherine. Nobody ever mothered her or helped her to understand how humans work. I started to cry. Will took me in his arms. He ran a gentle finger over first one wet eye then the other. He took a deep breath.

"Listen, Bee," he said. "All that apart, I have a request to make."

I suspected nothing more than a hole in a sock to mend or a button to replace on his jacket – but he went down on one knee in the white grass, holding my hand in both of his own.

"Beautiful Beatrice. My lovely, treasured Bee, I have wanted to ask you for so long, and this is perhaps the worst time in the world, but I can't help it. Please – will you marry me?"

Everything seemed to turn a slow somersault. For so many years I have loved and admired him as the big brother I never had, and ever since he kissed me I have longed for him in a different way, though I could never have said so. And now, despite the frightening news he had told me, I was standing on the cold grass in a state of dizzying happiness.

"Yes," I said. "Dear, beloved Will, yes. Oh, yes, *please*."

He got to his feet, then wiped imagined sweat from his brow. "Thank goodness for that. I was so scared you'd say no, I've put off asking you for months."

He took me in his arms and we stood close together, kissing for a long time in the clear, icy moonlight.

Oh, how I love him.

2nd November 1541

Katherine knew nothing of what was coming. I was not prepared, either. In shameful truth, I was still so blissfully happy that the threat of what might happen had faded from my mind. So this morning I was with Kitty and the Queen's other ladies, chattering and laughing as we practised dance steps to the music of a lute – and then there was a loud knocking at the door. The threat was back at once, hanging over everything like a black cloud, and my heart almost stopped. The lady who was playing the lute looked up in alarm, her fingers motionless on the fingerboard. The door burst open, and a group of the King's guards marched in. We fell back against the walls. The room seemed very full of these uniformed men with their armoured breastplates, and swords and helmets. Very big and hard and bright. Their leader said it was time for the dancing to stop. He told Katherine she is to stay in her chambers until her name is cleared of "certain allegations" – which, he added, "His Majesty is sure it will be." Then he called for all Katherine's servants to present themselves.

When every one of us was assembled, he said we were all dismissed. The only exception is Lady Rochford. She alone will stay with the Queen. But why Lady Rochford? She is a Howard, of course, but she seemed so shocked and dismayed that we thought she must know nothing about it. Katherine herself was shaking with fear and anger. "What have I done to deserve this?" she demanded. "For what reason does His Majesty imprison me?"

The leader of the guards gave her no answer. He and his men stood back, indicating that we should leave the room. We all filed out, leaving the Queen alone with Lady Rochford, who was ashen-faced and aghast, and kept uttering little moans. Katherine's lips were trembling, and we knew that when the men had gone, she would be in tears. Two guards were posted outside her door.

3rd November 1541

When Katherine knew the King would be at prayer in the Chapel Royal, she managed to dodge between the guards and make a run to see him – but the men chased her and caught her. They dragged her, screaming hysterically that she is innocent, back to her room.

I was so upset that I fled to the kitchens and sought out Will, who put down his knife among the half-chopped onions and came outside with me. I buried my head in his neck, my arms tight around him. The smell of onions added its harmless reason for tears and provided a small trace of comfort, but the shock of what I'd just seen had left me tremulous in mind and body. "It is not her fault," I wept, "not her fault."

Will said, "Her only fault was to let her relatives drop her into this bear-pit. She fancied other men, but how many girls do not?"

I thought guiltily of Robin for a moment. Will went on, "Cranmer probably means her no harm personally. He is not a vindictive man. But she is a Catholic."

Anger swept over me. "Why do people have to go on dying for different ideas of God?" I argued. Then I thought of something else, and looked at him. "Will, what is *your* God?"

He frowned, thinking about it, then he replied, "I believe in the God of the green leaf and the bird's egg, I suppose. The God who is in music and laughter and kindness. I do not care in which Church He is found. But Cranmer would burn me for saying that. So would the Pope. And so would the King."

We clung together for a little longer. Then Will said, "I'd better get on with the onions."

5th November 1541

In the council today, Cranmer and several of the councillors confirmed that the story told by Lascelles and his sister, Mary Hall, is true. Cranmer told Henry that the Queen, by taking a former lover into her service, had betrayed him "in thought, and if she had an opportunity would have betrayed you in deed".

Kitty's husband was there. He said Henry stared at Cranmer as if he could not believe what he had just heard. After a few moments his face crumpled and he began to weep like a child. Between his sobs he poured out his distress in a torrent of words, speaking of Katherine as his rose without a thorn, his true love. With tears running down his face, he asked if he must really believe this of her. The Duke of Norfolk stared down at his hands and met nobody's eye, and the rest of the councillors sat in agonized embarrassment. Chapuys, the Spanish ambassador, said afterwards that for a man of such courage as the King, it was extraordinary to see him so broken.

The King left this afternoon, with just a few attendants. He has gone to Oatlands, where he and Katherine were married, and where he was happy. He rode at full gallop.

Katherine has been told of the charges against her. From her window, she saw Henry ride away, and she is hysterical. Her uncle, the Duke of Norfolk, spent some time with her, but he was no help – we heard her screaming and crying. He came out shaking his head and said that his niece was threatening to kill herself. He gave orders for all sharp things such as scissors to be taken away from her.

Lady Rochford is frantic as well, tearing her hair and shrieking like a mad woman. It is whispered that she knew all about Katherine's previous affairs, and even assisted her in them. I suppose that is why she was the one chosen to remain with the Queen. She too is to be accused. Henry already knows she is treacherous, but he did not mind her betrayal of her own husband when it was to the King's advantage. This time it is different.

7th November 1541

Cranmer visited Katherine yesterday and again today, but she is still distraught and frantic. Later today she quietened a little – apparently the archbishop brought her a letter from the King, saying that if she will confess her crimes, he will deal leniently with her. Henry himself is still away at Oatlands.

Francis Dereham and Henry Manox have both been arrested and imprisoned in the Tower. People are being questioned closely about what they know. Several of them have testified that Dereham used to call Katherine "wife", as though they were a married couple.

Kitty says the Queen should admit that she was engaged to Dereham. It would count as an "existing pre-contract", so her marriage to the King would have to be declared illegal. In that case she could not be accused of adultery, because she had never been Henry's true wife. But Katherine has nobody to advise her. It is not in the Duke of Norfolk's interests to show her any sympathy. His only chance of staying in the King's favour is to claim that he is shocked by his niece's behaviour and wants to see her duly punished.

The wretched girl is still shut up in her rooms with Lady Rochford who, the servants say, is "raving mad" and clearly useless. Katherine will get no help from her or from any member of the Howard family. They manoeuvred her into the position of queen for their own purposes, but now they will throw her to the wolves in order to preserve their own skins. She is on her own.

11th November 1541

The King has come back to Hampton Court. He put on a theatrical pretence of good spirits. He commanded an evening of dancing and gaiety and flirted with the ladies as though he were twenty again.

Most of us found it an unpleasant sight, but we had to smile and appear to look happy.

Katherine has written a long confession to the King, pointing out that she was only eleven years old when Henry Manox started to pay attentions to her, and saying she was confused and upset by what he was doing. As to Dereham – she claims that she was glad to get away from him when she was called to court because he had raped her and she was afraid of him.

Cranmer, surprisingly, has suggested that there probably was a pre-contract between Katherine and Dereham, and he thinks her marriage to the King can be annulled. It seems that Will is right, and the Archbishop is not seeking to send her to the block. He merely wants her out of the way so that the Catholic influence on the King will come to an end. Katherine's worst enemy is her own uncle, backed by the Howard clan. All of them are desperate to wash their hands of any suggestion that they might have known Katherine was not as pure as Henry believed. They are all models of innocence. If there is guilt, then it is for Katherine to accept, and Katherine alone.

12th November 1541

Kitty is expecting a baby. She has known about it for a few weeks now, but she very sensibly feels that King Henry is in no mood to welcome anyone else's glad news, so she is keeping her pregnancy a secret for the time being.

Yesterday the King attended a council meeting that lasted until five in the morning. The debate continues today. A messenger came to say that Lady Rochford will be sent to the Tower to await questioning. And Katherine is to go to what used to be the Abbey of Syon, in Brentford, where she will be under house arrest.

13th November 1541

This has been a frantic day of packing and getting ready for departure – but with none of the holiday spirit that accompanies going on progress. Sir Thomas Wriothesley arrived and disrupted everything. He summoned Katherine to the Great Chamber and told us that if we knew anything about the Queen's "great offence", we must disclose it. Then he announced the four ladies who would go with Katherine to Syon. Chief of them will be Lady Baynton. Her husband, Lord Baynton, will go with them as well, since he is Katherine's chamberlain. I was not chosen. Secretly I am glad, for I have hopes that Will and I may snatch a few days to go and tell Elinor our news.

Wriothesley did not allow Katherine to take any of her court dresses, and he impounded all her jewellery. Sir Thomas Seymour will return it to the King. I remembered Lady Edgeworth's quiet comment when it was given to Katherine at Christmas. "It has been given to other queens." And now it has been taken back once more. Heaven knows if it will ever be given again.

Nobody would have thought it was a queen who got into the barge with some other women as they left for Syon. There were no splendid robes or jewels. Katherine was dressed in a plain, dark gown, with a hooded cloak. Her face was chalk-white and she did not look back at those of us who stayed behind on the jetty. I do not know if I will ever see her again.

16th November 1541

Lady Edgeworth made no objection when I asked if Will and I could go away for a few days. She put her hand on my sleeve and said, "Yes, you may. I will find another cook for a few days." Then she added, "My blessings on both of you." Will and I have not told anyone we are to marry, but she always knows what is going on. So we rode home from Hampton Court this afternoon.

Elinor was thrilled to see us – and to hear that we are going to marry. She clapped her hands together and said, "It has always been my dream! I would never have mentioned it to either of you – your lives are your own. But I am so happy."

Eva too was glowing with delight, and little Bella was capering about in excitement though she didn't understand exactly what was happening.

Daniel laughed and said, "You beat me to it, young brother William. I thought you'd take your pick of the court ladies."

"That's just what I did," Will said, and gave me a kiss.

We had a celebration dinner of rabbit pie and sweet little apples saved from the autumn crop. Then we talked about the terrible news of the Queen's downfall.

Eva was angry about what had happened. "There are such evil people at work," she said. "Jane Boleyn is one of them. Countess Rochford, as she still calls herself, though she sent her own husband to the block. She did much to bring about Anne's death, though she was a close relative. And the Duke of Norfolk. Catholic he may be, but not a good Catholic. What a poisonous, treacherous man. He will act the innocent now, and say he had no idea what his niece got up to in the Dowager Duchess's house."

"The other Howards are doing the same, to save their own skins." Will added.

It is all very grim, but Will and I are too happy to think about it much. We helped Elinor with some household jobs, then went out on our own, and sat together under the oak tree where I saw Agnes kissing her drover all those years ago. We plan to get married at Christmas.

20th November 1541

The privy councillors are questioning everyone who might know what Katherine has done in the past. The enquiry began on the day Will and I left Hampton Court, and it is still going on. Kitty says letters have been sent to all the English ambassadors in other countries, detailing the Queen's offences and asking anyone with information to come forward.

Will and I think it will not improve King Henry's reputation abroad. He is already regarded as a monster for the way he has treated his wives, and this can only make it worse.

The music master, Henry Manox, was the first to be interrogated. He admitted he had tried to seduce Katherine, but swore he had never done more than fondle "intimate parts of her body". He said he adored her, and suffered agonies of jealousy when she discarded him in favour of Francis Dereham.

The court then called Mrs Katherine Tylney, a chambermaid who had been with us on progress when Francis Dereham arrived. Her story of what had been going on was astonishing. She said when we were at Lincoln, the Queen had twice left her chambers late at night and gone to Lady Rochford's rooms on the next floor up. She took Katherine Tylney with her, and another maid called Margaret Morton. The first time the Queen did this, she stayed in the upper room until two in the morning. The second time, she was there almost all night. Mrs Tylney said she had to wait for hours outside the room with one of Lady Rochford's servants, and from the sounds that came to their ears, they had no doubt of what was going on.

Margaret Morton, the other servant, had even more to add. She said when we were at Pontefract and also at York, Lady Rochford had taken letters from Katherine to a man. Asked who this man was, she said she was fairly sure he was Thomas Culpeper.

This makes things much, much worse. Thomas Culpeper is one of the King's most favoured gentlemen. He is a cousin to the Queen and they have known and liked each other since childhood. But on that fated progress, the liking grew into something greater. Margaret Morton said she saw Katherine look out of her window in the house at Hatfield and smile at Culpeper who was gazing up from below. "I knew there was love between them," she said.

I cannot understand why the Queen was so reckless. Did she not understand what a dangerous game she was playing? The King's men found a letter from her to Culpeper when they ransacked his rooms. It was read out at the hearing. Katherine had written:

I never longed for anything so much as to see you. It maketh my heart to die when I do think that I cannot always be in your company. Come to me when Lady Rochford be here ... Yours as long as life endures, Katherine.

She cannot survive such damning evidence.

22nd November 1541

The hearing goes on. They called Lady Rochford, who was no longer screaming and raving but looked terrified. Her only hope of saving herself was to shift as much blame as possible to Katherine, so she spoke freely. She said the affair between Katherine and Thomas Culpeper began last winter, when the King was in his mood of black depression.

Lady Rochford made no attempt to defend Katherine. She said the Queen used to meet Culpeper in her own chambers at first, as the King had stopped paying visits to her bed. There was a panic one night when Henry felt a moment of desire and came to Katherine's rooms, only to find the door locked. After much knocking and shouting, it was Lady Rochford who let him in. I remember that night, because it caused quite a rumpus, but I had never suspected that Lady Rochford had bundled Culpeper out through a back way before admitting the King to his wife.

After that, Katherine and Culpeper met in Lady Rochford's rooms. That matches the evidence given by the two chambermaids, and she did not deny it. I can only suppose she thinks her best chance is to confess everything to the King and hope he is merciful. Will says if she withholds anything, she knows her stepson, the Duke of Norfolk, will reveal it. There is no closeness within the Howard clan now. Each one of them is scrambling to clear his or her name, with no care for anyone else.

Next to be questioned was Thomas Culpeper. I know him well by sight, as he was one of Robin's friends. They belonged to a group of particularly dashing and talented young courtiers, and the King liked them, admiring their panache and wit. Thomas, like the others, is confident and handsome, well aware of his own charm, and he must have brought a welcome respite to Katherine in the dismal winter months when the King was so depressed. Perhaps it flattered his vanity to have a secret affair with the King's wife. He will pay for it dearly, for Katherine condemned him without meaning to when she wrote one of her misspelled and untidy letters, warning him to be careful what he confessed to his priest when seeking absolution. Clearly, she had no faith in the secrecy of the confessional, and this raised some eyebrows at the hearing, though the Protestants permitted themselves a smile. She said that any priest who absolved Culpeper of things that "should pass betwixt her and him" would very probably pass on his knowledge to the King.

Not surprisingly, Culpeper is back in prison. So is Lady Rochford. They say that she has finally lost her senses and has fallen into complete insanity.

At the end of the day, a royal proclamation went out, saying that Katherine has forfeited her honour and will be proceeded against by law. She is in future not to be called the Queen. She will be referred to simply as Katherine Howard.

23rd November 1541

Wriothesley and Cranmer have gone to see Katherine at Syon. I don't know what she can say to them.

The Dowager Duchess who owns the house where Katherine grew up is in a terrible panic, we hear. She stripped the room Francis Dereham used to occupy, and took away all his papers, saying they were not for anyone else to see. She has been questioning William Damport, a servant whom she still employs, trying to find out who revealed what Katherine had been up to. I suppose she is afraid that she herself will be blamed. The Howard family, treacherous lot that they are, will not support her. The Duke of Norfolk, far from standing by Katherine, has been spreading it about that she had "prostituted herself to seven or eight persons".

I find it strange that Norfolk, of all people, was sent to search his stepmother's house for incriminating evidence. Henry must be very confident that the Duke will reveal whatever he finds, even if it damns his own family. He is probably right. Norfolk is terrified that Henry may start to see the whole Howard clan as enemies – but Kitty told me he has some Plantagenet blood, so he is never quite secure.

The main evidence comes not from the Howards but from the common people, who are anxious to reveal what they know so as to stay out of danger. Another of the Duchess's servants, William Ashby, told the Duke how his mistress had removed all Dereham's papers, and said she would hide them "in case they led to any trouble". He added that she had also been through papers belonging to William Damport. Damport was very friendly with Francis Dereham, so he is suspected of knowing more than he will let on. They have taken him to the Tower, and it is whispered that he is being tortured.

26th November 1541

The Dowager Duchess's efforts to clear her name did not work. She too is imprisoned in the Tower. She took to her bed after the Duke's visit and said she was too ill to see anyone, but the King's men arrested her all the same. Wriothesley and the Earl of Southampton have been to see her and found that she really is ill. She swore she knew nothing about what Katherine had been up to, and she wept bitterly. They asked her for details about how she had brought Katherine up – what clothes had been provided and what education? Had she talked to the girl a lot, had she formed any impression of her character? With truth, the Duchess said she knew almost nothing about Katherine Howard and certainly had not been in any way responsible for forming her present attitude.

The King is in a dreadful state. He is trying to turn his love for his pretty young wife to hatred, but the conflict is driving him close to madness. He shouted the other day for someone to bring him a sword so that he could kill Katherine himself. He calls her a wicked witch, but in the midst of his fury he sometimes bursts into tears. Lately he has tried to escape from it all by going out hunting. He takes nobody with him except the huntsmen and a small group of musicians to soothe him when they rest in some secluded place deep in the forest.

The sad thing is, Henry really did think Katherine was his perfect girl, loving and innocent. The loss of her must be a terrible blow, but his anger is equally terrible, since he knows that he has been fooled. He is taking no part in the investigation that is going on, but he will not do anything to stop it. He has unleashed the council bloodhounds, and he must stand back now until they have done their work.

1st December 1541

Francis Dereham and Thomas Culpeper have both been found guilty of adultery with the Queen. The Duke of Norfolk presided over the trial at Westminster Hall. He sentenced both men to be tied to hurdles and dragged through the streets to Tyburn, where they will be hanged, brought down while still alive and cut open. Their bowels will be burned in front of them, and they will then be hacked into quarters and beheaded. It is the worst possible death, designed to show what happens to men who think they may dally with the Queen of England, but it makes me shudder.

7th December 1541

Although sentence has been passed, Francis Dereham still protests his innocence. Culpeper gave up hope and pleaded guilty. He may have been wise in this, as we heard today what has been done to William Damport and Francis Dereham in the Tower. Last week, the torturers used a terrible instrument called the brakes to smash and tear out Damport's teeth, but he still would not give his friend away. Yesterday they tortured Dereham himself. He was amazingly brave and did not give way – but then they told him that Damport had blurted out every detail of Dereham's affair with the Queen. It was not true, for Damport had never spoken, but the belief that he was betrayed broke Dereham. He signed a confession of his flirtation with Katherine, though he still denied that he had committed adultery with her. The King read his confession, but he was all the more enraged by Dereham's defiance, and refused to change the sentence to a more humane death.

Thomas Culpeper, who admitted his guilt, is to die through beheading, which is a more merciful end. This is a terrible lesson for those caught in the King's displeasure. It is always a mistake to argue – particularly if you are a person of no status. Culpeper is a gentleman, and therefore can expect to be spared the worst humiliations.

Dereham, on the other hand, is nothing but an upstart commoner, and his protest has brought him nothing but agony and a protracted, dreadful death.

10th December 1541

Dereham and Culpeper were executed today. I do not want to think about it. Their heads have been set up on pikes above London Bridge.

15th December 1541

The Duke of Norfolk's worst fears are coming true. Cranmer, despite a trace of sympathy for Katherine after the way her family has thrown her to the dogs, is determined to see the end of the Howards. With the help of his right-hand man, Wriothesley, he is arresting one member of the Catholic clan after another. The Dowager Duchess is already in the Tower, and her daughter, Anne, has been arrested. So have Lord William Howard and his wife. This is absurd, as Lord William was not even in England when Katherine's supposed adultery took place. He is the governor of Calais, but they brought him across the Channel in such awful weather that several members of his staff were swept overboard and drowned. Lord William's sister, the Countess of Bridgewater, is also imprisoned in the Tower, and Cranmer has taken her children away to be brought up under his supervision, no doubt as good little Protestants.

Norfolk himself is far from safe. He knows this, and has written a letter to the King that was in turn put to the council. Kitty told me that he offered no defence of his relatives who have been arrested, and simply sought to save his own skin. He claimed the credit for searching the Duchess's house and finding papers that revealed Dereham's guilt and his stepmother's involvement. He said he had no love for his "traitorous nieces" (Anne Boleyn as well as Katherine Howard) and begged for "some comfortable assurance of your royal favour, without which I will never desire to live".

The King has given no sign that he is impressed.

22nd December 1541

The council has sentenced most of the Howard family to life imprisonment and the loss of all their lands and possessions. Lord William and his wife are included, though they were out of the country, and so are all those who could have known what was going on but did not say so. It includes Joan Bulmer, and both William Ashby and William Damport, as well as several other servants. The King is considerably richer as a result, since all their wealth and property goes to him, but he is no happier. He looks much older now. He must know that he will never attract a young girl again, and it may well seem to him that there is nothing to look forward to except the slow descent to his own death.

11th January 1542

Christmas was a grim affair. I could not help comparing it with the celebrations last year, when Katherine Howard was so rapturously enjoying her first – and only – Christmas as the Queen of England. The gifts and jewellery showered on her were taken back only a few months later and her gorgeous robes hang in some dark closet with pomanders to protect them from the moths. She herself is at Syon, waiting to know when she will die.

Will and I cannot ask the King's permission to marry yet. It would be tactless in the extreme to draw his attention to our own happiness and hopes for children when he is enmeshed in such disaster. We will have to wait until this whole dreadful business is over.

16th January 1542

Parliament met today to discuss the details of what should be done with Katherine Howard and also with Lady Rochford, who is still in the Tower. The King has said Katherine should be given some chance to defend herself in public, and this has been agreed. A group of members is to visit her in ten days' time to ask her if she will come to a hearing in the Parliament chamber.

30th January 1542

Katherine does not want to come to a hearing. The men who went to see her said that she seemed resigned to her fate. She told them she accepted that she deserved to die, and said she "submitted herself to the King's mercy". The Lord Chancellor was touched by this and said the Queen was "no mean or private person, but a public and illustrious one" and her cause should be judged with proper care. He suggested that a further group from Parliament should visit her again and tell her that the King, "her most loving consort", would accept it if she could find a way to declare herself innocent.

2nd February 1542

The new group went to Syon, but Katherine again turned down their offer of a hearing. I can only suppose she knows too well what actually happened and can find no excuse. She simply said she hoped to "make a good death" and leave people with an opinion of her that was not completely bad. Poor girl. She is little more than my own age, and nobody bothered to give her much guidance. It is hardly surprising that she fell so readily for men who offered her love and admiration. I cannot in all honesty wish I could be with her, as I am not sure that I could bear it, but I hope somebody can offer her some comfort.

The council, now dominated by the Protestant group, does not share the Lord Chancellor's scruples. Its leaders say the case against Katherine has been proved and no further talk is needed. They have sent a petition to the King asking that the Bill of Attainder against the Queen should be put through without any further delay. When that is done, her execution can be carried out.

7th February 1542

The Bill has been passed. King Henry went to Parliament to give his assent, and it has now become law. Both Katherine and Lady Rochford are to die, and all their lands and possessions will become the property of the King, who now seems in savage mood. He wanted to see the death of the Dowager Duchess as well, but the Parliament persuaded him to show mercy as she is old and ill. In two days' time, the Duke of Norfolk will go to Syon Abbey with some other councillors, to tell Katherine of her fate.

The King's grief seems to be at an end, or if it is not, he has turned it into anger and a kind of fierce gaiety that most of us find disconcerting. He has to face the old, implacable fact that he still needs to beget another son, so I suppose he is gathering his energies, such as they are, to try to attract yet another wife. He has long had a liking for Anne Bassett, Lady Lyle's daughter, who came to court to serve Jane Seymour, but she, though scrupulously polite, gives him no encouragement. I can hardly blame her. Henry will not find himself a popular choice among the ruling families of Europe, either. He is known as a man who kills or divorces his wives when it suits him, and no young princess will want to take on such a dangerous husband.

11th February 1542

I cannot imagine how the Duke of Norfolk could tell his own niece that she is to die on Tower Green next week, but that is what he did. Apparently she behaved with extraordinary self-control, and asked her uncle to tell the King that she hoped he would not punish the whole Howard family for her faults.

The Duke did not know the date of Katherine's execution, or if he did, he chose not to tell her. So Katherine was unprepared when the Lords of the Council arrived yesterday to take her to the Tower. One of the boatmen, still shaken by what had happened, told Will about it. He said the soldiers who went in to fetch the Queen had to drag her down to the barge by force. She'd backed away in hysterics when she saw them and flatly refused to leave the house. Neither cajoling nor bullying had any effect, and in the end they simply had to grab hold of her and bundle her out of the house, screaming and struggling in panic. The boatman said the barge she travelled in was a closed one so that nobody could see in. Katherine could not see out either. I am glad of that, for the rotting heads of Dereham and Culpeper are still impaled on pikes above London Bridge. At the Tower steps, the Constable greeted her with the same courtesy he had shown when she had visited on royal occasions as the Queen, but she was weeping and shaking and could hardly walk.

Strangely, the King did not sign the Act of Attainder, though he agreed it verbally. Perhaps he found this last step too much for him. The execution could not legally go ahead without his signature, and we had a few hours of hoping that Henry had decided to take some other way out. Then the council established that a Royal Seal saying *Le Roy le veut* – The King wishes it – is as good as a signature. Parliament will meet tomorrow, though it is a Saturday, to attach the seal to the document, and then the sentence will be carried out. They do not execute people on Sundays, so Katherine has until Monday morning to count her last hours away. She has said her clothing is to be given to the maidservants who have looked after her in these last weeks, as she has no money with which to reward them.

13th February 1542

I am glad I did not see it. The Duke of Norfolk, too, stayed away. Kitty was there with her husband, though I don't know how she could watch. The room Katherine had been kept in was the same one that Anne Boleyn had occupied. But Kitty is very much the court lady now, and she accompanies her husband without question if he requires it.

All the same, Kitty had been told one thing that she would rather not have known. On the final night of her life Katherine asked the Constable to bring the block to her room so that she could get used to the sight of it and practise, she said, how to kneel and offer her neck to the executioner. The Constable had been embarrassed by the request, but he did as she asked. I can only think that Katherine's desire to "make a good death" had become the only thing left that she could achieve, and she wanted to do it well.

The rehearsing did not help. Kitty said that as the uniformed Yeomen Warders of the Tower brought her out, Katherine was so faint with terror that she could hardly stand. They had to help her on to the black-draped scaffold – and yet, when she stood ankle-deep in its clean straw, her small, clear voice could be heard by all who stood in the hush of Tower Green among its tall, grey buildings. She said she accepted her death as just punishment, and offered her prayers for the King. She told the listening people to obey him in all things. Then she knelt at the block.

Kitty said she could not watch at the last moment, and turned her face away, but she heard the single, terrible whack of the axe. She said the breath went out of the crowd in something between a groan and a shout, and then there was a confusion of yelling and cheering and weeping. When she found the courage to look again, the Queen's ladies, with tears streaming down their faces, were wrapping the broken remains of their mistress in a black cloth.

The spectacle for the crowd was not over, for then they led out Lady Rochford. She was raving and screaming like a wild thing, Kitty says, and the King had signed a special act enabling the execution of an insane person. Strangely, she quietened at the sight of the black-draped scaffold and the now blood-soaked straw. Maybe she knew then that madness could not save her. She made a perfectly coherent speech and commended her soul to God. Then she knelt in her turn.

18th March 1542

Today, Will and I gathered our courage and asked the King for his permission to marry. He looked at us without much interest and said, "Marry. Aye, why not." Then he added, "You have my blessing."

He said that Will must remain in his position as chef at the court, but there is no queen to serve now so I have no place. He said, "Do as your husband bids you." Then he turned away.

5th April 1542

I wrote to my uncle and aunt in Norfolk to invite them to the wedding. I have sent them letters from time to time to say what I am doing, and my aunt has sometimes replied, but they knew nothing about Will. They wrote back with surprisingly warm congratulations and accepted the invitation. And, to my amazement, they have offered us the tenancy of the house I lived in with my mother and father. Their previous tenant has died, so they need someone to look after it. Provided that we meet the costs of any repairs and upkeep, my husband and I will inherit it when they die.

Will laughed. He said, "That's their idea of generosity, is it? We keep their property in order, and pay them rent for the privilege." But the rent is low, and there are big advantages. Elinor, Tom and the children need more space now. They can move into the big house, together with Eva, and Tom says he is happy to help with the rent. Daniel is going to marry a girl called Alice, and my uncle has agreed that they can take over the cottage and forge.

Now that I am not needed at court, I can use my time to make any changes in the house and help Elinor and her family to move in. The stable block that used to house Papa's horses and hounds will be wonderful for Tom. There is ready-made space for a forge, and he is thinking he may buy a couple of good brood mares and start up a line of his own horses. There is ample grazing for them, and good stabling.

I was startled at first by my uncle's offer, but God works in strange ways, and I feel now as if my dreams have come true. I am released from the court, with its dangers and corruption, and I can do something for Elinor to repay all the love and help she has given me. I am sixteen now, a grown woman about to marry the man I love – and yet I feel no different. I am still the ten-year-old who came across an unknown woman moving into a cottage and found a new mother.

12th April 1542

In my last days at court I was troubled about little Elizabeth. She had come to love Katherine Howard for her gaiety and easy friendship, but now, for the second time, she has lost the nearest person to her, and in the most brutal of ways. At three years old she was well aware that her mother, Anne Boleyn, was executed at the King's command. It took her a long time to recover her confidence and trust, but now her father has inflicted the same terrible death on Katherine. At eight years old Elizabeth's trust in her fellow humans has been destroyed again, and this time the destruction may be permanent. A few days before I left she still looked pinched and white-faced under her shock of red hair. When someone mentioned plans for the future she declared firmly, "I will never marry."

Her ladies clucked like ruffled hens and tried to soothe her, saying she would feel different in time, but I think Elizabeth spoke the absolute truth. As she sees it, the wedded state is too dangerous to contemplate. Poor little girl. I cannot blame her.

25th April 1542

We were married at Easter, in the chapel at Greenwich Palace. I wanted it to be in the local church, but everyone was shocked at the idea and said that the King would be insulted. I'm glad I gave in, because it was in fact lovely. I had not realized that so many people would come to wish us well. All the court ladies I have worked with were there in their best dresses. Elinor and her whole family came, and there were lots of meetings with people who had known her in her years at court, all eager to give the children sweetmeats and coo over little Bella. The King himself did not attend, and neither had we expected him to, but he called us into his presence afterwards and gave us a bag of gold. This will be a great blessing, as the house turns out to have been badly neglected. There are urgent repairs to be done to the roof and the outbuildings, and we were worrying about how to find the money.

My aunt and uncle came from their manor of Oxburgh in Norfolk with some of their Bedingfield relatives and stayed at court for a day or two. Of course, they took the opportunity to look around the house and were shocked by the way their previous tenant had neglected it.

When everyone had gone, Will and I took a couple of horses – Russet was sold last year as he had become too small for me – and rode across the fields and through the forest. In a grassy glade, where sun slanted between the trees, we were at last alone together. We did not come back until the owls were calling.

22nd May 1542

We are working very hard on the house. There is still a lot to do, but it is watertight now, clean inside and simply furnished, ready for its new life. Elinor, Tom and the children moved in yesterday with Eva.

2nd June 1542

Kitty and her husband were here today. Kitty's baby is due next month, but she looks well and happy. While Francis went with Will to be shown the house and outbuildings, Kitty and I sat down for a long talk. She told me the Duke of Cleves begged the King to take Anne back as his queen after Katherine's death. Of course, Henry refused. He likes her better now than he did, mostly because she was so obliging about the divorce, but that does not mean he is any more willing to go to bed with her.

At the moment, Kitty says, Henry's main interest is to find a husband for his daughter, the lady Mary. He thought the Duke of Orléans, heir to the throne of France, might do, but the French king demanded a huge dowry. Henry flew into a rage and said it was a deliberate insult. As a result, the French are now his arch-enemy again. He is convinced that they intend to invade England, so he has stepped up his building of fortifications along the south coast.

Henry has not forgiven King James for failing to meet him last year at York either. To make things worse, groups of Scots have been raiding the north of England, and Henry is mustering an army to invade Scotland in retaliation. I thought of Eva's account of the battle of Flodden Field. I so much hope we do not have to see another terrible slaughter. Perhaps it is because of Kitty's coming baby, but I feel for all mothers who nurse their children through the hard years of their growing up, only to see them killed in battle at the whim of a king. I do not think women will ever accept war as the great sport of nations.

I asked Kitty if there was any sign of Henry choosing a new queen, and she laughed. "Who will have him?" she asked. "He is hardly an eligible young bachelor, is he? Look at the size of him, not to mention his terrible record as a husband. Would *you* want to marry him?"

I shrieked with horror at the thought, and we collapsed into giggles as we always used to.

19th July 1542

Kitty gave birth to a baby boy last night. I went to see her today, and she was wonderfully happy. Her son is to be called Henry, of course. We both laughed, but she said, "Francis thought it would be tactful. The King is so angry with the Scots that a little flattery can do no harm. But it will take more than that. He's set on an all-out war, as far as I can see."

I myself had thought I was pregnant last month, but it came to nothing. Will was disappointed, but there is no point in letting the mind dwell on it. Perhaps a baby will come when we are not quite so busy. We are in a constant turmoil of building and repairing, cleaning and painting, making curtains to keep out draughts and stacking wood for winter fires. We need to get the main work done before winter begins.

26th August 1542

Envoys from King James of Scotland came, asking if there could be a peaceful way to stop the raiding across the borders, but Henry is bent on war. A large army had already gone to the north, and they crossed the border and burned farms and villages. As a result, the Scots attacked them on their way back, at a place called Haddon Rig. Henry is, of course, furious, and even more determined on a Scottish invasion. He has sent for the Duke of Norfolk to summon an army and march north from Newcastle.

The Duke is no doubt delighted. The King has ignored him since the Howard family fell from favour, but this is a chance to ingratiate himself again. Norfolk led the slaughter at Flodden and Henry knows that he is a formidable soldier.

14th September 1542

Daniel and Alice were married today. It was a simple wedding at the church across the fields, but we all had such a lovely time. This is Harvest Festival, and in the abundance of fruits and grain and vegetables, our autumn feast seemed natural and right. Daniel is taking over the horse-shoeing business from Tom, with his agreement. Tom has long wanted to use his skills to make decorative ironwork – finely wrought lamps and fire baskets, wall brackets and candle sconces. To his delight, the Church dignitaries have asked him to construct a large, intricate rood screen for the church where Dan and Alice were married.

Such decorative things are starting to be accepted in the new religion as they do not depict the Virgin Mary or the saints, so cannot be said to touch on Catholic "idolatry".

26th September 1542

The King has been wrangling with the Scottish envoys while Norfolk musters his army in Newcastle. The Scots took several English lords prisoner in the last skirmish and Henry wants them freed. He offered to pay a ransom for them – but in return he demanded Scottish hostages to be kept in the Tower and quite possibly tortured or killed if his requests are not met. He also insisted that James should visit him in London.

None of this is possible, of course. Understandably, the Scots do not like the hostage idea. Who would? King James does not want to come to London because his wife is about to have a baby and London is a very long way from Edinburgh. He offered to meet the King in York, but Henry is still smarting from James's failure to arrive last time, so he has refused. Kitty and I agree that our king has no taste for peacemaking at the best of times. These are not the best of times, and he is determined to go to war. He would have set out at once, but the Duke of Norfolk has said that he cannot move an army of 3,000 soldiers until the necessary supplies of food and (even more important, beer) arrive by sea from London. Apparently the ships are on their way, but they are not expected to reach Newcastle until next week.

17th October 1542

Yesterday Kitty came with Francis and baby Henry, who was much cooed over. He seems happy and contented and Kitty says he is no trouble. She has plenty of help, though, with a wet nurse to feed him and servants at hand to do anything needed. She chose well when she married Francis, who has both money and good sense. Kitty has never been rash.

Will asked Francis if he'd heard any more about the beer supplies for the King's troops in Scotland, and Francis told him that the ships brought only enough for two jugs per soldier per day, which was nowhere near enough. "You have to remember, an army is a rabble," he said, "kept in order with food, drink and thrashings. If any one of those things is missing, they will rebel or desert. At two jugs a day, the campaign will collapse within a week."

28th October 1542

Francis was right. The Duke of Norfolk led his men across the border and set fire to towns called Eccles and Kelso, as well as a number of villages, but the beer ran out after four days and the army withdrew to England. The Scots claim it as their victory, and King Henry is raging again.

27th November 1542

Norfolk's army is still in the northern border country, waiting for more beer to arrive, I suppose. Meanwhile, an army of Scots has attacked further to the west, in marshy flat land near Gretna called Solway Moss. The messengers said it was a terrible place to fight, a deep bog that had the men wallowing up to their waists in mud and water. It was hardly a battle at all, though ten English soldiers were killed and about twenty Scots. Several men from both sides were drowned. The Scots withdrew in disarray, leaving half-submerged cannon and useless weapons as well as dozens of floundering horses that could neither be ridden nor led out of the quagmire.

All the same, the Duke of Norfolk is claiming it as a triumph. He sent riders to report that his army is coming back with 1,200 prisoners, at least twenty of them noblemen of high standing. They are also bringing 120 guns, about two dozen heavy cannon, four wagonloads of lances and *three thousand* horses! People will be standing at the roadside to gawp and marvel.

16th December 1542

King James of Scotland is dead. It seems an extraordinary thing. Everyone saw him standing on nearby high ground to watch his soldiers at the disastrous battle of Solway Moss, less than a month ago. Some say he lost all heart when he saw them defeated and struggling to save themselves, and died of a nervous collapse. Others, less romantically, say he caught a fever. Either way, the Scottish king was on his deathbed when his wife gave birth to their first child. He was only 30 years old. Will said he probably died of gloom when he heard he had a daughter instead of the hoped-for son, but I told him that was not funny. Just think of James's wife, widowed and with a baby to bring up who will inherit the Scottish Crown.

The little girl's name is Mary Stuart. She has inherited the throne of Scotland and is even now the queen, at just a few days old. When she comes to rule, she will be known as Mary, Queen of Scots. Please God, let her live and thrive, for her mother's sake apart from all else.

23rd December 1542

The Scottish prisoners arrived in London four days ago. Those who are of the nobility were taken to the Tower, but for hospitality rather than imprisonment. King Henry has spent hours with them in private talks – though talks are never quite so private as anyone thinks. Everyone knows that the Scots lords will be released – but at a cost. They have to sign a contract agreeing that King Henry will be the guardian of the newborn Scottish queen, and that when she is old enough she will marry Henry's own son, Edward.

The Scots know they are beaten. Their king is dead and they are imprisoned, no matter how comfortably, in the Tower of London. If they refuse Henry's proposals, they have good reason to assume they will never come out again. If that happens, they will not be martyrs, for nobody in Scotland will know they died in the lost hope of keeping their country independent of England. So they have signed the papers.

I suppose they have a faint hope that fate may save them from this future royal marriage. Children lead precarious lives. The English prince might not live to be a man. Even better, from the Scots' point of view, Henry himself might die. But if neither of these things happen, Scotland will come under the rule of Henry Tudor's son.

Kitty says the King is purring with pleasure. "You can almost see him licking the cream from his whiskers," she remarked. He is sure now that he has solved the Scottish problem. When his son comes to the throne, it will be with the Queen of Scotland as his wife. He will rule both countries. Henry has won.

10th January 1543

Our Christmas at home was a joy. The children brought in holly boughs, and when Will could get away from the court we took pleasure in serving him good food that he had not had to cook. We sat in a blaze of candles around the big table that used to seem so empty when my father and I sat at one end of it on our own.

The Scots lords, released from the Tower, were invited – or commanded – to join the royal party at Enfield, and on New Year's Day Prince Edward, now five years old, was presented as their future ruler. Kitty says he made a well-rehearsed speech of welcome and behaved beautifully. The Scots could not praise him enough, she said, but then, they could hardly do otherwise. To add to Henry's satisfaction, he has signed a treaty with the Emperor Charles, agreeing that England and Spain together will launch an attack on France within the next two years. But Kitty had something else to tell me. Henry has his eye on a new wife.

I said, "Oh, no. Don't tell me someone is dangling another girl under his nose?"

Kitty shook her head. "Don't worry. This is different. It's Katherine Parr."

I couldn't believe it. I know Katherine quite well. It was she who bravely asked the King to release her cousin, Sir George Throckmorton, from the Tower on one of those nights when he was dallying with Katherine Howard at the palace in Lambeth. I said, "But she is married! Her husband is Lord Latimer."

"Yes, but he's old and ill now," Kitty said. "For months, she has been his nurse rather than his wife. He is not expected to live much longer."

Things tumbled about in my mind. Katherine Parr, of all people. What can she be thinking of? She's such a quiet, intellectual woman. And by no means a girl. "She must be thirty or more." I said.

"She's very attractive, though," Kitty replied. "All that auburn hair. And don't be fooled by her good education and academic talk – she's as romantic at heart as any other woman. She's wildly in love with Thomas Seymour, though he's a rogue."

That was even more of a shock. Thomas is one of Jane Seymour's two brothers. He is handsome and confident and thinks every girl must fall for him. Girls do, of course. I almost fell for Robin. I'd have thought Katherine Parr had more sense, but Kitty said, "She doesn't welcome the King's attentions. She was horrified when he started sending her presents."

A new suspicion struck me. "This isn't another of the Duke of Norfolk's schemes, is it?"

"Oh, no," Kitty said. "There's nothing political about it this time. Norfolk is still out of favour with the King in spite of the Scottish affair. It's not religious, either."

Katherine likes the new religion, Kitty says, but she can't join the Lutheran Church while her husband is still alive, because he is a devout Catholic. He fought on the side of the rebels in the Pilgrimage of Grace.

"And he didn't get executed?" I asked. It seems Latimer claimed that the rebels had kidnapped him and forced him to join them. Kitty laughed at my doubtful expression. "A likely story!" she agreed. "But he got away with it. The King must have been in a good mood that day."

26th January 1543

Elinor knows Katherine Parr well, of course. And Eva's knowledge of her goes even further back. She had worked with Katherine Parr's mother, Maud, when they were both ladies-in-waiting to Catherine of Aragon.

The court is like a tight family. Everyone knows everyone, and there are tales of old times, just under the surface, always waiting to be told.

As for Thomas Seymour, Elinor shook her head.

"He's the same kind as the Duke of Norfolk," she said. "A power-seeker. He and his brother Edward grabbed their chance to push their sister Jane into the King's notice when rumours were spreading about Anne Boleyn. They played their cards well and so did she. And it worked."

I thought again of that birthday visit when Papa took me to meet Jane Seymour and the King. To me as a ten-year-old, Jane was up there with the angels, regal and kind and perfect. I could not imagine her as an ambitious girl with scheming brothers. How little I knew then!

Elinor filled in some of the details. Edward Seymour, the elder of the two, did best out of his sister's royal marriage. Henry made him the Earl of Hertford and he's now Warden of the Scottish Marshes, standing high in royal favour. Thomas is furiously jealous of his brother, so he is desperate to claw his way into some privilege of his own. "That's why he is setting his cap at Katherine Parr," Elinor explained. "She's a woman of high standing in her own right, and when her husband dies she will be very wealthy. But Thomas Seymour will not stand a chance if the King wants Katherine for himself."

I would not be in Katherine Parr's place for anything. She is in love with a scheming imposter and yet seems fated to marry the ageing, obese, dangerous King of England.

16th February 1543

Kitty is pregnant again, and is very happy about it. Pregnancy seems to suit her. She looks contented, her face a little rounder than it used to be and always smiling. She tells me the King has given Katherine Parr another fabulously beautiful gown. He has them made for her by couturiers in Italy. Nobody at court has any doubt now that Henry wants her, though Katherine herself is no more than polite to him and receives each gift with humble astonishment at his kindness. Thomas Seymour can only watch and grind his teeth with jealousy.

2nd March 1543

The Duke of Latimer died today, so Katherine Parr is a widow for the second time in her life. She has inherited lands and money that make her extremely wealthy. The funeral is to be in St Paul's Cathedral. The King cannot make any proposal until the time of mourning is over, but everyone assumes he will want to marry her with as little delay as possible.

11th March 1543

An excited group of court ladies came to the house to chatter about the latest scandal without fear of overhearing. Katherine Parr's brother, William, wants to divorce his wife, Anne Bourchier, who has eloped with another man. William is so furious that he is demanding she pay the highest penalty, which is execution.

What excites the ladies is that Katherine is not taking her brother's side. Her sympathies are entirely with his wife. She went to the King and threw herself at his feet, begging for Anne Bourchier's life. Henry did not scold her but merely pointed out that a woman of high rank must die for such a crime unless she can persuade her husband to pardon her. Katherine is no fool. She saw the chance the King was offering, and said she would try to get her brother to relent – and Henry said if she can do that, he himself will pardon Anne. So it all turns on Katherine's powers of persuasion, and the whole court is agog to see what happens next.

Elinor says that Lord Parr, Katherine's brother, would be stupid to refuse. He must know of the King's interest in his sister, which may well advantage the whole Parr family. William will probably swallow his pride and outrage when Katherine makes this clear to him.

14th March 1543

William Parr was not at all willing to change his tune, but Katherine had prepared her case well – and she had an ace up her sleeve. She told her brother that the witnesses who had informed against Anne were lying, and she could prove it. She then said she would use her influence over the King to have these witnesses tortured, and added, "Then, by God's help, we shall know the truth." Lord Parr knew he was beaten. He has written a letter to the King saying he is willing to forgive his wife for the scandalous way she has treated him. There was much laughter in our house when the ladies poured out this story, and we raised a glass of wine to Katherine Parr's victory.

"She may well make a good queen," Eva declared.

23rd March 1543

King Henry has consoled Katherine's brother by appointing him as a member of the Privy Council. William Parr chooses to take it as a compliment, but everyone can see that the Parr family is being brought into royal favour as a preparation for the marriage Henry has decided on. The King is making sure that Katherine's relatives are too grateful to him to offer any opposition. What a cunning old tomcat he is!

23rd April 1543

Parliament granted William Parr's divorce. He has come out of it with a lot of solid benefit. All of his ex-wife's estates in Essex now belong to him, and today, as a further assurance of favour, the King made him a Knight of the Garter. So Lord Parr is looking extremely pleased with himself. The outcome for Anne Bourchier is very different. Her children have been declared bastards, with no rights to inheritance, and Anne herself has nothing except her lover. I hope, for her sake, that he is worth it. But at least she has her life.

Katherine, the ladies say, seems no more than modestly pleased that she was able to help her sister-in-law.

10th May 1543

Kitty and Francis called by with news that Thomas Seymour has been sent packing. Yesterday, the King told Katherine Parr that he liked her very much, and hoped they might have a future together. She said very respectfully that she had no desire to be Queen of England, then added that her affections were already engaged elsewhere, as she was in love with Thomas Seymour.

Francis says the King probably knew this, but he needed to have it confirmed before he could do anything about it. Then he acted fast. He summoned Thomas Seymour to his presence and said he had an important job for him. "Seymour looked pleased," Francis said, "until he heard what it was. The King has sent him to Brussels, on a permanent posting as ambassador to the regent of the Netherlands."

Kitty giggled. "He did it terribly well," she added. "Very official and congratulatory, as though handing out a great favour. Thomas had to thank him on bended knee. He was cursing and raging afterwards."

"So has he gone?" I asked.

"Yes, vanished," Kitty said. "He went the next morning. Katherine seems perfectly calm, you know the way she is. If she was upset, she didn't show it. She told us the King needed her, and her duty had to be to her sovereign."

"Henry will like that," Elinor said.

And yes, it seems he does like it. Kitty says he now shows his affection for Katherine quite openly. He puts a hand under her elbow if she walks beside him and touches her cheek with his lips. I shuddered and asked how she could bear it, but Kitty did not laugh. "She bears it because she has to," she said. "What would you do in her place? Wait for him to accuse you of treason and cut your head off?"

She is right, of course.

24th June 1543

This time, I'm sure I really am pregnant. I feel sick all the time, but that is a small price to pay for a new life. Will is delighted. We are so lucky to be in this big house. I was not particularly happy here as a child, but it will be a good home for a new generation of children. I pray all the time that luck will not desert me, and that the baby and I will survive this coming birth. I try not to let Will see that it frightens me a bit, but I expect he knows. I tell myself there is nothing to fear. We are young and strong, and our house is clean and airy now, with its rooms full of warmth and sunlight.

1st July 1543

Today a treaty was signed, promising that Mary, the future queen of Scotland, will marry Prince Edward. We were all invited to Greenwich Palace as there was a big celebration. It is several months since I was at Court, and I must admit, I enjoyed it.

Elinor and Eva were surrounded by old friends and Tom was among the huntsmen and court gentlemen he has known for so long. We took the children with us and they behaved beautifully, though they were a little overawed by their first visit to the court. Michael and Maria are almost into their teens now, and little Bella is six years old, a serious little girl whose hair is still as fair as when she was born.

Kitty looked tired, I thought. Her latest pregnancy shows clearly, and I saw her put her hand to her back as if it ached. I thought she needed to rest, so we went outside and sat on the grassy hill that slopes down to the river, in the same place where we sat all those years ago, on my tenth birthday. I told her about my own coming baby, and she kissed me and said, "With God's blessing, our children will grow up together, Bee."

We watched the boats go to and fro on the sparkling water.

"So much has happened," I reflected.

Kitty said, "And so much more waiting to happen."

There were daisies in the grass, but we did not make daisy chains this time. We are grown up and were contented to sit in the sun.

12th July 1543

This was the big day. King Henry VIII entered into his sixth marriage. He and Katherine Parr, widow of Lord Latimer, were married at the chapel in Hampton Court. I was not there, but I hear Anne of Cleves was one of the witnesses. She showed no sign of resentment or jealousy, but as Kitty said, why would she? Of the five wives the King has had so far, she is the only survivor, and it may turn out that she is the one who comes off best – though nobody knows what fate has in store for Katherine.

20th July 1543

People seem to like the new queen. She is open and friendly, and although she has a formidable intellect, she never makes anyone feel inferior. Religion is her greatest interest, though nobody is quite sure how far she leans towards Protestantism. The problem is, of course, that Henry has made his own religion. It stands midway between the old Catholic Church and Luther's new doctrine, and its main precept is that Henry himself stands at its head. For this reason, it is dangerously easy to be seen as a heretic. Catholics are heretical because of their belief that the Pope directly represents God's will, but Protestants can be equally heretical if they think they can access the truth of God without referring to any higher authority. Such independence of mind is seen as a refusal of the King's authority as head of the new Church and is severely punished. We saw that demonstrated this week in the most horrible way, possibly as a test of the new Queen's opinions.

The royal couple went to Windsor after their marriage, and there, in the Great Park before a crowd of people, the King had three Protestant "heretics" burned to death. Wriothesley and Gardiner, who perhaps suggested this event, were watching the Queen closely for any sign of protest or disgust, for the pair of them, both Catholics, suspect she is a closet Lutheran. No doubt Katherine had been told in advance about what was to happen and realized it was a test of her complete subservience to the King, for she watched the horrible proceedings with a completely expressionless face. What she thought in private remains her own business, and Wriothesley and Gardiner are none the wiser.

23rd August 1543

I am back at court. One of the first things that Katherine did after her honeymoon was to ask the King if his daughters, Mary and Elizabeth, might be allowed to come and stay, as she was longing to meet them. He agreed, and they are both here at Windsor. Naturally, extra help is needed with two more royal young women to be served, so I was asked to return. Will thought being busy would stop me from worrying about the coming birth. "The baby will like it better," he said. "No fun being stuck inside a worrying woman. And besides, the money will come in handy." He's right about that – and I am glad to be with him, working together.

Elizabeth is a joy. She is nearly ten years old and speaks several languages. She is well grounded in the classics, and the new queen is so impressed with her that she has taken over her education. Katherine Parr is a wonderful teacher – she and her young pupil seem to enjoy every minute of the lessons, exchanging opinions and discussing texts with great liveliness. Mary, a woman of 27 years old now, liked her at once. The two of them share a keen interest in theology, and are somehow rather similar as people, very self-controlled and careful, yet full of intellectual excitement.

Edward – still only five – is not allowed to come to court much in case he catches any dangerous infection, but he too has taken to Katherine. She is gentle and kind with him, helping him with lessons that he finds interesting. For once in the history of this turbulent family, all of them seem to be getting on well. The King is pleased to see his children being so skilfully taught. He is clearly impressed by his new wife's abilities, and by the obvious fact that his children adore her and are being well educated.

12th October 1543

This is Edward's sixth birthday, so there have been great celebrations. It also marks a stage in his growing up, as the King has engaged Dr Richard Cox, a fellow of King's College, Cambridge, to take charge of the royal boy's continuing education. With Dr Cox comes the unfortunate Barnaby Fitzpatrick, son of an Irish lord. He is to be Edward's whipping boy. A princeling cannot be struck or caned by a commoner, but he has to have his faults made clear to him, so the whipping boy gets the thrashing instead. Strangely, the two lads seem to have struck up a friendship in spite of this unpleasant arrangement. Edward has always seemed a rather cold child to me, or perhaps merely an over-cautious one, but it may be that in order to prevent anything unpleasant happening, he has promised not to cause his playmate any punishment. On that basis, of course, the whipping-boy system works well. Any privileged but kind-minded boy would shrink from having to watch his friend being beaten on his behalf, so he will always behave well. On the other hand, if the favoured lad has a cruel streak, he might treat himself every day to the pleasure of watching another boy being beaten on his behalf. I would rather not think about that.

16th October 1543

The Scots are enraged about the treaty of Greenwich, which promised their baby princess to the Tudor Prince Edward. They can see very well that King Henry has forced them into yielding their sovereignty, and they deeply resent it. A rider bringing letters to the King from Edinburgh got very drunk later that night, and was roaring, "He'll nae defeat us in sic a way! Yon Henry will rue his treaty yet!" Will said the gentlemen hustled him out of the way before someone told the King.

8th November 1543

Kitty gave birth to a little girl today. She is to be called Lettice, which comes from the Latin *Laetitia,* meaning happiness. My baby is not due until the spring, but I am happy to see how Kitty seems to take birth in her stride. It gives me great encouragement.

2nd December 1543

The drunken Scot spoke truer words than we thought. His Parliament has revoked the Treaty of Greenwich, which means the Scots have withdrawn their agreement to any marriage between Edward and the baby daughter of James V. To make things worse, the "auld alliance" between Scotland and France has been renewed. King Henry is raging. At one stroke the Scots have sided with his hated enemy, destroyed his hopes of ruling over a united Britain and declared his son not good enough for their princess. He was so angry that his face was the colour of a beetroot and I wondered if his heart would give way in such an explosion of fury. But anger in itself will not kill him – he is too well used to it. He gave orders at once to muster the biggest army England had ever seen, shouting that he will teach the Scots a lesson they will never forget.

11th December 1543

The King meant every word of it. Lord Hertford, the elder brother of Thomas Seymour, is in charge of a colossal force of men that will march north next week. There will be no Christmas celebration for them – they are to keep going until they reach Edinburgh, the Scottish capital.

20th December 1543

Kitty is pregnant once again.

"She's the brood-mare kind," Will said. "It comes naturally to her. She'll probably have one every year until her husband dies of exhaustion."

"What about Kitty's exhaustion?" I replied, but he just laughed.

19th January 1544

We were at Hampton Court for Christmas and the New Year, and despite what is happening in Scotland, Will and his kitchen staff were as busy as ever, producing the usual abundance of festive fare. Lord Parr, Katherine's brother, was created Earl of Essex and her uncle was appointed as her chamberlain. However, two weeks of over-indulgence in food and wine has had a bad effect on the King's health. This week he has had agonizing attacks of pain from his ulcerated leg. Katherine is unfailingly kind to him, changing the dressings patiently and doing whatever she can to ease his pain.

Meanwhile, the army has blazed its way north, wrecking and killing everything and everyone its path. The soldiers burned Edinburgh, destroyed the port of Leith and razed Holyrood Palace to the ground, and their mission is not finished yet. This "rough wooing" is set to go on until Scotland, like a disobedient wife, is brought to her knees in abject pain and misery.

I hope Henry's men do not find the widowed Scottish queen and her baby daughter, for there is little doubt that they will kill them if they do. She has gone into hiding, and no torture or extortion has managed to extract the truth of where they are.

7th February 1544

Today, the King declared a new Act of Succession. It declares that if he and Katherine Parr have a child, he (or even she) will rank second to Prince Edward as heir to the throne. Next will come any children that King Henry "might have by other queens".

Kitty and I exchanged glances but we did not dare to raise an eyebrow. Afterwards, where nobody could hear us, Kitty said, "Does he really imagine he could father a child with yet *another* wife? He is fooling himself. Any failure in that department is not with his wives, but with him." We both agree that his colossal size and general ill health make it unlikely that he can sire any more children.

Meanwhile, the army continues its trail of destruction in Scotland as it works its terrible way south again. Melrose and Jedburgh have been laid waste, and the border town of Berwick lies in ruins.

24th February 1544

The Spanish Duke of Najera has been here with a great train of people. Eva came to act as a translator, and the lady Mary's Spanish is excellent. I was able to help too. My Spanish has only been learned through Eva's diary and with her help, but it was useful. I took no part in the dancing, as I am big with my coming baby now, but Queen Katherine danced throughout the evening, though she had told us she was not feeling well. The Spaniards were much taken with her.

The lady Mary stayed on after the Spanish party had left. She is translating the *Paraphrases of the Gospel St John*, by Erasmus of Rotterdam, a great scholar who set out to create a Latin version of the New Testament. Queen Katherine is greatly interested in this, and she and Mary spend much time together, working on the translation.

Elizabeth has been sent away. Nobody knows why – she must have said something that her royal father regarded as disrespectful. The Queen is greatly upset about this because she is very fond of her stepdaughter. She begged and pleaded with the King to change his mind, but this time he would not give way. Poor Elizabeth. She seems fated never to have a proper home.

16th March 1544

My baby was born three days ago and she is beautiful. Elinor was with me, and although it seemed a long time of terrible pain, she said it was an easy birth. So I am lucky. Will and I had agreed that if we had a boy, he would be called John because Will's father was Mr John, the court jester. Since she is a girl, are going to name her Joanna. Will already calls her Jo.

I will not go back to the court for quite a long while because I want to feed my baby myself. It seems such a natural thing to do. All the titled ladies use wet nurses, as their husbands do not like them to suckle a child, but I hate the idea of handing my baby over to anyone else. I shall not miss the court goings-on. King Henry is working towards his long-planned invasion of France, as agreed with the Spanish emperor, and I feel we have had enough war. Henry's soldiers are still blazing their way through Scotland, determined to make sure that country is too weakened to make a strike against England while the King is leading an attack on France. I am too sleepy and contented to bother about all these battles. Whatever the rights and wrongs, they bring nothing but misery for the people who live there.

7th June 1544

What a long time since I last wrote! But these have been good months with little Joanna. She is a happy baby, always ready for her feed and taking an interest in everything. The first time she smiled at me, I caught her up and hugged her in sheer delight.

I have almost lost interest in everything else, but I was touched by the Queen's kindness to Lady Hertford, whose husband led the invasion of Scotland. Lord Hertford, who is Thomas Seymour's older brother, Edward, marched north with his army before last Christmas, and has not been home in all the six months since then. Lady Hertford went to the Queen in tears, saying that she feared she would never see him again. Queen Katherine asked Henry if the Duke could be sent home, and he granted her request. Will says the King is so taken up with his preparations to invade France that a small matter of that kind hardly matters to him – but if Katherine had not asked, Lady Hertford's distress would never have been noticed. I wonder, though, if Katherine put in a word for Edward Seymour because he is Thomas's brother. Does she still retain some feeling for that handsome adventurer?

8th July 1544

Yesterday the King announced that Queen Katherine will rule the country as his regent while he is away in France.

"As he did with Catherine of Aragon," Eva remarked. "It means he has complete trust in this new wife. That makes a change. I could never imagine Anne Boleyn in charge of England, or the Howard girl. And Jane Seymour would have been a disaster, because her brother Edward would have taken charge."

Elinor said, "Anne of Cleves could have done it. She's a clever woman. It wasn't her fault that her mother never told her the facts of life."

Thinking back, I realize that my mother never told me, either. I found out when Agnes threw a bucket of water over a pair of mating dogs. I asked what they were doing, and she said, "Making pups. If you stop the dog putting his seed in the bitch, it saves having to drown the litter when they're born." A crude way to be told, I suppose, but it never troubled me.

Katherine Parr will have her advisers, of course, among them Lord Hertford (Edward Seymour), back from Scotland after the Queen's plea on his behalf. Others include Archbishop Cranmer and Thomas Wriothesley, who is now the Lord Chancellor. "What a nest of vipers," Will said.

14th July 1544

King Henry and his army are on their way to France. Queen Katherine has gone with them to Dover. She has written a prayer for Henry that is to be said in every church in the country. I have always found it difficult to see how two warring countries can both ask for God's help to bring them victory. Katherine's prayer begins in the frail hope that peace can be found without the need for a battle, but it goes on, "Or else grant, O Lord, that with small effusion of blood and little damage of innocents, we to Thy glory obtain victory; and that, the wars being ended, we may all with one heart and mind knit together in concord and amity." I think that is a good prayer.

9th August 1544

When she returned from Dover, the Queen moved her household here to Greenwich. Elizabeth wants to join her. The King banished her from court in March, but Elizabeth has now written to Katherine, thanking her for trying to intercede on her behalf and saying how much she misses her company. Her letter begs the Queen to try again to change King Henry's mind. I hope he will.

Kitty's husband, Francis, is quite close to the "nest of vipers", as Will calls the councillors, and they get frequent reports from France. The King is moving towards Boulogne now, determined to capture that city. He is enjoying his war. The activity has improved his health and he is revelling in the days of riding and campaigning. He and his Welsh ancestors are fighting people, and it does him no good to sit about in velvet clothes with nothing to do but eat and drink. Like a hound or a hunting horse, he needs exercise and excitement.

21st August 1544

Henry granted Elizabeth's request – but she had not long been here when plague broke out, as it so often does at this time of the year. She and the Queen, together with Mary and Prince Edward, have gone to stay with the Countess of Rutland at her castle in Oakham. Kitty is with them, as her next baby is due very soon and Francis wants her to be out of danger from the infection. Rutland is out in the country beyond Leicester, far enough from London to be safe. Queen Katherine has given orders that anyone who has been in contact with a plague victim must keep strictly away. She has also told the courtiers they are not allowed to enter any house where there has been a case of plague. She believes the contagion can be carried in some way from person to person, so she is removing the royal children from any possible contact. It seems to be working, for a letter from Kitty says everyone in Oakham is healthy.

17th September 1544

Boulogne has fallen. Henry entered the city three days ago at the head of his army, flags fluttering in triumph. The Emperor had similar success in his attack from the south, and the French king has signed a peace treaty at a place called Crêpy. Perhaps Katherine's prayer will be granted and we can live in peace with France.

23rd September 1544

Kitty has had her baby. It's a boy and he is to be called William.

"Very nice too," my Will said.

With the cooler weather, the plague has burned itself out, and the Queen and her party are coming back to Greenwich. A messenger came to our house today, asking if I will return to the palace and help in the preparations for the King's return. I was going to refuse, but Will said, "Why not? You can bring Jo – there are plenty of servants to help look after her. And we need the help." I suppose he is right. It's going to be a rush to get everything ready for the royal return and Kitty is still lying-in after the new baby, so they are a pair of hands short. And anyway, my natural place is with Will, even though I'll miss Elinor and Eva and my own home.

25th September 1544

Oddly, I'm enjoying being back at the palace. The bustle and gossip of the court people is quite refreshing after the summer months of new motherhood – and I am treated with a touch more respect now that I have produced a thriving baby.

The Queen has been away for a few days with Mary at Hanworth. Mary has finished her translation of the *Paraphrases*, and we hear that Queen Katherine admires the work very much. She has persuaded Mary, despite her modest protests, to publish it under her own name. I think that makes good sense. The book will be all the more popular if people know it was written by a princess.

2nd October 1544

The King is back. And what a change in him! He looked years younger as he swung himself down from the great black horse he rides and held out his arms to Katherine. Suddenly I saw again what has always been magic about him – the sheer presence that leaves everyone excited and a little short of breath. While the mind considers him appalling, the heart leaps.

18th October 1544

Thomas Seymour has returned from Brussels. His tour as English ambassador in Belgium has ended, and he is walking around among us with his bright black eyes and jaunty beard, as cocky as ever. Everyone is agog with interest. The King has appointed him Lord High Admiral of England but, of course, that will not satisfy Thomas. His elder brother is the senior member of the Privy Council now, and the cause for jealousy is even greater.

Kitty is back with us, her latest baby being safe in the care of a wet nurse. She laughed on hearing of Thomas Seymour's new appointment. "That's clever of the King," she said. "Thomas will spend most of his time inspecting ships in remote places like Plymouth and Newcastle."

Katherine shows no sign of what she feels about the man she used to love – if, in fact, she feels anything. She addresses him with nothing more than formal politeness and shows no interest in his tales of life in a foreign capital.

7th January 1545

Christmas was a busy time, as usual, but we were all glad to see the royal family together and enjoying each other's company. Elizabeth, who is still only twelve, presented the Queen with her own translation from the French of a book by Margaret of Navarre, *Le Miroir de l'Ame Pécheresse* – The Mirror of a Sinning Woman's Soul. She had written it all out in small, faultless script, and the dedication on the title page read: "To the most noble and virtuous Queen Katherine." It was signed, with a message. "Elizabeth, her humble daughter, wisheth perpetual felicity and everlasting joy." Katherine was delighted. There is nothing she likes more than exploring ideas about religion and matters of the spirit, and her young stepdaughter is a tremendous pleasure to her. Elizabeth too seems happier and more content than she has ever done. These months with the new queen are perhaps the nearest thing to real mothering that she has ever known.

The King, on the other hand, is starting to pout and look discontented. The energy and good health he had built up during the campaign in France kept him active through the autumn and he hunted almost every day. Slowly though, as the days shortened and the rain and cold of November closed in, his gaiety evaporated. He is always prone to depression during the dark winter months, and this year seems set to be the same.

Eustache Chapuys, the Spanish ambassador, is very old now, and he too is not coping well with the winter. He has taken to a chair with small wheels fixed to it, as his limbs are shaky these days and walking is hard for him. He will be leaving the court soon to return to Spain.

Kitty is pregnant again. How strange it is that birth for her seems as regular and natural as any other function, when for the King and his various wives, it has been an elusive goal, set about with failure and bitterness. Speaking for myself, I am grateful for this rest time following Joanna's birth. I hope we will have a brother or sister for her at some point, but I do not want one baby after another, like peas in a pod.

4th March 1545

The King is both unwell and angry. He increasingly sees himself as attacked by members of the Protestant religion who fail to recognize him as its head. Catholics understand this, as it is a simple choice between Pope and King, and they practise their religion quietly among themselves. For the Protestants, the line between faith and heresy is alarmingly narrow. The larger Protestant Church founded by Martin Luther does not recognize the authority of Rome – but neither does it see Henry of England as its head. All across Europe the Protestant faith gains popularity through its idea that every human being can worship God and receive His guidance and mercy, independent from the authority of the Pope and the priests. The King sees this as disrespectful to himself and therefore treasonable. This winter he has imprisoned 23 people for "heretical" Protestant beliefs.

Among them is an unfortunate woman called Anne Askew. She applied to the King for a legal separation from her husband because he had bodily thrown her out of the house and would not let her come back, even to see her two children. Anne had appealed to Katherine, who listened to her story with compassion. But this time when Katherine appealed to the King about Anne's case, he had no sympathy at all. He said the woman was obviously a dangerous Protestant and sent her to the Tower, where she still is.

Will fears that Katherine was rash to have listened to Anne Askew. "They will put the poor woman on the rack," he said sombrely, "and who knows how many people she will name as traitors when her joints begin to tear apart?" I fear he may be right – and such information would have frightful results. I dare not think of what will happen if the King starts to see his wife as sympathetic to heretical Protestants.

17th May 1545

Eustache Chapuys, the old Spanish ambassador, has at last returned to his own country. Elinor and Eva came to say goodbye to him. Eva had tears in her eyes. She has known Chapuys since 1529, when he first arrived in England. He had been a great supporter of Catherine of Aragon through the years when Henry was finding a way to divorce her.

Eva told me once that Chapuys described Anne Boleyn as a "whore" and a "concubine". I thought of that when the King came out to the garden where Chapuys was sitting – frail in his chair that has handles so that a helper can push him – but Henry was kind to the old man. He thanked him for his long service and for the work he had done in bringing about a friendship between England and Spain. Eva and

Elinor exchanged glances, and I knew what they meant. There had been times when the King had hated Chapuys as much as he hated the wife he was trying to discard. But since then the ambassador has put in years of work to keep the peace between two countries and two rulers. He must be happy now to see that the King is in close contact with the Emperor. Since their joint attack on France, both of them are pleased and relationships are smooth. It's a good time for Chapuys to go home. His job, at least for now, is done.

4th July 1545

I am pregnant again! The new baby, God willing, will come next spring, not long after Jo's second birthday. "Perfect," Will said. "Aren't you clever?" He is such a good father to Jo. He tosses her in the air and catches her, and she shrieks with laughter. He says his own father used to do that to them when they were children, and he always loved it.

The Queen has become very studious. She is writing a book of prayers and meditations, and her face is serious and preoccupied.

28th August 1545

Charles Brandon, the Duke of Suffolk, died last week. He had been the King's closest friend, though he married Henry's sister, Mary, in a romantic fling that caused no end of trouble. He leaves two young sons, and the elder one, named Henry, has come here to be educated with Prince Edward. Elizabeth shares the lessons as well. She is never idle. When the boys go outside to practise archery or the tilt-yard skills, she takes up her lute and plays and sings, or puts in more work on a piece of intricate embroidery. She and the Queen share a passion for learning.

Queen Katherine has set up a school for the education of girls, centred around her own teaching. It is a new thing, for girls have always been thought of as creatures with just one use, as wives and mothers of children. Katherine contends that women can be of far more value to their children if they have learning to pass on to them. I think she does not accept that there is any great difference between the female mind and the male one. I myself share in some of her classes, and find her teaching wonderful. Needless to say, there is great competition to come to the court and benefit from the Queen's teaching.

One of the new pupils is Lady Jane Grey. Her mother, Frances Grey, is Charles Brandon's daughter. Lady Jane was named after Jane Seymour, and she is almost exactly the same age as Prince Edward. I like her very much. She is a quiet, clever child, but seems very frightened. Her mother is said to be a cruel woman who beat and whipped her daughters if they displeased her, even when they were little more than babies. Jane seems to be blossoming now in this coming together of young people in the court – all anxious to learn. Katherine sends them on to Stoke College if they merit further education and pays their fees out of her own purse. She never turns a poor student away. The motto she chose when she became queen was "To be useful in all that I do." She is putting that motto into very real practice, and I respect her more with every day that passes.

26th October 1545

The King has suffered some kind of sudden illness. For a moment this morning he staggered and almost lost consciousness. A great flurry of barber-surgeons arrived and he has been confined to his bed for some days. He is in no danger, it seems, but he is still not well enough to appear in public.

16th November 1545

Queen Katherine's book was published last week, to great acclaim. The universities of Oxford and Cambridge are so impressed that both of them have sent requests to ask her to be their patroness, and she has accepted. She is now recognized throughout the country as a talented, erudite woman in her own right.

The King is still unwell. Will said, "He is probably suffering from chronic jealousy." We both laughed, but there may be some truth in it. If so, the Queen will have to be careful.

27th November 1545

There is some nasty gossip going around, probably started by Thomas Wriothesley. He is a Catholic of the Duke of Norfolk type, and has always disliked Katherine Parr. I used to think Thomas Cromwell was a plotter and schemer, but Wriothesley is as bad, if not worse. He is spreading a rumour that Katherine is a rabid Protestant who shares the

Lutheran views held by Lady Hertford and by Thomas Seymour and his brother. This is desperately dangerous. If Wriothesley manages to slide the idea into the King's mind, there will be terrible trouble.

At the moment it seems that Henry has heard nothing. He is out of bed now, but his ulcerated leg has got much worse through the long time of inactivity. His temper is explosive, but he calms a little when Katherine sits beside him and talks to him. Meanwhile, she is busy with her next book, which is to be called *The Lamentations of a Sinner*. She has been telling us some of its contents. Yesterday, she said she had written a passage advising young women to learn of St Paul that they must be obedient to their husbands and learn from them. Evidently, she is being very careful.

This pregnancy is making me strangely tired. Will suggests I leave the court for a while. The King is not much disposed to hospitality or any kind of revels while his leg is so painful. "It's all very quiet," Will said. "And Eva would be glad of your company."

He is right. Eva is 60 years old now, and her fingers are bent with rheumatics. She does not complain, and Elinor and the children look after her well, but they have other things to do. Eva would like someone to talk to in the coming winter months. And we are at Greenwich just now, so Will can come home in the evenings if he is not too busy. Yes, I'll go.

15th February 1546

Will came home tonight looking troubled. "Someone has been telling tales," he said. "You remember Anne Askew, the woman who wanted a divorce, but ended up in the Tower instead? Someone has told the King she has made a new confession – and it mentions the Queen."

Who is this spreader of rumours? Will doesn't know, but gossip has it that an unknown person has been sending heretical books to Katherine. It is only a matter of time before the King starts to ask questions. And Wriothesley will be only too glad to supply the answers, true or not.

29th March 1546

My baby came earlier than she should. She had been lying the wrong way round, so it was a long, difficult birth. She did not live.

I have been ill since then. Will says we are young, and there is time for more children to come, but I grieve for my lost baby and have no energy. Little Jo is a consolation, yet I find I want to do nothing at all except the household tasks that need no thought. Elinor says to lose a child is a bad shock, and the body and mind need time to recover

18th July 1546

The summer sun has slowly made things better. The energy that would have gone into caring for a new baby has formed itself anew and I am hopeful again, trusting in nature for another child when the time is right. Eva, too, feels better in the warmth of these long days. She tells me I need not think I have to be with her all the time. So I am back with the court, in the Whitehall palace, because more than anything I want to be with Will. He shares my grief and my hopes, and when the pair of us and little Joanna are together I feel that we are a family.

There is horrible news, though. It was quite untrue that Anne Askew had said anything about the Queen, and last month Lord Chancellor Wriothesley persuaded the King to let him interrogate her afresh. When Anne would not give him the answers he wanted, Wriothesley personally supervised her torture on the rack. He was determined to make her tell him that the Queen has Protestant beliefs, but Anne would not speak, in spite of the terrible pain. She lost consciousness as her joints were torn from their sockets, but Wriothesley waited until she had been revived and then, with his own hands, went on turning the wheel of the awful machinery, to wrench her body apart even further. Anne still would not speak. When she was almost dead they laid her on the bare stone of the floor, and the Lord Chancellor went on questioning her for a further two hours. Anne did not deny her Protestant faith, but she would not say one word to implicate the Queen or her ladies.

She was burned at the stake two days ago, at the Guildhall in London. They had to carry her on a chair to her execution because her body was ruined by the torture. The executioner himself was perhaps horrified by what had been done to her because he hung a small bag of gunpowder round her neck, and as the pyre was lit it exploded. Anne Askew died instantly and without further pain.

28th July 1546

What I feared has happened. The Queen was sitting at King Henry's side, as she often does, with his sore leg resting across her lap to try to soothe the pain of it a little. She was talking about matters of faith, not unusually, being much taken up by the book she is writing about prayer – but perhaps it was coming too close to being a lecture. The King suddenly lost patience, and cut off her flow of words quite rudely, telling her to be quiet. I hope it is only through jealousy of his wife's growing fame as a religious thinker, as Will suggested. Katherine looked at him in surprise but obediently began to talk of inoffensive domestic matters. They went on chatting, and everything seemed normal again. When he retired to his room Henry kissed his wife as usual and bade her goodnight as affectionately as always.

But Bishop Gardiner had been listening. And Gardiner is very close to Wriothesley as the two of them belong to the Catholic faction that wants to see the end of this Protestant queen. This afternoon Henry was grumbling to some of his gentlemen about his wife's tendency to lecture him on religion, and Gardiner seized his chance. In front of everyone, he told the King that Katherine was teaching people dangerous ideas, suggesting that they had the right to think for themselves and did not intend to respect the authority of either the Pope or the King. He added darkly that Henry could "make great discoveries if he were not deterred by the Queen's powerful faction". He made it clear that this "faction" consisted of a group that backed Katherine's Protestant ideas and said that Henry should understand how dangerous it was to "cherish a serpent within his own bosom".

Those who heard him held their breath. The King stared at Gardiner as if he could not believe what he heard, then he got to his feet and hobbled to his private quarters, beckoning the bishop to follow him. They were there on their own for a long time. When Gardiner came out, he was smirking with triumph. He said the King has agreed to the drawing up of an accusation against the Queen, with a view to putting her on trial for her life. Katherine, thank goodness, does not know this.

29th July 1546

The council today questioned three of Katherine's favourite ladies, asking them whether the Queen had any books that are forbidden on the grounds of heresy. The ladies were shocked and said firmly that she had not. They were released, but we fear this is the beginning of something far worse.

Even now, Katherine does not seem to realize what danger she is in, or else she will not believe it. She does not seem to grasp the idea that the matters of faith she finds so interesting can also be matters of politics. Today she has been chatting to the King as usual about the finer points of theology. He listens to her very carefully now, with narrowed eyes.

"He's like a cat beside a mouse hole," Will said today. "Waiting to pounce."

4th August 1546

This evening the King was talking at length with his new doctor, a shrewd, clever man called Thomas Wendy. At the end of their conversation, Henry signed a warrant for the Queen's arrest. I did not know this had happened because I had gone down to the kitchens for a posset for the Queen and had dallied talking to Will. When I came up the stairs, I found a document lying on the carpet, just outside Katherine's chambers. It looked important, so I gave it to the Queen.

She read what it said – and burst into tears. "He has rejected me," she sobbed. "It is all over."

Her sister took her in her arms and tried to comfort her but Katherine was utterly distraught. We read the warrant and looked at each other, aghast. Were we destined to see a third terrible execution – yet another loved wife killed? We could do nothing to pacify Katherine – her hysterical screaming could be heard all over the palace.

After a while Dr Wendy arrived. He said the King had sent him to find out what the matter was, and he preferred to come alone rather than with the other doctors. I told him about finding the warrant on the floor, and he said, straight-faced, that he had given it to a member of the Privy Council, who must have dropped it. Will thinks Dr Wendy and the King planned the whole thing together. Whether that's right or not, Dr Wendy explained to Katherine that Gardiner and Wriothesley are plotting her downfall. She was overwhelmed by terror. She screamed like a rabbit with a weasel at its throat, on and on, and there was nothing we could do to stop her. The doctor himself could not help. It was appalling to see such a poised, self-controlled woman so hysterical.

Dr Wendy left us. He must have gone back to the King because a little later, Henry came in, and we were dismissed. He and Katherine were together for over an hour. We heard the screaming give way to sobs, then at last to the low murmur of voices. After he had left, she called us in. She was in control of herself as usual. She told us to get rid of any books that could be considered heretical, and we promised to do so.

We expected that she would go to bed then, but she said she had to see the King first. She asked Lady Lane to light the way with a candle, then turned to her sister and said, "Come with me." In her nightgown and with her hair loose, she made her way to Henry's bedchamber.

Lady Lane told us afterwards what happened. The King was still up, chatting with his gentlemen. He welcomed Katherine and was obviously not surprised to see her, though his gentlemen were. Then, in front of them as witnesses, he talked to his wife about her tendency to lecture him on matters of religion. "I could see it was all rehearsed," Lady Lane said. "He sat back when he had finished, offering the Queen a chance to say what she wished. And she did it beautifully."

Katherine assured her husband that if she had ever involved him in spiritual discussions, it was only to benefit from his superior knowledge and guidance. "I am but a woman," she said, "with all the imperfections natural to the weakness of my sex; therefore in all matters of doubt and difficulty I must refer myself to Your Majesty's better judgement as to my lord and head."

It was a masterpiece of diplomacy. Nobody will ever know whether Katherine's meek and submissive speech was of her own making or whether Henry had dictated its content, but it worked wonderfully well. The King smiled and said, "Then we are perfect friends, as ever at any time heretofore." And he took his wife in his arms and kissed her.

When she came back, Katherine told me to put the warrant back exactly where I had found it. In the morning it had gone.

5th August 1546

The outcome was really quite funny. I was cutting roses to put in Katherine's chambers when the King and Queen themselves came out to the garden with three ladies and sat down, chatting and laughing. Before long, Wriothesley came along the path at the head of a 40-strong squad of the King's guards, their helmets and cuirasses glinting in the sun as though they were marching to battle.

Wriothesley presented the warrant and announced that he had come to escort the Queen and her ladies to the Tower. There was a gasp among the ladies, who thought for a moment that everything had gone wrong – but the King got up and moved away a little, beckoning to Wriothesley, who followed him.

We could not hear what was said, but the Lord Chancellor fell on his knees, babbling explanations. Henry did not listen. He shouted in Wriothesley's face, "Knave! Arrant knave! Beast! Fool!" He commanded him and his men to leave the royal presence at once, and they scuttled out in disarray while we collapsed into nervous giggles. Even Henry permitted himself a smile, and he pulled Katherine to him and kissed her.

All the same, the Queen is most careful now. She discusses religious matters with other scholars, but as far as the King is concerned, she is nothing more than a dutiful wife.

2nd September 1546

It has been like old times. A treaty of peace has been signed between England and France, so Claude d'Annebault, the Admiral of France, has paid a state visit with a great entourage of people. Will and his helpers in the kitchen have been run off their feet, and we have all been up until the small hours, dancing and feasting and enjoying masques. The King went hunting with his guests, and the long dining tables were laid with gold dishes, set with jewels.

Now that the French party has gone home, the King and Queen are setting out on a short progress. Will and I do not have to go with them, which is good because it is pig-killing time and we will be busy at home, making bacon and ham for the winter.

25th September 1546

The progress was too much for the King. He has come back ailing and fretful, and although he makes light of it and pretends he is as healthy as ever, he can hardly walk. Orders have been given for two indoor conveyances to be constructed, upholstered in velvet, so that he may be pushed from room to room. He cannot go up or down stairs, and the carpenters have devised a cunning machine that can raise a seat strong enough to convey his vast bulk.

It seems to have come so suddenly, and everyone assumes that His Majesty is nearing the end of his life. I think this is an over-gloomy view – after all, Henry has been ill before and fought his way back to health. But the gossip is hardly concerned with the King himself. It is all about who will take the reins after his death. Prince Edward will inherit the throne, of course, but he is only nine years old. Somebody will have to guide him and take responsibility for the country. I keep hoping it will not happen yet. For all his faults, Henry is a secure and powerful monarch. Some of the men who are waiting like vultures to seize what they can frighten me more than the King does. Explosive as he is, we are used to him, and his word is law. When he leaves us, we will be staring in the face of uncertainty.

12th December 1546

This is going to be a grim Christmas, but King Henry is still a force to be reckoned with. He has uncovered a plot by the Howard family and is furious. How much is truth and how much is his imagination is difficult to say, but we learn that the Duke of Norfolk has been plotting to overthrow the present queen. He wants to replace her with his own daughter, Mary Howard, the Duchess of Richmond. Norfolk's son, now the Duke of Surrey, backed this plan – yet another Howard plot to lever a young woman into the King's favour.

This particular scheme is truly outrageous because Mary Howard was the wife of the King's illegitimate son, Henry Fitzroy, Duke of Richmond, who died so young. Did Norfolk really imagine that the King would take his dead son's wife as his mistress? The man must be insane. Henry's response was instant, ailing though he may be. He threw the Duke of Norfolk into the Tower, and his son as well.

"There's a cheery place to spend Christmas," Will remarked. Then he added, "If you ask me, the King should have done it years ago. Those two are a right pair of scoundrels."

2nd January 1547

Here at Greenwich, it has been a strange and silent festive season. All of us know it will be the King's last. He knows it too. On Christmas Eve he called both houses of Parliament together and delivered a carefully considered speech, making it clear that this was his final address to them. Something of Katherine Parr's thoughtfulness on religious matters seems to have taken root in him. For the first time he has accepted that the Protestant Church is here to stay, and that it must move on beyond the domination of his own power. He issued a plea for an end to religious discord, telling the members of his regret that "charity and concord is not among you". He deplored the fact that, "the Word of God is disputed, rhymed, sung and jangled in every alehouse and tavern". The fatherly, concerned tone of what the King said, coupled with the knowledge that they might not hear his voice ever again, reduced several members to tears.

Apart from the Queen, the lady Mary was the only member of the royal family at court for Christmas. Some members of the Privy Council were permitted, but nobody else was allowed. The quiet was eerie.

On the last day of 1546, the King dictated his will. Prince Edward inherits the throne followed by the lady Mary and "any children that Queen Katherine might yet bear him". One has to admire his undying optimism. He gave instructions that he should be buried beside Jane Seymour, who gave him his only son.

9th January 1547

The King rallied a little after making his will, and ordered that he and his household should be removed to Whitehall. Will and Joanna and I are with them, since nobody has suggested otherwise. Will is making nourishing soups laced with cream and brandy.

Two days ago an Act of Attainder was passed against the Duke of Norfolk and his son, the Duke of Surrey. They are both declared traitors and stripped of all wealth and possessions. Surrey will be tried next week, but there is no news of what will happen to his father.

19th January 1547

The Duke of Surrey was executed on Tower Hill this morning. Norfolk still waits in the Tower for judgement. It seems likely that he will wait for a long time, for the King can no longer deal with such things.

23rd January 1547

With the last of his failing strength, the King spoke to the privy councillors about the choice of men to assist the young prince in his regency. I thought he would name Katherine as the obvious choice, but he did not. The Lord Protector will be the Duke of Hertford, Thomas Seymour's older brother, who led the "rough wooing" in Scotland. Other advisers include Cranmer, Lord Lisle and, strangely, Lord Chancellor Wriothesley. Somebody suggested Thomas Seymour himself, but although the King was short of breath and could hardly speak, he cried out weakly, "No! No!"

Then he saw the lady Mary, who was in floods of tears, having only just been told that her father is dying. Nobody has told either Elizabeth or young Edward of the King's mortal illness, which seems dreadful to me. Surely they should have been given a chance to see their father for the last time? But perhaps Henry wanted to spare them distress.

They brought the warrant for Norfolk's execution to the King for him to sign, but he was drifting in and out of consciousness and could no longer hold a pen. "Norfolk has the luck of the devil," Will said. Neither of us smiled.

28th January 1547

It is over. At two o'clock this morning, Henry VIII, King of England, came to the end of his life. Two nights ago he recognized that he was failing, and asked Katherine to come to him. Kitty and I were among the ladies who accompanied her. The King thanked his wife for being "so faithful a spouse" after a life that had seen "so many changes". Katherine was weeping helplessly. The Lords of the Council were in the room, and Henry said they were to treat Katherine "as if I were living still". If she marries again, she is to have £7,000 for her use as long as she shall live, and all her jewels and ornaments. Katherine was so much further overcome that it was painful for him to watch her. He said gently that she should leave, and we helped her to her rooms. She lay on her bed, crying her heart out. What a strange marriage it has been. Katherine married the King out of duty, but she came to have a very real love for him.

At the end Henry sent the doctors away. He was asked if he wanted to make his confession or receive the last rites, but he managed a faint shake of the head and murmured, "Only Cranmer … but not yet."

By the time Cranmer came, the King could no longer speak. The archbishop took his hand and asked him to give a sign if he "put his trust in God, through Jesus Christ". He felt the dying man tighten his failing grip in reply.

Henry Tudor was 55 years old. It seems a short life for a monarch whose reign has left no man, woman or child in his kingdom untouched.

30th January 1547

It is only today that Elizabeth and Edward have been told of their father's death. The Lord Protector, the Duke of Hertford, has taken charge of them both in Enfield, where he broke the news. They are both dreadfully upset, as I would be on finding that such an event had happened without a word of it being communicated. If the idea was to spare them pain, it was surely mistaken. Prince Edward is to be proclaimed King tomorrow.

17th February 1547

Royal funerals are always a gradual business. The King's body has been taken to Syon Abbey, where Katherine Howard was kept in the weeks before her execution. The sealed lead coffin was carried on a litter covered in cloth of gold and bearing a wax effigy of King Henry. The Lords of the Council followed, and directly behind the coffin walked the King's great black horse, riderless now.

There is a frightful story about what happened the next day. The coffin was kept overnight in the ruined chapel at Syon. Henry's men had destroyed the chapel in his dissolution of the monasteries. In the morning, it was found that the lead panels of the coffin had split apart after the jolting of the journey. Plumbers were sent for at once to make repairs – and one of them had a dog with him. The dog was seen to lick up the blood that had seeped from the coffin, and a shiver of horror ran through everyone. I have looked up Eva's diary. In 1532 Friar Peto predicted that if Henry cast off Catherine of Aragon and married Anne Boleyn, the dogs would lick his blood. Just superstition, of course, and yet it lingers uneasily in the mind. Eva crossed herself when she heard, and closed her eyes. She said nothing.

The cortège moved on to Windsor. Elinor and Eva both went to the funeral but I stayed with the Queen and her other ladies, since by tradition a woman may not attend her husband's last rites. I was glad to escape the event as it would have been deeply upsetting. I have often been horrified by King Henry's actions, but without him the world is somehow less.

Henry was laid to rest beside Jane Seymour. The lords of his household broke their staves of office and cast the pieces into the vault, to signify that their service to him was finished. The herald blew a fanfare on his trumpet and shouted, "*Le roi est mort! Vive le roi!*" The new young king did not hear, for he was weeping in Enfield.

25th February 1547

I am pregnant again. I hardly dared write of it when I first knew, being full of a superstitious fear that this new, small life would not survive the King's death. But when Will suspected it, he put his arms round me and said, "Don't be afraid, my sweetheart. Life ends and new life begins. It has to be like that, or the world would stop." I tell myself not to be cock-sure, but I can't suppress the belief that this time, it will be all right.

2nd March 1547

Katherine Parr is deeply hurt that the Privy Council has refused to let her see Prince Edward. These powerful men are now in complete charge, and the Queen Dowager, as Katherine is now known, has faded into a shadowy figure that can be ignored. She is soon to leave court and move to the Old Manor at Chelsea. She is immensely wealthy, but in terms of influence, she has become invisible.

Lord Hertford, Thomas Seymour's older brother, now rules the council. To cement his position, he made the young King sign "letters patent" that give Hertford the right to appoint Privy Council members and to consult them only when he wishes to. Thus he has made himself king of the country in every way except in name. He is now to be known as the Duke of Somerset, and other members of the council are gleefully grabbing privileges as well. Katherine Parr's brother, William, is the Marquess of Northampton. Wriothesley has become the Earl of Southampton.

There are whispers that the King's will was dictated or even possibly written by other persons. Henry's life ebbed away more quickly than he had perhaps anticipated, and it may be that he left the unpleasant task of handing his power to others a little too late. Now that his influence is gone, the gentlemen of the council have become a selfish rabble, and the effect is starting to be felt across the country. The common land that has always been freely shared for the grazing of animals is being fenced in for the sheep farming that the big estate owners find so profitable, and people are distraught. These "enclosures", as they are called, will rob countless people of their livelihood.

King Henry was not above taking land and property, of course. When he overthrew the monasteries he declared his ownership of countless abbeys and granges, with all their fertile acres, and handed them out to his friends. But he did things for large reasons and on a large scale, and this mean-minded grabbing would never have been his style. These men have no style. I find them disgusting.

Thomas Seymour is back in this country, jostling for power as always. It infuriates him that he is not a member of the council, so he is once again trying to marry his way into power. We all thought he would set his cap at Katherine, since she was so in love with him and is now a very rich widow, but he is aiming higher than that. He is writing letters of admiration to Elizabeth.

5th March 1547

Elizabeth has turned Thomas Seymour down. Her nurse, Mrs Ashley, saw the letter and told everyone what was in it. "Very dignified, but put him in his place, good and proper." She is a terrible gossip, especially when her adored young mistress has done something to boast about.

Will said, "Young Lizzie knows better than to tie herself up with a rogue like that," but I am not so sure. Elizabeth has refused to consider Thomas's cheeky offer, but she is growing into a lively girl, aware of her attractiveness. She might well fall for a man with charm, and if Thomas has nothing else, he certainly has charm in abundance. Meanwhile, he will probably fall back on his second choice – Katherine Parr.

26th March 1547

I smile to see my last entry. That is exactly what Thomas Seymour did. He proposed to Katherine and, to the dismay of the few people who know, she has accepted him. She is still officially in full mourning for her husband and it would be extremely incorrect to marry again so soon, but Thomas doesn't want to wait. Of course not – the sooner he is married, the sooner he will have wealth and power.

29th March 1547

Thomas Seymour's scheming developed quickly. We would not have known what he was up to, but a man called John Fowler got very drunk in the kitchens last night and showed Will a handful of gold coins.

"Nice work!" he said proudly. "Bet you wish you could get a job like that, eh? Looks as if I've struck it lucky."

Will topped up the man's glass and said, "Go on?"

John Fowler, who is Thomas Seymour's nephew, is in the service of young King Edward. The royal boy is kept very well guarded. Nobody can speak to him without the council's permission. But Seymour offered Fowler a fat bribe to ask Edward what lady he would like to see as a wife for his Uncle Tom.

The boy didn't understand that he was supposed to plump for the ex-queen. He thought about it carefully then suggested his cousin, Mary, or perhaps Anne of Cleves. John Fowler reported this back to Seymour, with a hint that Edward is kept very short of pocket money. Seymour sent Fowler back the next day, equipped with a bag of gold pieces (a good number of which he kept for himself) to put the question more plainly. Edward's eyes lit up when he saw the coins. He agreed at once that Katherine Parr would be the ideal wife for his uncle.

The next day Thomas Seymour told Katherine that he has the King's permission to marry her. Edward is only a young boy, but he is the King of England. His word is law.

11th April 1547

I went to see Kitty last week. She is lying-in with her new baby. When we had finished admiring him, she told me something very interesting. Thomas Seymour wants to make himself the guardian of his young cousin, Lady Jane Grey, who has been studying with Katherine Parr. He thinks young Lady Jane might in due course be the perfect wife for Prince Edward, so he proposes that he should make himself the girl's guardian. She would then live permanently with him and Katherine when they are married, and be considered their daughter in legal terms. That would put Seymour marvellously close to the throne.

Lady Jane's father, the Duke of Suffolk, objected on the grounds that there was no guarantee that his daughter would be properly cared for and chaperoned, but Kitty thinks he is simply holding out for a better deal. Seymour is offering him a lot of money in exchange for rights over his daughter. However, Lady Jane is also her father's best asset, and he will not hand her over without a cash reward that is big enough to be worth while. I am appalled by such horse-trading, but what more can one expect of such men?

28th April 1547

Thomas Seymour and Katherine Parr are now married. It is supposed to be a deep secret as Katherine is still in mourning. She and her new husband are living apart for the time being, hoping to keep the rumours down, but the Duchess of Somerset has found out, and is on the rampage. She is the wife of Edward Seymour, Thomas's brother, now the Duke of Somerset. It was she who, when she was merely Lady Hertford, came weeping to Katherine to ask her help in returning her husband from the campaign in Scotland, but that is forgotten now. Her husband is running the country, and she is outraged that Katherine should have married without asking his permission.

29th May 1547

Katherine asked Lord Somerset to her house in Chelsea and confessed that she and Thomas Seymour are married. He already knew, of course, and was simmering with fury. He berated Katherine for her insolence and disrespect and slammed out of the house. So she and Thomas are even further away from being accepted by the Privy Council.

2nd June 1547

Thomas Seymour wrote to the lady Mary, asking her to use her influence with the council on his behalf. That was a big mistake. As Will put it, "He picked the wrong person there." Mary is a stickler for correct behaviour, but she never knows much about what is going on, so she was shocked and appalled to hear that Thomas had married Katherine. She sent him a very stiff letter, refusing to support him, but worse, his action has destroyed her friendship with Katherine. Mary's strict Catholic principles cannot condone what she sees as morally corrupt behaviour, so she wants nothing more to do with her erstwhile friend. What's more, she is going to prevent Elizabeth from seeing the ex-queen if she possibly can, because she now regards Katherine as a bad influence.

I find it extraordinary that Katherine Parr, with all her intelligence and learning, should let herself be so taken in by a man whose only aim is to claw his way into wealth and power. He is leading her into such folly.

10th June 1547

Katherine has written to Lord Somerset, asking him to give her all the jewels traditionally worn by the Queen of England, as she is entitled to wear them until young Edward is old enough to marry a queen consort of his own. She is within her rights, as the King promised them to her on his deathbed, and the Duke must know it. But his wife loathes Katherine, and she will resist any idea of letting her wear the royal jewellery. Will says the Duke is terrified of his wife and always does as she says, but this time he is caught between the Duchess and an equally determined ex-queen, and he does not know what to do. While he thinks about it, the jewels remain in the Treasury.

21st June 1547

Katherine has been back to Court for a formal visit – that, of course, is why she wanted the state jewels. All her ladies were there. She was wearing a magnificent dress with a long train that required someone to hold it, and she turned to the Duchess of Somerset as the senior lady and asked if she would be the train-bearer. It was a test of power, and we all knew it. To be chosen as train-bearer to the queen is normally seen as an honour, but the Duchess was outraged. She said it would be unsuitable for her, the wife of the Lord Protector, to stoop to such a service for the mere wife of her husband's younger brother. What she meant was, she sees herself as the acting Queen of England.

Katherine had lost the battle for status, but she turned away with unruffled dignity and several ladies were quick to offer their services. Ever since then, the Duchess has been keeping up a tirade of hurtful remarks and scandalous insinuations. At one point she said the King only married Katherine Parr when he had "brought himself so low by his lust and cruelty that no lady who stood on her honour would venture on him". And she has made her husband refuse to hand over the queen's jewels.

8th August 1547

Perhaps Somerset has been having pangs of conscience. He has awarded Thomas the rank of Captain General and Lord Protector's Lieutenant in the South of England, and given him the manor of Sudeley, together with its ancient castle. Thomas is now a member of the peerage – but he is still seeking to get closer to the centre of power. Via the obliging John Fowler, he has kept up a supply of pocket money to young Prince Edward, and the boy has done what he can to help Thomas's cause. He wrote to Katherine, promising that when he was able to, he would make sure she was well provided for. He apologized that he could not write as often as he would like, for he was hardly left on his own for more than a few minutes. Letters are smuggled in and out by Fowler. It is just as well that the Lord Protector does not know this.

18th September 1547

We have been at home for most of the summer, but Will and I have been asked to be permanent members of staff in Katherine's Chelsea house. It is not so rural as Greenwich, but the surrounding manor has walled gardens that are excellent for growing fruit and vegetables.

Eva and Elinor do not need so much help now. The house has its servants, and Elinor's daughter, Maria, is fourteen and very practical. She is pretty, too, and has a great ambition to come to court. Her brother Michael is quite different. He has been helping Tom in the forge since he was old enough to hammer a length of hot iron. He is not interested in the doings of court people – his main interest is in making things, and I admire him for that.

Will and I have agreed that we will not move to Chelsea until after my new baby is born. Katherine is agreeable to that.

9th October 1547

My baby boy came fast and quite easily, early in the morning while the birds were singing at dawn. He is dark-haired, and Eva said, "What a little Spaniard he looks!"

We have not been able to decide on a name, so I asked Eva if we could call him after someone in her family that she would like to remember. "My uncle Rod," she said at once. "I loved him so much, and he was a wonderful man." So our little son is Rodrigo Valjean. What a resounding name that is! Somehow I feel he will grow to fit it.

14th November 1547

The Chelsea house is very big, and a lot of work has been done to renovate it. Will likes its three kitchens, and Joanna ran up and down the staircases and through the rooms that stand empty, loving the echo of her own quick footsteps. Maria has come with us, because she sees this as a chance to make a first contact with court life, and I am so glad.

It will be good to have her help with the children, and I hope it may lead to what she wants for herself.

Katherine Parr looks contented and happy. Her new book, *Lamentations of a Sinner*, is finished. It has been printed, and all those who have read it are full of praise. Perhaps this is a sinful thought, but I do feel some satisfaction that the Duchess of Somerset cannot claim to be capable of any such achievement. Katherine is established in her own right now as one of England's major thinkers. For a woman, that is an astonishing achievement.

4th January 1548

Elizabeth is here, not just for a visit but to stay. She seems greatly relieved. She told me life at court had become intolerable. The council had fixed absurdly rigid courtesies that insisted she must go down on one knee to her young brother Edward whenever she met him, not just once but *five times*. As a girl of fifteen, that must have been irksome.

She is to resume her education, pursuing the reading and learning that she enjoyed so much in the early days of Katherine's reign. She has brought her own lady-in-waiting, the wonderfully gossipy Mrs Ashley, so there is no great increase in the household work, and Will is only too happy to be cooking for bigger numbers. Katherine is delighted to be teaching again. After the months when her royal household was recognized as a centre for the education of girls, it obviously gives her great pleasure.

12th February 1548

Lady Jane Grey has come to join Elizabeth. Her grandmother is with her, so she is well cared for and chaperoned. Her father's hesitations over Thomas Seymour's scheme have been soothed, we suspect because enough money has now changed hands. Thomas has bought himself an asset that he hopes will pay off when his girl marries Edward and becomes the Queen of England.

Lady Jane is not unlike Elizabeth to look at, with the same red hair and arched eyebrows, but she is three years younger. She seems watchful and scared, and Will calls her "a skinny little rabbit". She reminds me a bit of myself at that age, but she has had a far worse time of it than I did. She told me a little yesterday of the beatings she had had to endure from her mother ever since she was tiny.

I join her and Elizabeth for lessons when I have no other duties as my love of learning has never left me since my days with Mr Thornton. Elizabeth requested a change of tutor not along after she came here, and Katherine was happy to agree. We now have the famous scholar, Roger Ascham. Lady Jane is an eager pupil. Mr Ascham seems concerned about her nervousness and encourages her to speak her mind, and yesterday Jane suddenly burst out with a great list of what she had been through. She said whatever she did in the presence of her parents – "whether I speak, keep silence, sit, stand or go, eat, drink, be merry or sad, be sewing, playing, dancing, or doing anything else," had to be done "as perfectly as God made the world".

The tutor asked gently what happened if there was any falling short of these standards, and she went on, "I am so sharply taunted, so cruelly threatened … with pinches, nips and bobs and other ways…" Tears threatened, but she struggled on "… I think myself in hell." I put my hand over hers, and she gripped it tightly. After a few moments, we went on reading Plato.

Thomas Seymour is here as well, of course. I am a little uneasy about the glances that run between him and Elizabeth. She obviously finds him attractive – what girl does not? In an academic household devoted to books and learning, he walks about like some glossy animal, waiting to be admired.

5th March 1548

Katherine Parr is expecting a baby! It comes as a great surprise to everyone, but as Will pointed out, "This shows it was not her fault if she and the King had no children." I am glad Henry did not know. It would have been such a blow to his pride.

Mrs Ashley, Elizabeth's nurse, is concerned about Katherine's pregnancy. "She is 35 years old," she says. "That is late for the birth of a first child. I do hope she will be all right."

She went on to say she is sure that something is going on between Elizabeth and Katherine's husband. "Why are both of them always missing at prayers?" she asked. "I think I need to be absent myself one morning and see what I can find."

I will keep an eye open as well. I have no wish to curtail Elizabeth's pleasure in a first-ever love affair, but this is frightening. What if she too should become pregnant? The idea is too awful to contemplate.

7th March 1548

Mrs Ashley stayed in Elizabeth's room yesterday morning, despite the girl's entreaties that she should go to her prayers. Thomas Seymour walked in without knocking, and he wore only his nightgown and slippers. Elizabeth was still in bed and shrank under the covers, Mrs Ashley scolded Thomas severely and he left, angry about such temerity from a servant.

15th March 1548

Thomas goes to Elizabeth's room every morning. He only enters if the girl is still in her bed or wearing her nightclothes. If she is up and dressed, he goes away again. Mrs Ashley stays in Elizabeth's room when he comes, but the pair of them have started to behave as though she were not there. She says he tickles Elizabeth when she is in her bed and she squeals with laughter. If she up and wearing nothing but her nightgown, he slaps her familiarly on the buttocks. One day he caught her to him and tried to kiss her. "I put a stop to that," Mrs Ashley said firmly. "I told him he should be ashamed of himself."

Katherine is so taken up with her pregnancy that she has become dreamy and smiling, lost in a world of her own happiness. Thomas has told her that Elizabeth likes a romp, as all children do, and she seems to think that the adolescent girl under her roof really is no more than a child. Sometimes she comes to the room herself and joins in the tickling and the laughter. There was one extraordinary day when she and her husband chased Elizabeth down to the garden, and tore the flimsy nightgown she was wearing to shreds. The girl came back to her room panting and laughing, covering herself with the dangling strips that were all that remained of her gown. Mrs Ashley was horrified – but what could she say?

To me, it is quite obvious that Elizabeth is full of desire for the handsome man who teases her. She is becoming very indiscreet about the way she behaves with him. She cannot refrain from touching and kissing him. It cannot go on like this much longer.

21st March 1548

Last week Thomas started to show signs of being worried about Elizabeth's passion for him. He knew that Katherine must notice the girl's incautious behaviour sooner or later, so he decided to shift the blame on to Elizabeth. Perhaps he was trying to get out of the situation, but if so, he did it all wrong. He told his wife that he thought Elizabeth had become undesirably attractive. Then he said that he had seen her through a window with her arms round a man.

Katherine sent for me and Mrs Ashley, and asked what was going on. Neither of us said anything against Thomas Seymour, but Mrs Ashley pursed her lips and advised Katherine to question Elizabeth herself – which she did.

The resulting rumpus could be heard all over the house. Voices were raised. Elizabeth wept and shrieked that she had never done anything wrong. But Katherine had thought the thing through. She knew there were only two men in the house, apart from the servants, who live a separate existence. One was the irreproachable tutor, Roger Ascham. The other was Thomas Seymour himself.

When Elizabeth had gone weeping to her room, Katherine called Mrs Ashley and me to her room. Her face was very pale, but she told us her suspicions and that we must at all costs protect the girl.

"Thank goodness she knows," Mrs Ashley said afterwards. "Now perhaps it will stop."

6th April 1548

It did not stop. And this morning it came to a head. Katherine realized that Thomas and Elizabeth were missing and walked through the house, looking for them. She found them alone in a room, embracing passionately. She said nothing, just took in the scene then turned away. She sent for Mrs Ashley and me and told us Elizabeth was to leave the house as soon as possible. She did not weep. She seemed as cold as stone.

4th May 1548

Katherine had a very formal leave-taking with Elizabeth yesterday. We were all there except Thomas Seymour. The former queen made no reference to the reasons for Elizabeth's departure and expressed neither affection nor regret. Her manner was that of a teacher saying goodbye to a student who has completed her course.

"God has given you great qualities," she said. "Cultivate them always, and labour to improve them, for I believe you are destined by Heaven to be Queen of England."

Elizabeth stared at her, white-faced, and her mouth trembled a little. She managed not to cry, but she could not speak. She kissed Katherine and dropped a respectful curtsey. Then she turned and left the room.

5th May 1548

Katherine did not come to see Elizabeth depart this morning. Mrs Ashley is very angry that her young mistress has had to pay so dearly for an escapade that she thinks is entirely the fault of Thomas Seymour. Unfortunately, she has been telling people that he always loved Elizabeth and would have married her rather than Katherine Parr. As a result, the gossips all have it now that Thomas has never loved Katherine and has been unfaithful to her with countless other women, many of whom have borne his illegitimate children. Thomas, of course, is both embarrassed and enraged, but the damage done to Katherine and her reputation as a cultured, erudite woman is far worse. She did not deserve this.

20th May 1548

Since Elizabeth departed, Katherine has done her best to pick up the threads of her damaged marriage. She went away for a few days at Hanworth, and when she came back, she announced with great joy that she has felt the baby she is carrying move inside her. Thomas is away at court just now, but she sat down to write to him and give him the glad news. He has been behaving himself better, I am glad to say.

11th June 1548

Today Katherine told us that her baby will be born at Sudeley Castle in Gloucestershire, the residence that Thomas's brother gave him after the King's death. She assumes that Will and I and the children will be going with them as part of the household, and I have no objection to that – I will be glad to be with her. So we are busy packing. It is like the old days of going on royal progress – but I suppose we will not see that again until the young King is old enough to go out and meet his subjects.

Thankfully, Lady Jane Grey is still with us. After the crisis with Elizabeth she was terrified that all teaching would cease and she would have to return to her cruel parents. She is a sweet girl, and very clever. She loves Katherine, who has treated her with a kindness she has never known.

28th June 1548

Sudeley Castle is beautiful. It stands in lovely countryside, and Thomas Seymour has quickly endeared himself to the local nobility by offering good hunting and boundless hospitality.

There has been a letter from Elizabeth, which I can only guess to be a deep apology. Katherine nodded as she tucked it away with her papers but said nothing. The lady Mary has written too, saying she is pleased to hear of the coming baby. Evidently she has overcome her disapproval of her old friend's marriage, and that is very welcome.

Thomas has received a message from John Fowler, who must be still quietly supplying the boy king with pocket money, for he enclosed a letter from young Edward. It said the Duchess of Somerset had just given birth to a son.

Will laughed. "How she would love her boy to rule the country!" But that will never happen. Although Jane was queen for two years, the Seymours are not of royal blood, and there are signs that Edward Seymour, Duke of Somerset and Thomas's elder brother, is heading for a fall. We hear a lot of rumours that the other lords resent the arrogant way he has put himself in the position of unofficial king.

Thomas has no cause for complaint. Sudeley is quickly becoming recognized as a court centre in its own right, popular with the local nobility. Perhaps Thomas Seymour can at last accept that he has achieved as much as he can – but somehow I doubt it.

26th July 1548

Sir Robert and Lady Tyrwhitt are here. Sir Robert used to be an Esquire of the King's Body to King Henry, as Kitty's father was. He and his wife stayed in Katherine's household after the King's death, and Katherine made him her Master of Horse. He is a member of the Privy Council and owns a vast estate that used to belong to Lincoln Cathedral. They both seem genuinely fond of Katherine and anxious to help her.

The gossipy Mrs Ashley was imprisoned after Elizabeth was caught in her affair with Thomas Seymour and left Katherine's house. The Privy Council then sent the Tyrwhitts to take charge of Elizabeth and find out exactly what had been going on. All attempts to make her admit that Thomas had been plotting to marry her and make himself king failed. Elizabeth would not sign any "confessions" drawn up for her and attacked them furiously for arresting Mrs Ashley. Sir Robert says he was much amused by her perceptiveness and quick wit.

Katherine's baby is due before long now, so the other guests who have been filling the house throughout the summer are tactfully starting to depart. The Tyrwhitts will be staying, and Lady Jane Grey is still here. She is very much one of the family.

30th August 1548

Katherine has a baby girl. It was a long, difficult birth, but the child survived it and seems to be doing well. She will be called Mary, after the lady Mary, who I am sure will be delighted. Katherine is very weak after the agonizing hours of labour, but her doctors and Mary Odell, the midwife, are confident that she has suffered no permanent damage. She looks wonderfully happy to be a mother, and is so proud of her little daughter.

3rd September 1548

Dear God, please help us take care of her, if it be Thy will.

Katherine has a high fever and is delirious most of the time. The doctors can find no way to ease the fire that is devouring her. We lay cold cloths across her forehead, but waves of heat come from her, and she raves incoherently.

A letter has come from Thomas's brother, the Duke of Somerset, congratulating Thomas and Katherine on the birth of their daughter. As his own wife produced a boy six weeks ago, he could not resist adding a touch of patronising regret that Katherine's child was not a son.

None of that matters. I so much want her to live.

5th September 1548

This morning Katherine's fever worsened. She was gripped by confusion and fury, thinking that she was back in the moment when she found her husband embracing Elizabeth. Thomas was sitting by her bed, looking desperately worried, but she glared at him and said, "Those about me care not for me, but stand laughing at my grief."

Thomas was shocked. He asked us if we thought his wife would be comforted if he lay beside her and took her in his arms. Lady Tyrwhitt pursed her lips, but the doctor who had been there through the night thought it could be a good idea. Thomas lay down beside Katherine and tried to embrace her, but it did no good. She pushed at him feebly and burst out that she had wanted to talk to her doctor alone but could not do so because her husband was always there. Thomas's face crumpled, though whether in grief or resentment I did not know.

Lady Tyrwhitt glanced at me, and we left the room. She went back later but I had to feed my own baby. For him at least, I am of some use.

6th September 1548

The fever has burned itself out but Katherine is exhausted. We can all see that her life is flickering out like a spent candle. She murmured weakly that she must make her will. I brought writing materials for her secretary, and he leaned towards her to catch the faint words. She spoke slowly but with clarity.

"I, Katherine Parr … lying on my deathbed, sick of body but of good mind and perfect memory…" I was weeping too much to hear the rest.

7th September 1548

Katherine Parr, most gracious of ladies, died this morning between the hours of two and three. She left everything she has to Thomas Seymour.

The story seems ended. Anne of Cleves still lives, but Henry and all his other wives are dead.

Afterwards

I did not think I would write in this diary again, as I want no more to do with kingship and the court. But today, 20th March 1549, Thomas Seymour was executed for high treason. He had been found guilty of trying to gain control of the throne by pushing Lady Jane Grey as the young King Edward's bride.

Katherine's baby daughter, seven months old, is an orphan. She has been disinherited because of her father's crime and owns nothing. Nobody wants her. Somerset and his wife will not take her, though she is their niece. Neither will they make an allowance to anyone else for her upkeep.

Will and I would gladly adopt Katherine's baby to be part of our own family, for no payment, but we do not count. My father was only the royal huntsman, and Will is the son of a court jester. There is nothing we can do but watch the powerful at play and cry. Or laugh.

Historical note

Henry VIII was famously married to six different wives, but none of them – apart from Catherine of Aragon – lasted for more than a few years.

Catherine of Aragon and Henry were married just before Henry was crowned King of England in 1509. Their marriage lasted for nearly twenty years, and it seems that it was a happy one, at least at the beginning. After he married Catherine, Henry is reported to have said, "If I were still free, I would still choose her for wife above all others."

Catherine gave birth to five children, but only one of them survived for more than a few weeks – a girl, Mary, not the hoped-for boy who could continue the Tudor line. By the time Catherine was in her thirties she was no longer able to have children and Henry wanted an end to the marriage. Henry had set his heart on a new, younger wife, and by 1526 he was wildly in love with Anne Boleyn. Anne was ambitious and clever, and she had seen that the King's favours could be short-lived, so she kept Henry at arm's length. This astonished him, and increased his determination to marry her.

In 1527 Henry began to try to arrange a divorce, which proved extremely difficult and took six years to achieve. Before he could marry Catherine, back in 1509, he had needed special permission from the Pope, as head of the Catholic Church, because Catherine was his brother's widow. Now Henry argued that the marriage should never have taken place and could be "annulled" – declared invalid. The Pope wouldn't give his permission – it would have meant going against the previous Pope's authority (who had allowed Catherine and Henry to marry in the first place), and secondly he needed to keep the peace with the powerful Emperor Charles V, who was Catherine of Aragon's nephew and who held most of Europe. Finally Henry made himself head of the Church in England and got his divorce without permission from the Pope. These must have been sad and humiliating years for Catherine: Henry went so far as to imprison their daughter, Mary, when she protested against the divorce. Henry's actions not only affected Catherine but the whole country. Breaking away from the Pope's authority meant that Henry would go on to reform the Church in England, taking away land, wealth and power from the monasteries, and England would eventually become a Protestant country.

Anne Boleyn's uncle, the Earl of Norfolk, saw that his family could gain immense power in the court if his niece should become queen, so he and his supporters were strongly in favour of Henry's divorce from Catherine.

In 1532 Henry granted Anne a peerage in her own right. Anne was not popular with the people, but she began openly to plan for her marriage to the King. Early in 1533 she became pregnant.

Although he had still not divorced his first wife, Henry married

Anne in a secret ceremony within a few weeks of knowing she expected a child. The Pope threatened to excommunicate him, but by now Henry was planning with Archbishop Cranmer to establish a separate Church that would be answerable only to the reigning monarch of England, and not to Rome.

A few weeks later Cranmer took on himself the authority to judge the King's case and declared Henry's marriage to Catherine null and void. With this final break from Rome, the Church of England was born – and Henry could consider himself a free man.

Anne Boleyn was crowned on 1 June 1533. On 7 September of that year, she gave birth, not to the longed-for son but to a girl, Elizabeth, who would become Queen Elizabeth I of England. None of her subsequent babies survived and Henry began to tire of his new wife, who was proving no more capable of providing a son than the discarded Catherine.

The three brief years of Anne Boleyn's marriage saw Henry's love for her turn to loathing. He began to look elsewhere, and in 1535 he fell in love with the meek and submissive Jane Seymour. However, with two wives still living, another divorce was out of the question. Abetted by his new adviser, Thomas Cromwell, Henry began to think of a more drastic solution.

Just over three months later a court was appointed to investigate charges that Anne had committed treason against the King by having illicit relationships with several other men, one of them her own brother. She was arrested and taken to the Tower of London.

At her trial Anne swore that she was innocent of the charges. Her eloquence moved many people, but it could not save her. Both she and the men accused with her were sentenced to die. Anne Boleyn was beheaded on 19 May 1536. Henry VIII announced his betrothal to Jane Seymour the next day, and married on 30 May. In 1537 Jane gave birth to a boy, Edward, but she died of childbirth fever a few days later.

Although Henry now had a son, this was just one boy, and he still needed a wife who would give him more children. After several young women had turned him down, he married a German princess, Anne of Cleves, in 1540, having never seen her except in a portrait by Holbein. When they met in the run-up to their marriage, he took an instant dislike to her, and the marriage ended in an uncontested divorce after only a few months.

The Duke of Norfolk, uncle of Anne Boleyn, had another niece, Katherine Howard, a very pretty girl of sixteen. Once again, Henry was attracted by such a lively young woman and married her as soon as his divorce from Anne of Cleves had gone through. He called Katherine his "rose without a thorn", believing her to be as innocent and fresh as she looked. But Katherine was a Catholic and the Protestant faction wanted to be rid of her. When rumours of her previous affairs with other men turned out to be true, she, like Anne Boleyn, went to the block in 1542, after just two years of marriage.

Katherine Parr was married to a sick and elderly husband when she caught the King's eye – and she was also in love with Thomas Seymour, Jane Seymour's brother. Henry sent Seymour abroad on a long-term post and married Katherine as soon as her husband died. Katherine accepted this as a duty to her king, though he was now ailing and hugely overweight, but she became genuinely fond of him and cared for him until the end of his life. She then married Thomas Seymour, her first love, and bore him a child, but died of puerperal fever.

In 1547 Henry died and was succeeded by his nine-year-old son, Edward VI. The six years of the boy's reign ended with his death in 1553. Catherine of Aragon's daughter, Mary, became queen, but she died after only five years, in 1558.

Anne Boleyn's daughter, Elizabeth, then came to the throne and ruled wisely and magnificently for 45 years. Perhaps in abiding fear of the fate that had overtaken her mother, she never married, and the Tudor dynasty came to an end with her death in 1603.

Timeline

1485 Catherine of Aragon is born.

1491 Henry VIII is born as Prince Henry, son of the first Tudor king, Henry VII.

1501 Anne Boleyn is born.

1509 Henry VII dies.

Prince Henry is crowned King Henry VIII and marries Catherine of Aragon.

Jane Seymour is born.

1515 Anne of Cleves is born.

1516 Catherine of Aragon has a daughter, Mary, later to be Queen Mary I.

1521 Katherine Howard is born (cousin of Anne Boleyn).

1525 Henry VIII begins to tire of Catherine, who has failed to give him a male heir and is unlikely to have any more children. He falls in love with Anne Boleyn, and plans to seek a divorce from Catherine.

1526 The King's "great matter" about his divorce begins. Divorce is illegal within Catholic England, but Anne Boleyn has powerful allies. The Pope fails to give judgement.

1531 Henry VIII separates from Catherine of Aragon.

1532 Henry grants a peerage to Anne Boleyn. Archbishop Cranmer advises him that the "great matter" may be decided by the King and the English clerics, without reference to the authority of Rome.

1533 Anne Boleyn becomes pregnant, and Henry VIII marries her secretly although he is still married to Catherine of Aragon. Following a judgement from Cranmer, Henry divorces Catherine, and the Protestant Church of England is established.

Anne Boleyn is crowned Queen of England. On 7 September she gives birth to a daughter, Elizabeth, later to be Queen Elizabeth I.

1534 Anne Boleyn's next baby is stillborn. Relationships between her and Henry VIII begin to deteriorate.

1535 Henry VIII falls in love with Jane Seymour and seeks to free himself from Anne Boleyn, who fails to give him a son.

1536 Catherine of Aragon dies.

Henry appoints a court to judge Anne on charges of adultery with several other men, including her own brother. She pleads innocence, but is condemned to death.

On 19 May Anne Boleyn is beheaded at the Tower of London.

Henry VIII announces his betrothal to Jane Seymour and marries her on 30 May.

1537 Jane Seymour dies after giving birth to a son, Edward, later to be Edward VI.

1540 Henry VIII marries Anne of Cleves, but divorces her the same year.

Henry marries Katherine Howard.

1542 Katherine Howard is beheaded.

1543 Henry marries Katherine Parr.

1547 Henry VIII dies.

Henry's son by Jane Seymour is crowned Edward VI, at the age of nine.

Katherine Parr secretly marries Thomas Seymour (Jane Seymour's brother).

1548 Katherine Parr dies in childbirth.

1553 Edward VI dies.

Catherine of Aragon's daughter is crowned Queen Mary I.

1557 Anne of Cleves dies.

1558 Queen Mary I dies.

Anne Boleyn's daughter, Elizabeth I, comes to the throne and rules for 45 years. She never marries.

1603 Elizabeth I dies and the Tudor dynasty ends.

Look out for these other royal
stories by Alison Prince

My Royal Story

A
Tudor Girl's Diary
1501–1513

CATHERINE OF ARAGON

Alison Prince

It's the year 1501. Eva has come to London from Spain in the retinue of her friend, Catherine of Aragon, who is to marry Arthur, the eldest son of King Henry VII. But when Catherine meets Arthur's charismatic younger brother, Prince Harry, Eva watches the pair of them and wishes that princesses were free to follow the wishes of their hearts...

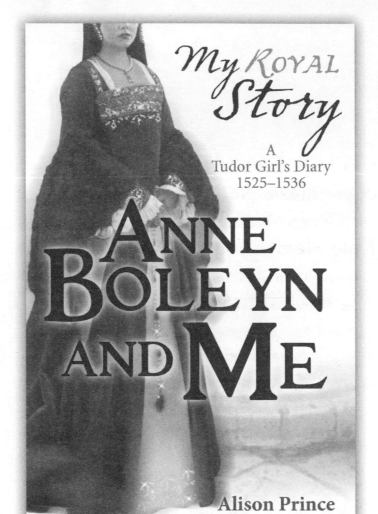

It's 1525. **Elinor** is lady-in-waiting to
Queen Catherine. **Anne Boleyn** is also one of the
Queen's ladies until she attracts the eye of
King Henry. Elinor watches and listens,
and writes down all she sees in her journal –
a witness to Henry's desire for a son that
tore his family and his kingdom apart...

Experience history first-hand with My Story –
a series of vividly imagined accounts of life in the past.

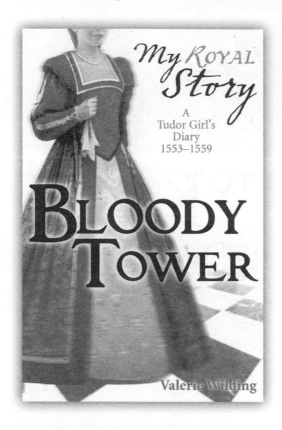

My ROYAL
Story

A
Tudor Girl's
Diary
1553–1559

BLOODY
TOWER

Valerie Wilding

Tilly lives in **turbulent times**. It's the 1550s;
when Queen Mary ousts **Lady Jane Grey** to
win the throne, her executioners are kept busy. Even
Princess Elizabeth is **imprisoned** in the Tower.
As Tilly watches the **plots** and politics of the
Tudor court unfolding, she waits for her chance
to deliver a very **important letter**...

My Story

An Elizabethan Girl's Diary 1583–1586

TO KILL A QUEEN

Valerie Wilding

It's the 1580s. Queen Elizabeth's enemies plot to kill her and place Mary Queen of Scots on the throne. While Kitty's father works on secret projects for Elizabeth, her brother's mixing with suspicious characters. As Mary's supporters edge closer by the minute, Kitty fears the worst ... that they'll all be thrown into the Tower.